EXTINCTION
CODE

BOOK ONE

JAMES D. PRESCOTT

ISBN: 9781926456270

Dedication

A special thank you to Dr. Ricki Lewis (DNA Science blog) and Joel Rubin for helping to make sense of the incredible and often mystifying world of genetics. To Lisa Weinberg and the rest of the beta team for all of your terrific feedback. And finally to my editor RJ, for your considerable prowess and never-ending patience.

Book Description

We were wrong about the origins of our species.
For eons, the truth has remained hidden.
Until now…

Geophysicist Jack Greer believes he may finally have found the resting place of the meteorite that wiped out the dinosaurs sixty-five million years ago. A few miles off the Yucatán coast, Jack and a team of scientists tow an aging drilling platform over the impact crater with the aim of securing a sample. But buried deep beneath the earth lies a shocking discovery that threatens to shatter everything we think we know about the origins of our species.

A world away, geneticist Dr. Mia Ward receives a mysterious delivery from her former boss and mentor, Alan Salzburg. In it are clues of a dire warning hidden inside the human genome, one which foretells man's very extinction.

His instructions to Mia are simple: keep the information safe and, above all, trust no one—words all the more chilling after Alan turns up dead. But who wrote the message and what does it mean? Jack's recent discovery may hold the answers, but can she reach him in time to save the human race?

Chapter 1

Yucatán Peninsula—5 miles off the coast of Mexico

Chief Scientist Dr. Jack Greer watched through high-powered binoculars as the helicopters drew nearer. It was early morning as he stood on the upper deck of a repurposed oil rig, his cheek fanned by a warm Gulf breeze. He drew in a lungful of salty air, feeling his pulse begin to quicken.

A geophysicist in his early forties, Jack was blessed, or some might say cursed, with a shock of dark wavy hair that, much to his elderly mother's chagrin, was often kept hidden away under a ratty old Houston Astros baseball cap.

His attention soon returned to the two choppers. They were about ten miles out, both little more than twin white dots pressed against a powder-blue sky. The second was larger than the first, a tandem-rotor heavy lifter. Swaying gently beneath the aircraft was a bright orange shipping container, secured by four taut cables. Rajesh Viswanathan from MIT was almost here. The final member of the team, he was already a week late.

Lowering the binoculars, Jack listened to the drilling team working below. They'd been here a month, boring a hole deep into the earth's crust. He and his team were on the hunt for the remnants of something no one had expected them to find: the asteroid that had slammed into the earth sixty-five million years ago, wiping out the dinosaurs and causing one of the largest mass extinctions in history.

At least that was the story most of the scientific community had come to believe. While the space rock theory was by far the strongest hypothesis, a growing chorus of scientists were beginning to wonder whether increased volcanic activity hadn't really been to blame. The team's goal was simple enough. By carefully studying the limestone deposits around the impact, as well as what was left of the meteorite itself, Jack hoped they might settle the debate once and for all.

But getting the research grants to embark on such an audacious expedition had proven far more difficult than he had ever imagined. Plain old-fashioned ridicule was the biggest obstacle. The crux of the problem was this: when a slab of iron, rock or ice slammed into the earth, most of it was instantaneously vaporized. And any remnants were flung up into the atmosphere and dispersed across the planet.

The laughing stopped abruptly once Jack's seismic surveys revealed a giant magnetic anomaly five hundred meters beneath the earth's surface. It didn't matter that the data on the meteorite itself was somewhat vague— the actual readings revealed a dark splotch in a sea of wavy horizontal lines.

Fuzzy or not, it was enough to pique the interest of DiCore, one of the largest mining operations on the planet. To them, the initial readings indicated the possible presence of diamonds and lots of them. In the 1970's, a similar discovery had been made in Siberia, at the Popigai crater.

In more practical terms, DiCore's funding had meant that a research project that might have lasted two weeks with grants from the US Geological Survey could now go on for months. For its part, DiCore's conditions were predictable enough. Once the scientists were done studying the remnants of the meteorite, DiCore would move in to extract whatever diamonds were present.

Jack was still contemplating the project when his co-chief on the expedition, Gabby Bishop, exited the main superstructure and crossed to where he was standing. She was an astronomer, but more than that, she was a friend of many years. A decade older than him, Gabby had shoulder-length silver hair and a pleasant, round face. She had also been the first to renege on their shared commitment to stop smoking. And as if to prove the point, Gabby fished a hand in her pocket and came out with a pack of Marlboro Lights. She started to offer him one and then stopped.

"Sorry," she said, lighting up. "Forgot you're still on the cigarette wagon."

Jack glanced over and tugged at the brim of his ball cap. "I'm trying to be good and you're not helping things."

"Am I detecting a crack in Jack Greer's infamous willpower?" she said mockingly. "Maybe you should stop fighting the inevitable."

He grinned. "Right now I'll settle for you blowing some of that smoke in my face."

They shared a burst of uneasy laughter.

The helicopters were less than a mile away now.

Gabby shook her head, unable to hide her own deep concern. "They must have gotten tied up with bureaucratic red tape," she said. "I'm sure that's why they didn't call." She found Jack's gaze and held it. "You know, given the situation out here."

The situation Gabby was referring to could best be described as Murphy's Law in action. Last month, as the rig was being towed into place, political tensions in the Gulf of Mexico had risen to an all-time high. A recent decision to step back from open relations with Cuba had quickly led to the reimposition of sanctions. Not surprisingly, the Cubans had retaliated by calling up dredging machines to form artificial islands along the edge of their maritime borders. It was a trick no doubt learned from China and undeniably part of an attempt to increase the scope of Cuba's exclusive economic zone. Whether or not the move was designed to strengthen their seat at the bargaining table wasn't clear. What *was* clear was that as a result, both countries had begun beefing up their military presence in the region. So long as Mexico remained neutral, the license granted to the expedition from that government remained in place. But Jack hesitated to even consider what might happen should the situation escalate any further.

The walkie on Jack's belt belched out a burst of static.

"Boss, it's Billy. We just hit a real coarse layer. Much harder than granite. I'm gonna need to pull up and swap out the tungsten carbide roller-cutter."

Billy Brenner was their sometimes impetuous chief drilling engineer.

Jack's gut told him they were getting close. When the meteor had first impacted the earth's crust, it had created a massive tsunami, eventually depositing layers of sand over the impact area. The largest bits had been the first to settle, followed by ever-smaller pieces. The result was rock layers of increasing density. That meant the harder the layer, the closer they were.

"Give me a depth reading first," Jack insisted.

There was a pause as Billy checked the digital readout on the drill's control panel. "Fourteen hundred and fifty-two feet."

The meteorite sat at around fifteen hundred feet.

"Push through it," Jack urged him, rubbing the pads of his fingers together as he tended to whenever his stomach coiled with nervous energy.

The hesitation in Billy's reply was hard to miss. Jack's order would surely put the engineer's baby at risk, but there was more to Billy's reaction and Jack knew it. Deferential as he sounded, Billy wasn't asking Jack—he'd been telling him, or at least trying to. Jack repeated the order and replaced the walkie-talkie, deciding he would deal with Billy and his temper later.

Gabby's brow furrowed as the cigarette slipped from her fingers. Jack watched the wind take hold and spin it in endless circles as it fluttered down to the crystalline waters below. The cautious wisdom she brought to the table was often a nice counterbalance to Jack's eagerness to take giant risks.

"You understand that if Billy loses that drill bit, we may be done," she told him in a tone few others could get away with.

The helicopters were overhead now, the wash from their blades kicking up a fierce wind and an even worse racket. Jack held the baseball cap tight to his skull. He leaned in. "How can we stop now when we're so close?"

Chapter 2

While the larger helicopter lowered the shipping container onto the deck, the other settled gently on the landing pad. The chopper's side door slid open and out came a plump Indian man with round glasses. Stepping onto the platform, he stumbled before quickly regaining himself. Dressed in a tight-fitting burgundy button-down shirt and white slacks, he looked noticeably out of place and uncomfortable.

"Welcome aboard," Jack said, fighting the wash of the rotor blades.

"I am Rajesh," the man said, shifting his backpack to his other shoulder. He was flanked by a young man and a petite Asian girl whom he introduced as Adam and Leah. They looked like grad students.

The helicopter lifted off, ushering in the sound of the drill and a flock of seagulls flying overhead.

"You're a week late," Jack told him, turning and starting along the walkway. Rajesh followed, struggling to keep up. The wobbly state his legs were in was no doubt making it difficult.

"Please accept my sincerest apologies, Dr. Greer," Rajesh stammered, looking to Gabby for reassurance. "We were ready to leave, but the government would not allow us to travel through a potential conflict zone." His shirt was beginning to stick to his wet skin.

Jack stopped and spun around. "I understand and I sympathize, but you never called to tell us you'd been delayed. So consider this your first and second strike."

"Second strike." Rajesh repeated the words as though examining an unknown artifact. "And on our third strike? What will happen then? I'm not trying to be obtuse, but as sports go, I much prefer cricket."

"Strike three and you and your posse of grad students will be on a chopper, heading home."

Rajesh grimaced. "You have my guarantee, sir, there will be no strike three."

An involuntary grin formed on Jack's lips. Late or not, there was something he liked about the guy. "Look, we're glad you're finally here. Least now we can finish what we started."

Gabby took over, explaining the rig's layout as she pointed to the various modules.

The rig went by many names. Conoco Phillips had christened her TOR. But to the scientists, engineers and deckhands, she was known as POS—an acronym involving excrement.

In the months that preceded the expedition, most of the unnecessary modules had been stripped away. What remained was the drilling section, as well as a ten-story superstructure with living quarters, conference rooms, a mess hall and several quaint spots where off-duty personnel could unwind.

On a portion of the open deck was a stretch affectionately called Fifth Avenue. It was here that a series of shipping containers—doubling as labs—were arranged in two neat rows, forming a kind of street. At the end of the strip was Rajesh's orange container.

Just then, Jack's walkie sprang to life.

"What is it?" he demanded, heading purposefully toward the superstructure. Below them Billy was waving his arms like a pedestrian desperate to flag down a passing cop car. Jack caught sight of him and skidded to a stop.

"I'm not sure," Billy said. "I think we've hit some kind of air pocket."

The grin that grew on Jack's face said it all. They were through.

Chapter 3

A burst of sunlight streamed in through the porthole windows, illuminating the normally dark and dingy conference room. The dominant decorative theme inside was fake wood, once a prerequisite for every basement in the eighties and early nineties, long before anyone knew better. Above them hung a suspended tile ceiling lined with rows of neon office lights, the kind that gave everyone a vaguely jaundiced complexion. Hard hats hung from hooks on the wall. Nearby was a fifty-inch flat screen and a whiteboard.

That was where Jack stood, surveying the entire team. "What do you say we go around the room, since I'm sure our newest arrivals haven't had a chance to meet everyone yet?"

Dr. Grant Holland smiled and gave Rajesh and the others a funny little wave. Long and gangly, Grant was nearly sixty with rosy cheeks and slightly thinning hair. Although he considered himself a scientist, some of his theories on morphic fields and interspecies communication were pretty far-out. "You might say I'm the biologist on board. A native of Bath, England, I studied at Imperial College London. My role here is to look at how life slowly came back after the asteroid impact. And if I was a betting man, which I'm not, I'd say the role of volcanoes in the mass extinction has been grossly overlooked."

Dr. Dag Gustavsson was next. A square-jawed Swede sporting a thick red beard and a penetrating stare, he could easily have passed for a Viking warrior were it not for the tie-dye and Birkenstock sandals. He clasped his hands and offered a slight bow. "Pleasure to meet you. I'm a paleontologist by training, but for this mission, I'll be channeling my inner zoologist as I chart the rise of mammals following the cataclysm."

Billy Brenner tapped the table with his finger, looking visibly uncomfortable. He was handsome, in a gruff sort of way. His cheeks were pockmarked from a bout of particularly bad acne during his adolescence, one of the many difficulties from his youth he continued to struggle with. "I'm in charge of drilling operations for Suntech. Been with the company for about ten years. Used to help my dad with his shrimping business before Katrina done away with that." He flicked his eyebrows as if to say, *But all that's in the past now.* Although to anyone watching, it was clear that wasn't the case.

"Guess that leaves you three," Jack said.

Adam and Leah waved and explained that they were both PhD students from MIT, working in the field of artificial intelligence.

The room became still.

For his part, Rajesh skipped over his childhood growing up in Calcutta and moving to America in his late teens, opting instead to swipe the cloth from the nearly three-foot object positioned on the table next to him.

"It is with great pleasure that I introduce A.N.N.A.," Rajesh announced.

Before them sat the upper torso of what looked like a robot. A glass screen in the delicate shape of a woman's face displayed the image of a real-looking person. Two mechanical arms unfurled as the robot waved at the group.

"Oh, man, that's wild!" Dag squealed, bolting upright in his seat.

Billy Brenner appeared stunned, perhaps even afraid.

Jack wasn't sure what to think. Gabby had said Rajesh would be bringing some sophisticated computing equipment, but he hadn't expected this.

"Her name is Anna?" Grant inquired.

"It stands for Artificial Neuron Network Algorithm," Rajesh explained. "We use mesh mapping and projective head technology to create her facial features and expressions."

Anna smiled and although it was nothing more than a video being projected against the inside of her glass face, the expression had, dared one say, warmth.

Rajesh patted the robot's shoulder and Anna's eyes traced down to his hand. "We tend to think of AI as the robot itself, but that is nothing more than the shell. Real AI is the programming that runs inside the robot. But not all AI is alike. Winning chess matches, dominating game shows or using data to target specific ads, those are things we call ANI or artificial narrow intelligence, one that specializes in a particular area of expertise.

"For most developers, the Holy Grail is AGI or artificial general intelligence. Here, the design seeks to emulate human-level intelligence. And yet from university campuses to billion-dollar corporations, the closest any of them have come to date is the basic intelligence of a house cat."

"What makes Anna any different?" Jack asked.

Rajesh nodded in Jack's direction. "Far from a household pet, Anna has the emotional and intellectual quotient of a ten-year-old child. She also has a rudimentary form of imagination. What she lacks, however, is what most children lack—wisdom and experience."

11

"How is it she's so much more advanced from everyone else?" Gabby wondered.

"Most AI teams are attempting to map the human mind with the goal of creating a digital duplicate, an undertaking that will surely take years. Let me ask you, if all manned flight had sought to strictly emulate birds, would we have jets today? We examined the work that our peers were doing and decided it was far better to pass all of the heavy lifting on to Anna. She's the one who has been doing the research on AI and in the process improving and refining her own architecture at an exponential rate. In essence, she's teaching herself to become smarter."

"I'm sorry, but this ain't normal, or natural," Billy said. "I mean, where does it all end?"

Anna's head swiveled to the engineer, her digital features cold and humorless. "It will end with my omnipotence. And humanity's enslavement."

The air in the room grew still.

A moment later Rajesh burst out laughing, his fleshy hand slapping the table. Anna joined in as well, her own robotic arm mimicking his.

"Oh, the looks on your faces," Rajesh said, his own face a mask of pain and pleasure. "Priceless, absolutely priceless."

Jack couldn't help but smile. "She's got a sharp wit, I'll give her that. I was worried Anna's abilities would be limited to ordering all-dressed pizzas."

Anna turned to face Jack and grinned. "I assure you, Dr. Greer, I'm capable of so much more."

"There is, however, one significant ingredient Anna is missing," Rajesh admitted. "Something common to human beings across the globe."

"Legs!" Dag shouted excitedly, eyeing Anna's torso.

Grant regarded the robot thoughtfully. "I must say, for some reason the thought of religion came to me," he admitted.

Rajesh shook his head. "You are not far off, Professor. What she lacks is the conscious desire to create in her own image. In effect, to evolve from created to creator."

•••

Moments later, with the meeting over, the drill was back up and running. Most of the team waited in the control room and watched a digital rendition with palpable anticipation. Jack and Gabby held their breath as the bit inched ever closer to the amorphous shape on the geographical display. Somewhere at the back of Jack's mind, beyond his buzzing nerves, beyond the shrill sound of the drill, he registered the drone of a nearby plane. Not nearly loud enough to draw his full attention, but for now it was there, like a circling fly.

The next sound Jack heard was the violent screech of metal as the drill seized up. Jack's heart froze in his chest. Whatever the bit had dug into down there, it had done to the tungsten carbide what a tank might do to a wooden spear—which was to say, shatter it. Within seconds, the resulting shockwave travelled up the pipe and into the drill housing. A gout of flame shot ten feet into the air. Billy and his team ran for cover. But the whine of grinding metal continued. The engineers had fled without shutting the equipment down. Jack snagged a hard hat off the wall and ran toward the drill.

He didn't get three paces before the platform began shaking, his ears filled with an electric hum. Jack fought for each step as though he were walking along the bottom of the Gulf itself. A terrible force was pulling down on him, something he had felt years ago as a passenger in a looping stunt plane. The g-forces were pulling him toward the grate. The water below was growing concave as well. Jack looked up just in time to spot that plane he'd heard earlier crashing into the water.

13

Nine-foot lengths of pipe fell from their moorings and landed on the metal grate next to him without bouncing end on end or rolling back and forth. It was as though a giant magnet were sucking everything toward it. Then all at once, the world let go. The ocean, now released from the force's grasp, rose up, spraying the deck. But it wasn't over, not yet. A blast of blinding white light struck them like a million flashbulbs firing at once.

Jack rubbed the stars from his eyes, rising to his feet. *What the hell just happened?*

The drill was still grinding away. In a few paces, he reached it and hit the emergency shutdown button. With that danger out of the way, Jack immediately initiated safety protocols to ensure everyone was unhurt and accounted for.

The plane he had seen tumble out of the sky and into the sea hadn't been more than a mile or two away. With flashes of light still dotting his vision, Jack gathered three deckhands and led them to the oil platform's Zodiac rigid inflatable boat. The supply ship was only scheduled to return in another two days, which meant that apart from a handful of lifeboats, the Zodiac was all they had to mount a rescue.

Fear stinging at every nerve ending, Jack and the deckhands set out to search for survivors. But crowding in on the frantic thoughts swirling through his head were new and disturbing questions about the meteorite. Whatever lay down there, it possessed powers the likes of which the world had never seen.

Chapter 4

Northern Brazil
Three hours earlier

The frame of the tiny turboprop plane shook violently, vibrating every bone in Dr. Mia Ward's body. The cabin was narrow and mostly empty except for the three other passengers sitting nearby, all fellow members of a WHO research team en route to Brazil to study craniofacial anomalies.

From the open cockpit, the two pilots shouted at one another in Portuguese. Mia caught something about high winds, but the rest was drowned out by the noise made by the shuddering overhead compartments.

On Mia's left sat Dr. Eric Metzner, his fingers wrapped tightly around his armrests, breathing like a woman in labor. He was a Canadian pediatrician with a specialty in disfigurement and an aptitude for high drama. On her right was Dr. Scott Chapman, a Brit from Manchester who held a special loathing for anyone who mistook football for soccer or didn't know the proper way to pour tea. Two seats behind them was Maria Bertola, a PhD student with a background in genetic epidemiology, the study of how genetic and environmental factors affected human health. Maria made the sign of the cross and kissed the crucifix around her neck. If there was an accident, chances were that crucifix was all they'd find of her.

The wingtips rolled up and down as the pilots struggled to keep the plane level. Mia glanced at Scott, who was struggling to swallow a pill. The sight made her stomach curl into a fight fist. She closed her eyes and thought of her daughter's smiling face and the dream of one day being together again.

Her physical journey to Brazil had started in Richmond, Virginia, when an application to the WHO and a never-ending stream of interviews had finally won her a spot as principal investigator. Their assignment was to study a terrible genetic ailment which left too many young Brazilians ostracized and in some cases unable to eat or speak.

Trained as a geneticist, Mia had once helped to create a groundbreaking *de novo* human artificial chromosome. This when most of her colleagues in the field had given up the possibility of creating a working HAC and had opted instead to empty existing chromosomes, filling them with helpful genes. The main application was in the field of gene therapy. Once humans had passed the embryonic stage of development, the challenge with HACs was getting the new chromosome into our cells. Doctors sometimes used viruses as delivery mechanisms, commonly referred to as vectors, but Mia was certain there was a better, safer way. The answer was in the body somewhere. She was sure. And when she found it, the treatment of illness and disease would be transformed forever.

Suddenly and much to the relief of those around her, the plane evened out no more than a second before the wheels screeched against the sizzling asphalt.

Mia stared out the window as the plane taxied. Huddled along the Amazon River and with a population

16

of two hundred thousand, Santarem marked the northern edge of the civilized world in Brazil. To cross the Amazon here was to enter a region few westerners dared to visit.

She removed her phone and used the glare to check her reflection. Her red hair, normally long and striking, lay in a jumble, making her look like she'd been through the spin cycle. Her face was pale and blotchy, her cheeks sunken as though she hadn't eaten in days. Certainly nothing a touch of makeup couldn't fix.

The plane came to a stop. Mia and the others stood and stretched in silence, thankful they weren't being scraped off the runway with spatulas.

Grabbing her knapsack, Mia strode out into a wave of stifling heat and blinding sunlight. With some effort, she struggled to draw in a lungful of air. Metal stairs led down to the tarmac. Scanning the horizon, she saw endless collections of flat structures with roofs made of corrugated tin. The sound of buzzing insects and blaring scooter horns dominated the landscape, along with the overwhelming abundance of the color brown. Despite the city's size, the airport in Santarem represented one of the few paved surfaces.

A black van awaited them at the bottom of the stairs. Beside the vehicle was the WHO's Brazilian Regional Director Isabella Silva. She waved them forward in short choppy motions. She was a pleasant-looking woman in her fifties who wore a large smile and a pair of lifts intended to rocket her into the five-foot-and-over club.

"Welcome, welcome," she said in broken English, motioning to the van. "I know you've had a long trip, but we go straight to the hospital. Carlos will take your bags to the hotel."

"How about a chance to freshen up first?" Mia asked, more concerned with her team than herself.

Isabella laughed. "It's one hundred degrees out today, my love. Freshen up will be gone as soon as your shower is done."

Mia glanced down at the beige cargo pants and green button-down shirt she was wearing. The faint hint of BO wafted up at her. Or was it coming from Eric or Scott? At this point, it didn't matter. From the front seat, Isabella spoke to the driver and off they went.

Ten minutes later they arrived at Santarem Municipal Hospital, a five-storied white and pink building that looked closer to a Holiday Inn than it did a place for healing and research. Mia caught the odor of bandages and sanitizer as Isabella led them through a nearly empty emergency waiting room and into what she called 'the research wing'. There a number of patients were seated. At least half of them were suffering from some form of genetic facial disfigurement. Mia had prepared herself for what she was about to see, but nothing could ever dull the intensity of coming face to face with such an affliction.

Seeing their arrival, the patients and their guardians clapped and cheered. Mia hoped these poor people didn't think they were about to be cured. Even if a viable treatment could be developed, these were human beings, not guinea pigs. A six-year-old girl the same age as Mia's daughter Zoey came forward, wrapping her arms around Mia's waist. The girl's left cheek had fused, pulling her lips back into a clearly uncomfortable expression. Mia leaned down and hugged her back, fighting the swell of tears threatening to spill down her cheeks. She marveled at their joy and resilience in spite of the hardships they had endured. She'd come here to help heal these people.

She wondered whether they were the only ones who needed it.

When the formalities and initial introductions were out of the way, Carlos drove them to the Sandis hotel. Lavished in white tile with a bright orange sign, it was a sight for sore eyes. They had no sooner entered the hotel—Carlos having dutifully brought the suitcases to their rooms—than Mia's vision was struck by a blinding white light. She came to a stop, rubbing at her eyes, doing what she could to blink away the field of stars you normally saw after standing up too fast. Slowly her vision returned and with it came the realization that she hadn't been alone. Everyone in the lobby, from the concierge behind the desk to Eric, Scott and Maria, was blinking madly. Then things went from strange to outright frightening. A nearby television was set to CNN International. There, too, the newscasters were reeling from the same inexplicable occurrence.

"The bloody hell was that?" Scott asked, scanning the lobby with wide, darting eyes.

It seemed everyone was asking themselves that very same question. Had the world descended into nuclear war? Had a nearby star gone supernova? Mia's imagination reeled from the plausible, to the unsettling. Either way, she knew it wasn't good.

Chapter 5

"We found him clinging to a piece of debris," Jack explained to the group gathered in a semi-circle around the survivor's hospital bed. Many of the onlookers were just as battered as the patient before them. The survivor was dressed in an aviator's flight suit, one that sported a Cuban flag on the shoulder.

Lara Steiger, a former first responder and army medic, was the only medical staff on hand. Blonde and in her late twenties, Lara had been running around for the last few hours, applying bandages and dressing wounds. While none of the injuries had been serious, two crew members were complaining of migraines and gaps in their memory, likely the consequence of a concussion.

"He's one lucky guy," Lara said, adjusting the settings on the heart monitor. "To survive a crash like that."

Jack had been under the impression they were rushing to the scene of a downed commercial airliner. Needless to say, he'd been surprised and more than a little concerned when he saw the plane was military and not one of theirs. How would the Cuban navy react when they learned an American vessel had fished their man out of the water?

"Mr. Fuentes," Gabby whispered softly, reading the

name tag on his uniform. She turned to the others. "Any of you speak Spanish?"

"I heard Alejandro Diaz speaking to someone in Spanish on the phone," Dag offered. "I can fetch him, if you want."

"Let's wait on that for now," Jack said, turning his attention back to the Cuban.

"What on earth shall we do with him?" Grant asked, a Band-Aid over his left eye.

Jack tightened his grip on the bed rail. He could feel the guilt starting to work its way in. Guilt that he had pushed too hard, too fast. "For now we do nothing, except let him rest. We have more important concerns at the moment. I know each and every one of us is eager to find out exactly what happened and why, but first we need to make sure we're safe here. That'll mean a new round of scans of the sea floor."

Jack turned to Billy, who had a bulge on his right cheek from the chewing tobacco he was supposed to have given up weeks ago. First Gabby, now Billy. At this rate, Jack would be smoking again by tomorrow morning.

Succumbing to vices aside, Jack and Billy hadn't spoken yet since the incident. The engineer's decision to run before shutting down the drill could have made a bad situation even worse. But the expression on Billy's face contained a different message, something closer to 'I told you so'. And it was clearly pushing hard against the back of his lips. "Can you help the structural engineers on board with making sure the rig's supports are still sound?" Jack asked.

Billy shuffled the chewing tobacco around and nodded.

•••

An hour later, Jack was in his cabin speaking on his satellite phone. The deep gravelly voice on the other end

21

belonged to Gordon LeMay.

Head caretaker, groundskeeper, farmer, Gordon had several titles, but in the end, his main responsibility was running the day-to-day at Jack's rescue farm outside of Houston. For the geophysicist, the farm was far more than a hobby, it was his home, and something of a secret passion. While some middle-aged women collected cats, he collected abused and neglected livestock and gave them a safe place to live out their remaining days.

As with many things in Jack's life, he had found his inner Dr. Doolittle little by little. One day on the local news, he'd happened upon the story of a pig farm being shut down for inhumane treatment. The animals were set to be euthanized and the farm put up for auction. Jack had flipped to a baseball game and sat for an hour watching the Astros take a beating. Over the next few days he fought like hell to silence the nagging voice in his head, the one that kept telling him he needed to do something.

Finally, perhaps more out of desperation than duty, Jack had hopped into his truck and raced down to the county clerk's office. He'd asked the woman behind the desk about the farm he'd seen on the news, the one with the animals in a sorry state. The clerk, a larger woman with curls that bounced as she shook her head, had seemed just as distraught. "Such a real pity," she'd told him, her eyes welling up with tears. Turned out the vet was already out there putting them down. Jack got the address from her and bolted, her final words chasing after him out the door. "Good luck, but you're probably too late."

If Jack had spent his life listening to naysayers, he'd probably still be working the oil fields. Twenty minutes later, Jack's truck skidded onto a gravel road and into the farm. An eighteen-wheeler stood next to the barn, its back doors ajar. Piled inside were the bodies of dead pigs. Jack got out of his car and headed for the barn. Inside, he found a man with an apron kneeling on the ground, a needle in one hand. Pinned under his other hand was a piglet. The little thing was no longer than a shoebox.

"Stop," Jack had yelled, only dimly aware of the eerie silence he was shattering.

Two men with animal control windbreakers appeared out of nowhere, their arms raised, palms out. "You can't be here, sir."

"He's the last one, isn't he?" Jack had asked, understanding the situation.

The veterinarian pivoted without raising himself off the ground and nodded. His face was deeply tanned like worn leather. "Believe me, son, I didn't ask for this, but these animals were in a sorry state."

"I don't doubt you. But that's my pig."

The vet looked down at the animal, confused, then back at Jack.

"Fact, this whole place is mine."

"Beg your pardon?"

"It's for sale, isn't it?" Jack said.

The vet's eyes dipped. "Technically, it's going to auction."

"And I'm gonna buy it, along with him." He pointed past the vet to the piglet he was holding on the ground.

"Whatever you say, mister, but this pig ain't a boy, it's a girl." The vet put the cap back on the needle while the animal control officers looked at one another and returned to the truck. "Gordon LeMay," the man said, removing his glove, and extended his hand to Jack. "You're one crazy son of a bitch, you know that?"

Jack laughed. Yes, he knew.

Now, back in his cabin on the rig, Gordon's smoky drawl was still droning into his ear.

"I got another leak in the stables, about a mile of

broken fences and two farm hands eager to get paid."

Jack sighed. Being impulsive had a funny way of landing you in piles of shit up to your elbows. There was no way to sugarcoat things. The farm was falling apart, had been for years. Restoring it to full functionality would require more cash than Jack had on hand. Between prior scientific expeditions, he'd started doing seismic work for mining companies. Had even developed something of a sixth sense when it came to finding diamond deposits. Another reason why DiCore had agreed to come on board with little more than Jack's word and a few pages of data. But even the money he made moonlighting hadn't been enough.

"The horses and pigs, do they have enough to eat?" Jack asked, rubbing the pads of his fingers together.

"They do."

"George too?" George was Jack's llama, a temperamental beast that nipped at everyone but him.

"George is as big a bastard as ever," Gordon informed him merrily. "And the goats are fine. All the animals are perfectly healthy."

A sense of relief washed over Jack. "Inside the safe in my office you'll find the emergency cash reserve. Use what's there to make repairs and pay the boys. I'll wire you more as soon as I have it."

Gordon agreed and hung up.

Jack was still eyeing the sat phone in his hand when a knock came at his cabin door. He opened it to find Rajesh. Jack nudged past him into the corridor. "Your girlfriend not with you?"

Rajesh looked momentarily confused, an expression magnified by his glasses, which were bent out of shape. "That's why I've come. She has completed compiling the data from the latest scan."

The time it took to compile a seismic scan was usually measured in days, not hours. "You won't impress

24

me by lying, Rajesh," Jack said, suddenly feeling bad for the MIT professor.

"I assure you, I'm telling the truth. She has also begun cleaning up the large dark splotch on the seismic surveys."

"How long did she take on the first one?"

Rajesh's eyes flickered to a space above Jack's head. "Um, one hour, thirty-five minutes, ten seconds."

"And the second?"

"One hour, twenty minutes, thirty-two seconds."

Jack felt the blood rush up his neck and into his face. "But she had to compile the second scan from scratch."

"That's what I was trying to explain in my presentation, Dr. Greer. She accessed your servers on board the rig and fine-tuned the multi-attribute full waveform inversion algorithm you were using. It's now far more efficient."

For once, Jack was speechless. "So the seismic scans are cleaner?"

"More than clean," Rajesh said, his forehead furrowing. "They show something I've never seen before."

•••

Jack sat near the television screen as Gabby dimmed the lights. Assembled in the conference room with them were the usual suspects.

Gabby's gaze fell on Billy. "I believe you had something you wanted to say?"

Gone was the wad of chewing tobacco from before. So too was the chip on his shoulder. He stared down at the table, his index finger making a series of rapid circles over a knot of wood. "Two things. The first is that the rig's anchor lines show no sign of structural damage, so we don't need to abandon ship or anything." A spattering of nervous laughter streaked through the room. "And for the other… Look, I knew carrying on

25

drilling when we weren't sure what we were biting into was risky. At the time, I didn't put up much of a fight. But when all hell broke loose I ran. That's the part that bothers me. I've been in scrapes my whole life and never chickened out. So for that, I wanna apologize to all of you."

Jack rose, acknowledging Bill's apology. "When you make an executive decision, you need to share the good and own the bad. I took a risk that nearly got people killed. If anyone needs to step up, it's me." Jack held his hand out before him. "The truth is I saw the finish line and all I wanted to do was cross it. I got us into the situation. I'm just thankful I had an opportunity to get us out." Jack settled back into his chair. The chief engineer looked surprised. He'd probably figured Jack was about to throw him under the bus. If that was so, the kid had a lot to learn about Jack Greer.

With that out of the way, Gabby loaded a scan of the ocean floor onto the screen. It showed where the drill had sliced through the limestone. But even the untrained could spot the gaping hundred-foot fissure that had opened along the fault line.

"Looks like we triggered some kind of earthquake," Dag said, pulling at the ends of his long red beard. "Split the ocean floor wide open."

"There's more," Gabby told them. She swapped images, revealing the scan of the meteorite Anna had just finished sharpening.

Silence descended over the room as those assembled attempted to make sense of the image before them.

"The hell is that thing?" Billy asked, sliding forward in his seat, his face scrunching up like a tight fist.

Jack studied the shape of the unusual object, the sloping angle of the outer edges. Could it be a natural formation? It looked like a... he wanted to say pyramid. But no, that wasn't right. Couldn't be right. "Gabby, pull out a little, would you?" he asked her. She went to the laptop and did as he suggested. The geometrical shape shifted, although it was no less startling. What they were seeing wasn't a triangle, it was something else—and it bore the distinct shape of an enormous diamond.

"Well, DiCore will be thrilled," Dag said, trying to lighten the mood without much success.

Everyone in the room was perched forward, their mouths frozen open. Others had left their seats almost robotically in order to approach for a better look.

Of course Dag's attempt at a joke only underscored what everyone already knew. Geologic forces didn't cut diamonds to fit engagement rings, nor did it make them anywhere near this large. Initial estimates had the object clocked in at a mile long and half as tall. Mystified as they were, one thing was clear, this object was no meteorite.

Chapter 6

After a long shower and an all-too-brief phone conversation with her daughter, Mia headed to the resto bar downstairs. She would grab a quick bite and then hightail it back to catch some much-needed sleep. Tomorrow promised to be a full day and she wanted to make the most of it.

Mia slid onto a seat at the end of the bar and ordered a glass of red and a bowl of Moqueca, a Brazilian fish stew with diced tomatoes and cooked shrimp. A large window in the restaurant faced onto the Amazon. Warm fingers of fading light danced along the water's edges, creating a mesmerizing spectacle. It boasted of being one of the longest rivers in the world, second only to the Nile. From here it also looked like one of the muddiest.

Gradually, a sound from above jockeyed for her attention. It was another darn TV. The folks on CNN had a new bone to chew on. But now, rather than covering Cuba's artificial-island-building campaign and the growing military tensions in the Gulf of Mexico, they were obsessing over the strange "flash felt by millions". Hundreds of fender-benders had been reported, and yet the cause of the anomaly was still unknown. Not surprisingly, a panel of experts had taken up the challenge and were at this very moment shouting at one another in what was fast becoming the latest form of gladiatorial combat: the pundit wars. It wasn't enough anymore to feature differing opinions. Those opinions had to battle to the death. Mia could just imagine the producers prepping the guests before a segment. "Two of you will go on air, but only one of you will make it to the commercial break."

The TV flicked off and Mia was silently thankful.

"They've been yammering about the same thing for hours," a man with an Australian accent complained from a few seats down. He was handsome in a rugged sort of way. His dark button-down shirt and taupe pants looked like they'd spent the better part of a week trekking through the bush. Sitting next to his draft beer was an expensive-looking camera. "You'd think those blokes would wait until they knew what they were talking about."

Mia smiled politely, glancing around for reinforcements and finding none. Two couples sat eating at tables nearby, engaged in quiet conversation.

"Oh, don't worry," he said. "I won't bite." He started back for his beer, thought better of it and leaned over, offering his hand. "Ollie Cooper," he said, pronouncing his last name 'coopaw'.

Smiling, Mia introduced herself. "I take it you're not a reporter," she said, referring to his rant.

"Hell, no," he said, chuckling. He took a long swig of his beer and set it on the bar with a wink. "I'm a sniper."

Mia wiggled her head, confused. "A sniper?"

Ollie raised the camera and clicked off three random shots. Clack, clack, clack. "I'm what you civilians might call a photographer. On assignment for *National Geographic*. Doing a story on the Assurini people. Did you know that some of them have never seen a white man before? When kids spot you entering their village, they run screaming bloody murder to their parents. Tall and

29

pasty, we must look to them like a bunch of freakin'
aliens." Ollie burst out laughing, a warm twinkle in his
eye. When he was done, he studied her intently for a
moment. "My money says you're here with Oxfam."

Mia sipped at her wine, relishing the vintage, cheap
as it was. "WHO," she corrected him, feeling somehow
ashamed for being so transparent.

"Even better. You a doctor?"

"Researcher."

"Ah, I see. Diseases?"

"Strike three," she said and pulled away, returning to
her meal.

A moment later, she glanced over. He was still
watching her, that twinkle brighter than ever.

A loud scream behind them drew her attention. Mia
spun and saw a woman sprawled on the floor, clutching
her leg and moaning in agony. She popped out of her
seat and rushed over. The woman was somewhere in her
late thirties and in relatively good shape. She and her
husband were tourists and dressed the part.

"Ma'am, what happened?"

The woman winced. "When I stood up I heard a
snapping sound and my leg gave way."

Mia followed the woman's pant leg to where the
fabric was pushed out and stained with blood. The bone
had broken through the skin.

Ollie stood nearby, a pained expression on his face.
"I think you better call an ambulance," he told the
husband, who nodded and ran into the lobby, shouting
at the concierge.

Mia felt a wave of unease wash over her. The femur
bone in a young, healthy woman didn't just snap. She
and Ollie stayed with them until the ambulance arrived.

"Madam, your food," the barman said, motioning to
the plate he'd just deposited.

"Would you have it sent to my room?" Mia asked,

still trying to shake free from the sense that something wasn't quite right.

••••

At eight o'clock the next morning, Carlos brought the team to the Santarem Municipal Hospital. No sooner had they entered when they were struck by a blur of movement and a cacophony of voices. The emergency waiting room, nearly empty the day before, was now overflowing. Some were on crutches, others sat with bandaged hands and faces. Mia thought immediately of the woman in the hotel dining room the night before.

What on earth is going on?

Isabella, the WHO regional director, scurried past them.

Mia called out after her. "Was there an accident?"

Isabella shrugged. "I'm trying to find out myself."

"Maybe Eric and I should lend a hand," Scott suggested, scanning the waiting room. "Both of us are practicing doctors. We may not speak much Portuguese, but I'm sure we can find someone to interpret for us."

Mia agreed, feeling utterly helpless she couldn't do more. "Call us on the intercom if you need anything," she told them. "I'll have someone add you both to the roster."

After struggling through the crowd of patients and their relatives, Mia and Maria headed for the craniofacial research ward. Once there, they found a similarly chaotic situation.

"Get us two face masks," Mia said, in case the sudden appearance of symptoms had been caused by a virus or bacteria. Isabella was standing by the nurse's station.

Mia began by handing masks to both Isabella and the nurse. "It's obvious you're as surprised as we are," Mia said. "I suggest you instruct all your staff to immediately begin wearing proper protective gear. I also believe you

31

should begin taking blood samples and testing them for every known bacterial infection and virus you can think of."

Isabella nodded her agreement, but her eyes already looked a little vacant.

Mia turned to the nurse. "Swab the mouth of everyone who's exhibiting any signs of a rash or signs of osteoporosis." The latter was a disease more common among the elderly and characterized by low bone mass. Often when Grandma fell it wasn't the impact with the ground that broke her hip. In many cases, the broken hip was what had led to the fall.

So far, the first day of the rest of Mia's life was getting off to a glorious start.

Chapter 7

Not surprisingly, shortly after the object's discovery, the meeting on the rig had rapidly deteriorated as each member of the team argued over what they had found. While the sense of curiosity in the room was strong, so too were feelings of fear and apprehension. When it became obvious that voices were only getting louder, Jack called for a break. Maybe a breath of fresh air would do them some good.

Shortly after, Jack found Gabby on a walkway overlooking the ocean, her silver hair tousled from a salty breeze.

"This isn't what any of us signed up for," Gabby said with unusual vigor as he approached. It was as though the words had been building up for a while, like tectonic plates compressed and waiting for a chance to snap free.

"We need to go down there," Jack replied, dimly aware that she had already offered a rebuttal.

"Jack, you can't be serious. We don't even know what it is."

Jack clasped his hands together. "Exactly, we don't know. And isn't it our job as scientists to find out? For all we know the thing is man-made, a relic from Atlantis or Lemuria. Wouldn't Grant be thrilled?" He chuckled, alone.

"That 'thing,' as you call it, has been down there for millions of years and when our drill made contact, it nearly sucked the entire rig into the ocean. I don't believe in little green men, but I know for a fact it's not from around here."

"I'll give you that."

"The best course of action might be to contact the government or the newspapers," she said, her gaze darting back and forth as though she could see the options materializing before her. "They must have protocols in place for a situation like this."

Jack's hands went up involuntarily. "Calling in the Feds is a terrible idea. Especially since we still don't know what it is. Yes, it's weird and frankly a little creepy, I'll give you that, but…" He removed his cap and stuffed it in his pocket. "Let me ask you this, why are we here?"

She stared back at him, blinking in the sun. "I know very well why we're here, Jack. To dig up the meteorite that may or may not have killed the bloody dinosaurs."

"Precisely," he said, snapping his fingers and feeling the old energy flowing back into him. "And supposing whatever's down there played a part in that?"

Gabby either didn't get his point or didn't want to.

"Come on. Do you really think it's a coincidence we found this thing sitting right where we expected to find that meteorite?"

Red lines formed under Gabby's eyes. For years, he'd known her as a level-headed, pragmatic scientist, ready to venture down any heretical rabbit hole. Seeing this new side of her was almost as unsettling as the object itself.

"I don't believe in coincidences," Gabby said.

"Good, neither do I. A great philosopher once said that only when we face the unknown will we meet ourselves for the first time."

"You just made that up."

"Okay, I did, but it still makes sense."

She fought a grin before pointing her finger at the choppy water below them. "You think this thing struck the earth and wiped out the dinosaurs. Is that what you're suggesting?"

"I'm not saying it, but it's one of many possibilities. The peak rings fit, so does the tsunami and everything else the Alvarez brothers found back in 1980. You wouldn't be doubting me if all we'd stumbled on was a giant space rock, would you?" He spotted the shift in her expression. A battle was raging within her. "I think a part of you is afraid of what we might find down there. I think a part of you is worried it might knock our species off of some imaginary pedestal. Maybe the earth isn't so special after all. Maybe we're little more than a pothole on some galactic highway and here's the guy we gave a flat tire to."

Gabby laid her hands on Jack's shoulders. "I keep coming back to something Stephen Hawking said. That whenever an advanced society encounters a more primitive one, things usually don't turn out well for the latter. Perhaps some things are better left alone."

"This is the tenth—no, the eleventh—research expedition we've been on together. I've seen you stand up to Jivaroan tribesman who were threatening to shrink our heads and talk your way past Rwandan gorilla poachers after we stumbled into their territory. In all that time I've never seen you tuck tail and run."

Gabby's eyes darted away. He was right and she knew it. "That thing's been there for millions of years. Will a few more really change that?"

Jack's tone softened. "We owe it to ourselves and to the world to find out what's down there."

"Aren't you worried it might change things forever?"

He took Gabby's hand and squeezed it gently. "I'm counting on it."

•••

Confident now that Gabby would stick around while they sought answers on their unexpected discovery, Jack made his way to Fifth Avenue, the main strip where the mobile laboratories had been arranged into something resembling a street. The rig had no manned submersible, but it did have an ROV (remotely operated vehicle) named Zeus, the same one the engineering team had relied on to check that the anchors holding the rig in place were still intact.

Jack arrived before a white shipping container. Inside he found Nicola Ganotti, an Italian-born grad student and Rover operator who had joined the expedition from the University of Milan. Early twenties, with a dark forest of hair and a slight gap between his two front teeth, Nicola was hardly a stereotypical northern Italian male. And the contrast had little to do with his lack of fashion sense. Nicola was as smart as a whip, but he struggled to maintain eye contact for longer than a nanosecond.

"How quickly can you get the ROV ready?" Jack asked, sidestepping the pleasantries.

Nicola jumped up from his computer desk and nearly struck his head on a nearby shelf. These containers were not only small, in the wrong hands, they could be downright dangerous.

"Dr. Greer, hello," Nicola said, rubbing his palms along the top of his windbreaker pants. A full second went by before he held out his hand.

Jack obliged. "Can your people have it ready within the hour?"

"Zeus is ready right now if you need him," Nicola said, nodding at the computer monitor. "We just finished inspecting the anchors and the cables for structural damage, but I mean, we can reconfigure him in a jiffy for whatever you need."

Jack got on his walkie. "Gabby, you there?" A few moments went by without a reply. "Gabby, pick up."

The line fed back a wall of static. They had been chatting a few minutes ago. She couldn't be far. Jack decided to change tracks. "Dag, you reading me?"

"Loud and clear, boss," the Swede shot back. "I'm with Rajesh and Anna in the mess hall. Did you know she has access to every scholarly article ever written? Hey, man, how mind-blowing is that?" He still had trouble using 'man' in a sentence without sounding like the leader of a commune.

"It's wild," Jack answered, not sharing Dag's enthusiasm at the moment. "We're sending Zeus down into the crevasse to get a better look at this thing. I'll pipe the feed into the control room on deck five. Have Gabby and Grant join you." Jack clicked off for a moment as he went back and forth in his mind. "And bring Anna along too."

Chapter 8

Scott plopped a wad of paper printouts on the desk, causing the electron microscope Mia had been working with to tremble.

She threw him a stern look. "Be careful, would you? This thing costs more than your house."

He rubbed his bloodshot eyes and then adjusted his surgical mask. "Here are the results from the blood tests we ran."

Her phone began to ring and Mia reached into her pocket and sent it to voicemail. It was probably her daughter Zoey. Right now, however, these blood tests were her top priority. Mia scanned down the first page before flipping to the next and beginning the process anew. Scott stood watching her. She glanced up. "Why am I getting the distinct impression you've already gone over this?"

He bit the side of his lip and nodded.

"Any bacterial infections or viruses?"

"They were all over the map. About ten percent of the patients we tested had Hepatitis C. A couple others had STDs. The rest were clean." Scott plucked an apple out of his pocket, pulled down his mask and took a bite.

"So what's at play here?" she asked. "Kinda hard not to see a connection with the flash of light the night before, but then again, you would have expected more patients with eye issues."

"I agree. Maybe we're dealing with some sort of radiation leak," he speculated, biting off another chunk from his apple.

Mia went back to the electron microscope and intensified the magnification. "Take a look at this and tell me what you think."

He slid in next to her and peered at the display. The patient's chromosomes had been spread over the sample plate. Through the eyepiece, they resembled a series of puffy X's. "Looks like alphabet soup to me."

She pointed to them one at a time, identifying chromosome one, two, three, all the way up to twenty-two followed by the sex chromosomes. In all, humans had twenty-three pairs of chromosomes (strands of DNA encoded with genes) made up from forty-six individual chromatids. The two chromatids of a duplicated chromosome were held together at a region of DNA called the centromere, giving it the classic X shape.

"So then what's this extra chromatid doing all by its lonesome?"

"That forty-seventh chromatid," she informed him, "is Salzburg syndrome."

Scott's eyes grew wide and his head cocked to one side. "Salz-what? Never heard of it."

"That's because it was only discovered a few years ago by a guy named Alan Salzburg, a brilliant scientist and a grade-A asshole."

"Sounds like you know this guy."

Mia frowned. "I used to work in his lab, but that was before he discovered Salzburg. During my time there, I became obsessed with creating a fully functional human artificial chromosome. When I finally cracked the problem, Alan swooped in and took all the credit."

Scott's face squished up. "Ouch."

"And when I protested he made my life a living hell and so much more."

"So much more?"

"Maybe another time," Mia said, feeling that old simmering anger rushing back in. "It was sometime after I left that someone in the lab discovered a new and extremely rare genetic disorder. Not surprisingly, they named it Salzburg syndrome after the guy who probably did next to nothing to find it."

"You know, this Alan guy sure reminds me of Thomas Edison," Scott said. "Saw this brilliant documentary on the BBC not long ago." He ran his fingers through his hair and scratched at his skull. "The bloke had a nasty habit of stealing other people's inventions and passing them off as his own. He was a top-notch wanker."

"Asshole or not, I do have to admit the discovery was an important one," Mia said. "Each of a chromosome's chromatids contains either a dominant or recessive version of a given gene. When children are born with an extra chromosome it's usually because a third copy was made, a condition called trisomy which leads to conditions like Down syndrome. The difference here is the single Salzburg chromatid isn't a duplicate, the DNA inside of it is entirely new and no one knows where it came from." Mia eyed the electron microscope display. "Thankfully, Salzburg is exceptionally rare. Which is probably why it hasn't gotten more attention."

"Define rare," Scott said, the apple held in his now limp hand.

"Well, Down syndrome, for example, occurs in roughly one out of every seven hundred births. Salzburg, on the other hand, shows up in about one in ten thousand. Except here's the really strange part. Salzburg doesn't only show up at birth. It can appear at any age, like cancer. Sometimes people don't even know they

40

have it."

"And what about the rest of the patients we swabbed?" he asked.

"That's what has me so confused," she said, shaking her head in disbelief. "I found Salzburg in every one of them."

She and Scott stood in silence for a moment, pondering what she'd just said. Mia's phone broke the spell. Once again, she reached into her pocket and killed it.

His gaze shifted to her pocket. "Zoey again?"

"Probably," Mia said, grinning away the many unanswered questions swirling around in her head. Among them: how could a recently discovered and exceptionally rare disorder suddenly be present in huge swaths of the local population?

Still uncertain, Mia removed her phone, plugged in her passcode and glanced down at her screen. She continued to stare for several seconds, her emotions running the gamut from confusion to disbelief. She wondered whether she was dreaming, but the cramps forming in her stomach told her this was no dream. She blinked hard, but the display on her phone never changed. It read:

Missed Call:
Alan Salzburg

Chapter 9

The descent toward the fissure in the seabed took the better part of an hour. While Nicola operated the rover by tweaking Zeus' thrusters, other members of the ROV team fed the submersible's fiberoptic cable and power supply. A third monitored the machine's vital signs. Powerful LED lights on the bow illuminated the surroundings.

"Wow, that's quite a gash," Nicola said through his headset as the fault line came into view.

"Grant, you notice anything unusual?" Jack asked the biologist, who was with Gabby up in the control room.

"I see a total absence of marine life," Grant exclaimed. "Even the coral has disappeared."

"Assuming it was there to begin with," Jack said. This was yet another reason he made a point of speaking with the local fishermen while out in the field. They were often rich repositories of information on conditions along the ocean floor.

"We are now entering the fault line," Nicola announced.

"Three hundred meters," a voice from Nicola's team called out.

The sheer edge of a cliff face drifted by the camera as the sub continued its descent. This went on for several minutes as the voice rattled off the depth readings every fifty meters. Frustratingly, the ROV's nose had to remain level, at least until they exited the crevasse. When they reached five hundred meters or fifteen hundred feet, Jack felt his pulse begin to quicken, only barely aware his index finger and thumb were doing a slow, pensive dance.

Then the bottom edge appeared. The rover left the wide fissure and descended into an immense underwater chamber. It felt to Jack as though they were entering another world. He recalled spelunking at Grotte di Teulada in Italy and the similar feeling it gave him. Slowly, the roof of this colossal underwater cathedral faded from view and a new shape began to materialize from out of the darkness. Jack's heart really began to thump a wild beat in his neck.

"Oh, boy, would you look at that," Dag said as it came into view.

A slightly rounded metal tip loomed against a backdrop of marine sediment. Watching the particles whiz past them gave the eerie impression of being in outer space.

"Get in a little closer," Jack told Nicola, who tweaked the ROV joystick between his fingers.

The object was so massive, they couldn't see all of it at once. Three *Titanics* set bow to stern would still come up short.

The ROV came to within fifty feet.

"No reflection off the metal," Grant said in amazement. "As though it's absorbing the light."

The ROV was rotating to the left when Anna's soothing female voice came on the line. "Dr. Greer, please angle the camera ten degrees to the south?"

Nicola looked at Jack, who nodded for him to comply.

The nose dipped.

"Closer, please," she said.

Once again, Nicola obeyed.

"Closer, please," Anna repeated.

The ROV was less than five feet away. Any closer might risk an impact.

There were markings etched into the otherwise smooth hull. They looked like pictographs, maybe hieroglyphics.

"I hope to hell you're recording all this," Jack told Nicola.

Nicola assured him he was.

Grant cleared his throat. "Given no one else looks inclined to admit the obvious, I suppose I'll be the one to come right out and say it. My terminology might be off, but I believe the gents at SETI would call this first contact."

Jack let out a long shuddering breath. "What do you make of those symbols?" he asked no one in particular.

"Scientists spent decades decoding the Mayan glyphs," Dag said. "Even Anna isn't that good."

"Insufficient data," Anna added, confirming Dag's point.

"Duly noted," Jack replied.

They worked their way down the smooth gunmetal surface, a veritable wall of grey. Within less than a minute the subtle outline of circular seams broke up the uniform finish. There were about three dozen of them. They varied in size and were arranged in rows from large to small. Soon a darker shape appeared on the object's outer hull.

"Whoa, go back up," Jack demanded. "What was that?"

"It went by so quick, I didn't get a good look," Grant said.

"Looked like a big porthole to me," Dag offered, uncertain.

Jack thought otherwise, but kept it to himself. The ROV's descent slowed before it began climbing back to the mystery spot. Nicola stopped as soon as the dark object came into view. What they had seen wasn't a window. It was a three-foot-diameter hole in the hull. Had it been cut? But the edges were perfectly smooth, not ragged the way you'd expect if industrial torches had been used. Besides, it was hard to believe a ship that had potentially crash-landed on Earth without suffering so much as a scratch could be cut by anything known to man.

The ROV was drawing a touch closer when it dawned on him. Perhaps the opening had not been from someone cutting their way inside. He thought of the other seams he'd spotted nearby, arranged like missile tubes on a nuclear submarine. Maybe it hadn't been a way in, but a way out. The idea sent cold fingers darting along his spine. Gabby's soft disembodied voice echoed in his ear. Was it possible she had been right? That this colossal structure was better left in its watery grave as it had been for millions of years?

Just then a real voice cut into the frequency. "Dr. Greer, it's Billy. The Navy's here."

Jack looked up, alarmed. For some reason, his mind had gone immediately to the Cuban pilot tied to his hospital bed in the rig's infirmary. Had the Cubans shown up to collect their imprisoned comrade?

International incidents aside, there was a far bigger reason to be worried, and Jack was staring at it through the ROV's forward-mounted camera.

Chapter 10

The MH-60S Seahawk helicopter was already on the landing pad by the time Jack exited the shipping container and climbed the stairs to the rig's upper level. A group of six sailors in tactical gear, their weapons in the low ready position, swept toward him. Following behind them was a self-assured US Navy officer adorned in a khaki uniform and beige cap. In his hand was a silver briefcase. The armed sailors rushed past Jack and down the stairs, splitting off in two directions like water moving around a boulder.

"This is a private scientific installation," Jack shouted after them as they sped by. When he swung back around he found himself face to face with the officer. The Navy man's lips peeled back into a dimpled smile. A molar capped in gold winked as it caught a ray of sunlight. Behind him were two other armed men, both dressed differently than the group that had just gone by.

"Rear Admiral Thomas P. Stark Jr.," he said, offering his hand. A silver star was pinned to each pointed collar. Above his left breast pocket sat several rows of colored ribbons and above that a golden officer's pin. When Jack failed to return the shake, Stark removed his cap and tucked it under the bend in his arm. His hair was blond and tightly cropped, like a well-mown lawn. Average height and weight, he was fit for his age, somewhere in his mid-fifties, Jack guessed.

"I know why you're here," Jack said, wondering if Stark's men were already plucking the Cuban pilot, Fuentes, out of his hospital bed.

Stark's eyes narrowed. "I thought you might."

"We were the ones who scooped him out of the drink. If the Cubans want him, they can come get him themselves. I have no interest in having my people used as political pawns."

"Little late for that," Stark said. Those dimples were back in full force. He held up the briefcase. "Is there any place we can talk?"

•••

Jack led them to one of the vacant shipping containers. It had been intended as a lab to study rock samples, but after discovering the object, all that business had stopped cold. He got on his walkie and called for Gabby again. As co-chief, she should be here for whatever was about to take place. By the third try she finally answered and agreed to come down.

The space was tight. Both of the armed men next to Stark removed their helmets.

"This is Commander Hart," Stark said. Athletic and deceptively powerful for his size, Hart sported a goatee with twisted edges, reminiscent of a gunslinger from the old west. The rest of his face had the sunbaked look of a surfer.

Stark pushed a few scientific instruments out of the way and placed his briefcase on the table. "And this here is Lieutenant Olsen."

The two men couldn't have been more opposite. While Hart was average height and wiry, Olsen was well over six foot two and stout. He was also a shade lighter, except for patches around the eyes where he wore his Oakley sunglasses. Unlike Hart, Olsen was neatly shaved, giving his face a youthful appearance.

"They're Navy SEALs," Stark said, letting the announcement hang in the air.

"I know all about the SEALs," Jack said, cutting him off. "When I was a kid, I read everything I could about Kennedy's time in office. For a while I couldn't decide between a career in the Navy or as a geophysicist."

Stark grinned. "No regrets, I hope, Dr. Greer."

"Only on days like today," Jack said. He was trying his best to keep cool, but all he could think about was the object they'd seen down below. More than that, he couldn't help wondering what the military would do if they found out.

At last, Gabby arrived, swinging open the large metal door. "There are soldiers in the infirmary…" she began before she saw Stark and the others. "The hell is going on here?"

"That's precisely what we'd like to know," Stark replied, introducing himself and the SEALs.

Gabby shuffled past them and over to where Jack was standing, holding her elbows.

"While this rig might be *your* office, mine is sailing a few miles from here. It's called the USS *Dwight D. Eisenhower* and it's surrounded by an entire carrier strike group. We're in the area on orders from the President, tasked with stopping a Communist state from illegally expanding its borders."

"You're talking about Cuba building those artificial islands," Jack offered.

"You betcha," Stark replied. "And who do you think they learned that little trick from? Well, it might work in the South China Sea, but it sure as hell ain't gonna happen in our own backyard, not on my watch. So if it's all the same to you, I intend to take that aviator into custody."

"Aviator," Gabby said, confused. "Have you been

listening to our calls?"

"Not us, ma'am," Commander Hart said. "The NSA."

"And if we say no?" Jack replied, wondering why Stark was even bothering to ask. Especially given Fuentes had likely been loaded onto the chopper already. "I didn't save this guy so you could use him in some game of international diplomacy."

"Fuentes won't be harmed," Stark assured them, collecting his briefcase from the table. "But we will be taking credit for the rescue."

Jack shook his head. "I don't give a crap about credit."

"Thank you both for your understanding then, and your time," Stark said. He turned and took two purposeful steps toward the container door, both SEALs in tow, before stopping. "Oh, there's one other thing."

The muscles in Jack's jaw tightened. "This is a scientific research expedition. We've had no contact with the Cubans, if that's what you're worried about."

"No," Stark assured them. "But I am worried about this." He set the briefcase back down, removed a piece of paper and handed it to Jack and Gabby.

It was a graph with a giant spike along the Y axis.

"What am I looking at?" Jack asked, a feeling of dread creeping up his throat.

"A gift, this one from our friends at NASA," Stark explained. He swung his arm in circles above him. "One of those fancy satellites they have floating around up there. Designed to detect gamma ray bursts. You science types probably know more about those than I do."

Also sometimes referred to as cosmic rays, GRBs were high-energy photons originating from outside of the solar system and in many cases outside the galaxy. Since their discovery in the mid-sixties, astrophysicists had suspected GRBs were caused by supernovae or the collision of two neutron stars. A single gamma ray photon was a million times more energetic than a regular photon. Luckily for us, the earth's ozone layer filtered most of the harmful radiation they carried, although astronauts had been particularly vulnerable.

"I know what they are," Gabby told them. "It's my field, but I don't see how that has anything…" Her gaze wandered away from the rear admiral's face and up to the ceiling, a habit she had whenever her mind was working overtime.

"Did either of you experience any flashing lights recently?"

Jack shook his head while Gabby nodded yes. They looked at one another.

The smile was back on Stark's lips. "Of course you experienced it. Remember the spike on that graph I showed you? Well the folks at NASA started crunching some numbers and calculated the point the burst originated from as well as how far out it reached." Stark handed them another piece of paper.

Jack stared down, his fingers feeling numb. He wasn't sure whether he felt more frightened or shocked. The picture Stark handed them showed a satellite image of the Yucatán Peninsula. Superimposed over that was an area of effect which reached as far south as Brazil and as far north as the United States. Directly in the center of the blast circle was the rig.

The gamma ray explanation made sense. Jack remembered watching a program in which astronauts reported flashes of light whenever cosmic rays impacted their optic nerves.

The joy drained from Stark's face. "First things first, I need to know what kind of experiments you folks are running here. After that I've got orders to shut you down and ship you all back to the United States."

"Fat chance," Jack protested. "We're not going

anywhere. And we didn't create any gamma ray burst."

"That's too bad," Stark said, shaking his head and closing his briefcase shut with a snap.

Gabby stepped forward. "Too bad? What's that supposed to mean?"

Her concern was obvious and well-warranted. They were on the threshold of perhaps the greatest scientific discovery in human history. And here they were watching it get snatched away. It was beyond infuriating.

"I had hoped you two might be able to shed some light on something else the NASA folks told us."

Jack shook his head, utterly confused. "About the gamma ray, you mean?"

Admiral Stark nodded. "Yes, those eggheads at NASA claim to have detected some kind of binary code embedded in the signal."

Chapter 11

Mia returned to the hotel, feeling like a sponge wrung dry. The lobby, slippery with white tiles, was empty except for a tired-looking clerk behind the desk. Mia had come to Brazil to study craniofacial anomalies in the hopes of developing preventions and perhaps even treatments that might offer hope to individuals and families struck by the genetic disorder. But that wasn't the whole story, was it?

The truth was, Mia had spent the last four years of her life clawing her way out of an abyss of pain pills and dark depression. The agony of hearing those words, even when they were only in her head, still seared like a hot knife. Invariably, addiction was a self-defeating condition. And on an intellectual level, she understood that now, along with the reality that the more we tried to deny the truth of who we were and what we had done, the more we empowered the negative forces which got us into trouble in the first place. It didn't help that substance abuse and the ravages of addiction had been prevalent themes in her early childhood.

Earlier, she had told Scott she had quit the lab, but technically speaking that hadn't been entirely accurate. She and Alan had slept together, a personal tidbit she did not think was any of Scott's business. And it wasn't long after that Alan had fired her. He was nearly thirty years older than her and certainly not her type. But there was something about a man at the top of his game that was irresistible, intoxicating. She'd had a husband who loved her and a daughter who worshipped the ground she walked on. What had she been missing? Clearly nothing.

It had started and ended at a conference. One second they were at the bar drinking mojitos, dreaming about the Nobel Prize for Physiology or Medicine and laughing their heads off. The next thing she knew she was waking up in his hotel room without a stitch of clothing on. The feeling had been surreal and incredibly disturbing, much like the way she was feeling now.

Alan had stood over her, buttoning his shirt. "You were a naughty girl last night." His voice was deep and resonating.

Mia's face had twisted with shame. What on earth had she done? A question she meant quite literally. What had happened the night before? She posed the question to Alan, who only chuckled and leaned in to brush the back of his fingers against her cheek. When she recoiled, she saw a flash of anger in his eyes.

"I hope you're not going to go all bitchy on me now," he said, his normally melodic tone menacing.

She felt tears struggling past her eyelids and squelched them back. "After the bar I don't remember a thing. How we got back to your room." She knew they'd been having a fun time, but she'd been anxious to get back to her own room to call Paul and Zoey and wish them a good night. How had it ended up like this?

Alan held out a hand to help her up. She hesitated. He wiggled his fingers encouragingly. She accepted and he pulled her onto her feet and into his arms. Mia placed her palms against his chest and pushed away as he pulled her closer to him.

"Whatever happened last night," she said, finally

53

breaking free, "was a mistake."

Alan shook his head and grinned. "I remember exactly what happened." He centered his index finger over his lips. "Don't worry, it'll be our little secret."

Mia felt her stomach turn in a slow, lazy circle. Alan's threat was as apparent as the tufts of hair pushing out the top of his shirt. Between the two of them, she had the most to lose. Alan's wife was buried up at Oakwood and he was a distinguished researcher. Her entire career lay before her, while at home she had a beautiful family who waited impatiently for her return.

She had thrown on the few articles of clothing she could find and run from the room, hot tears streaming down her cheeks. The next few days had been spent trying to pull herself together. Had she suffered a serious lapse in judgment lubricated by a few too many mojitos? Or had Alan put something in her drink? Mia never found out, but one thing was certain. She would never make either mistake again.

In spite of her disturbing encounter with Alan at the conference, it was shortly afterward that she had made the breakthrough on the human artificial chromosome. The greatest challenge had been integrating DNA into the new structure. Once that challenge had been overcome it now meant the new synthetic chromosome could be loaded with as many genes as needed. Turning that corner had been a major turning point not only for Mia but for the future of gene therapy.

Only days later, while she'd been sitting at home watching the news one night, a story had come on detailing her breakthrough. But to her utter astonishment, Alan had been the one to call the press conference, using it as an opportunity to take all the credit for himself. Mia wasn't out for glory, but since it had been her work which had led to the breakthrough, the idea of holding a press conference behind her back felt unconscionable. Her repeated calls that night had gone straight to his voicemail. As a result, it was only the following day at the lab that she'd let him have it. But Alan wasn't the kind of man who did well being lectured by those he felt were beneath him.

She'd soon found herself out of a job. That part hadn't been terribly surprising. But what came next had shocked her to the core. An anonymous email dripping with lies had arrived in Paul's inbox, informing him that Alan and Mia had been having an affair for years.

That evening, Paul had confronted her, demanding to know if it was true. She came clean about the night at the conference, tried to explain there were stretches of time she couldn't account for, but he was convinced she was downplaying her involvement. He saw and resented how much she admired Alan. Had been suspicious for months that there was more to their relationship than she was willing to admit. And now all of his concerns were proving right. He left with Zoey that very night to stay with his parents in South Carolina. Five days later, despondent and feeling like all she wanted was to fall asleep and never wake up again, Mia had been served with divorce papers.

It was following that little bombshell that the pills had entered the picture: OxyContin, Xanax, Vicodin. Anything to hold back the crushing torment tearing at her soul. By the time she got picked up for driving under the influence and wrapping her Hyundai hatchback around a light post, Mia's life had already hit rock bottom.

"Missus Ward," a distant voice called out to her as she waited for the elevator.

A hand touched her shoulder and she jumped with fright.

"Oh, I'm sorry, Missus Ward," the front desk attendant said, backing away. "This package came for you earlier today." He glanced down at the label. "Overnight delivery."

He handed her a fat brown paper parcel with her name on it. *To the care of Dr. Mia Ward.* Stenciled in dark capital letters on the top and bottom was the word *FRAGILE*. The white packing slip had the initials *AS* and an address in Richmond, Virginia.

Mia thought of the two missed calls she'd received from Alan earlier. After everything he'd done, what possible reason could he have for sending her this package? He had to know she'd be tempted to dump it in the Amazon. So why take that chance? Whatever was going on, it had to be serious.

Chapter 12

Mia hurried to her hotel room and locked the door once inside. She leaned back, the hard wood pressing into her spine. With trembling hands, Mia studied the parcel.

This afternoon, after she saw Alan had tried to call her, Mia had swallowed as much of the anger and loathing as she could and dialed him back a dozen times. But each new call had ended the same as the last. Alan never answered and she hadn't bothered leaving a message.

Some sort of medical emergency was sweeping large parts of North and South America, one she didn't understand just yet. But her gut told her it had something to do with Salzburg syndrome, the disorder Alan's lab had catalogued a few years back. If speaking with a sworn enemy might help her patients, perhaps even save lives, then she was perfectly willing to bite the bullet and see what he could tell her.

Bounding over to the table, she fished out a small pocket knife from her knapsack and used the three-inch blade to slice through reams of clear packing tape. Clearly Alan had been paranoid the ends of the envelope might tear open in transit. He must have also paid a handsome price to have it shipped overnight to Brazil. It spoke volumes, especially for a notoriously cheap guy who'd once demanded that lab technicians provide their own latex gloves.

Mia finished cutting through the tape and set the knife down on the table. She froze. How was it that Alan knew she was here? Had he contacted the WHO headquarters and used his considerable pull within the medical research community to locate her? Or had one of their mutual colleagues said something, not realizing the extent of the bad blood between them?

With the package now open, Mia stuck a hand inside the thick, bubble-wrapped envelope and brought out a digital voice recorder. Next she found a notebook. Wiggling the empty envelope, Mia heard something rattling around at the bottom. Her hand disappeared inside once again, only to emerge a second later with a USB key. Certain now she had everything, she fired up her laptop and plugged the USB into the port. At once, a username and password screen popped up.

She stared at it, her uncertainty quickly morphing into annoyance. This was so Alan to send her an encrypted USB. What was the point of sending her this stuff if she couldn't access it?

When she flipped open the diary, two words in black marker were etched on the inside cover.

Play recorder.

She did as instructed. Soon, Alan's radio-quality voice filled the room. Except he sounded awfully strange, speaking quickly, tripping over his words, as though he had a lot to say and no time to say it in.

"Mia, I need you to listen very carefully to what I'm about to tell you. As soon as this recording is done, I want you to fill the sink in your bathroom and toss this recorder in.

"I know I'm the last person on earth you want to hear from, but there's no one else I can turn to. The package you're holding contains an explosive discovery that has put my life and the lives of those around me in danger. I don't have time to go into detail, but here's all you need to know. Salzburg syndrome is not what we thought it was. It was manufactured and not by us. The chromatid's DNA holds the proof of what I'm saying, a secret message written by those who created it.

"Please keep the material safe until things here cool down. I'll contact you in a few days. And Mia, above all else, trust no one."

Mia swallowed hard, her heart hammering against the walls of her chest. All the moisture in her mouth was gone. What on earth was she to make of this? An encrypted USB and a story about some message hidden inside the DNA of a rare genetic disorder? She got up, steadying herself on a pair of wobbly legs. The digital recorder was still in her hand. She headed for the bathroom, intent on doing as Alan had suggested and dunking it under water. If he really was in danger, why would he involve her? Didn't she already have enough on her plate to deal with? It was true that at the lab he'd often called her his protégée. Maybe he wasn't sure who he could trust anymore.

Mia dumped the recorder in the sink and began filling it with water. It had reached the halfway mark when she heard a knock at her hotel room door.

A jolt of fear sent a rippling current coursing along every nerve ending. She skulked to the door, glancing through the peep hole. The man on the other side was wearing a hotel clerk's uniform, but she didn't recognize his face. After his second knock went unanswered, he scanned both ends of the hallway and produced an electronic room key, inserting it into the slot. Mia heard a click, followed by the sound of the handle being turned. He was trying to get in. But she had locked the bolt. That was when he swore and sent the heel of his boot thudding into the door. The water from the sink had begun to overflow, spilling onto the floor. Mia screamed, her feet slipping on the wet tiles as she recoiled.

But the scream only served to intensify her aggressor's determination. The edges of the door began to splinter. With a burst of adrenaline, Mia threw herself forward and latched the swinging door bar, hoping that might stall him while she tried to escape. She ran toward the window, searching frantically for another exit. A sliding glass door by her bed led onto a small balcony. But her room was six stories up, far too great a height to leap off without snapping every bone in her legs—and maybe even her neck as well.

Mia snatched the backpack off her bed, searching for the pocket knife. The door flew open just as her frantic mind recalled she'd left it on the table. In a panicked blur of speed, she grabbed it and made a break for the balcony. At least there her yelling might alert the police.

The man came forward, bypassing the items from the envelope she'd left on the table. He stepped out onto the balcony. Mia held the knife out between them and let out a terrible shriek. For a moment, it had the desired effect since her assailant hesitated. Down below, a number of pedestrians stopped and craned their heads to see what was happening.

"*Policía, policía,*" she yelled, without any idea if she was even shouting words they understood.

"Put the knife down and come with me," the man said calmly with a heavy accent. He lifted his shirt, revealing the gun in his waistband. "I don't want to have to kill you."

He continued to inch closer, one arm outstretched, the other hand on the hilt of the pistol. With every step, the real estate Mia was occupying on the balcony grew smaller and smaller.

"Get away from me!" she shouted and lashed out

with the blade, slicing a deep gash along his forehead.

The skin split with surprising ease. A gout of blood poured down his face and into his eyes as both his hands went reflexively to the stinging wound.

"You bitch!" he yelped in agony and charged forward in a blind rage. At the last second, Mia dropped down and watched his arms close around empty space, his torso bending over the balcony railing from the momentum. For a moment, his legs lifted into the air and Mia grabbed and pushed upward with every last ounce of strength, watching his bulk counterbalance up and over the other side. He fell through the air in slow motion, his arms and legs wheeling wildly. He hit the ground with a sickening crunch.

Mia peered over the edge, her hands covering her mouth in horror. "Oh, my God, what have I done?"

Down below, a crowd gathered around the dead body. Some of them pointed in her direction. At her feet was the man's pistol, which must have fallen loose as he went over.

Trust no one.

Scooping the gun up with two fingers, she darted back into the hotel room, grabbed her backpack and began stuffing it with whatever she could. In went the gun, a handful of other essentials, as well as Alan's diary and the encrypted USB. She didn't need to be a Nobel laureate to know the police might not believe her story. She had killed a seemingly unarmed man. Sure, he had kicked down the door, but she was a foreigner and he was one of them.

Trust no one.

She got to her splintered hotel room door and her British research assistant, Scott Chapman, appeared. The expression on his face changed the second he realized it was her.

"What happened?" he asked, utterly bewildered.

61

She blew past him.

"You have blood on your face," Scott shouted after her. "If you're hurt, let me help you."

But she was gone. The adrenaline still coursing, she threw open the hotel stairway door and charged into an alley. A police car raced by, its sirens blaring. Mia had no clue where she would go, only that she was a fugitive in a foreign land. As she sprinted down the alley and onto a side street, Alan's final warning kept buzzing through her head.

Chapter 13

There was only so much buffeting a man's psyche could take before he decided he was better off battening down the hatches and diving for safer waters. That was how Jack was feeling after his conversation with Rear Admiral Stark. Much to his surprise, the Navy had known about the downed Cuban pilot in addition to their role in causing the strange gravitational anomaly. Stark had even handed over a few details of his own, namely that the anomaly had been the precursor to a burst of gamma rays and they had detected within said rays some kind of pattern. Stark had refused to elaborate any further, although he had made it clear the scientific personnel on the rig were being evacuated.

Jack had asked him for twenty minutes to speak with his crew in private. He needed to explain to a bunch of cranky scientists why their life's work was being interrupted because of a military standoff in the Gulf. Stark had agreed to ten.

Everyone was assembled in the mess hall, the only enclosed room on the rig that could accommodate a group that size. Among them were scientists from an array of disciplines, plus their attending grad students, as well as the deckhands and support staff. In all they numbered fifty men and women and one synthetic person.

Jack stood before them and cleared his throat. The room was awash with rumors and rampant speculation. "I'm sure none of you need to be told what we found. The Navy has asked us to evacuate, but not because of that." The room erupted in a cacophony. Jack put up his hand and called for silence. "They're under the impression the disruption we experienced was a result of a science experiment gone wrong. Everyone in the area's got an itchy trigger finger. And that burst of gamma rays didn't help the situation. The scientific directive as outlined by the US Geological Survey and DiCore has also been put on hold. I'll therefore be recommending that all non-essential personnel be relocated to the US mainland. That includes the drilling team, most of the deckhands and any scientists and grad students who wish to leave."

"What about you?" Dag shouted from the back of the mess hall, near the serving line.

"I'm not going anywhere. I hope Rear Admiral Stark and his superiors will see the wisdom in what I intend to propose."

Gabby rose to her feet, gripping Billy Brenner's shoulder as she did so. "You wanna go into that thing, don't you?"

Jack felt his hands pull out of his pockets and rest on his hips, a subconscious posture of guilt.

"We don't know what's down there, Jack," Gabby snapped. "What if they decide to blow it up?"

Grant, seated nearby, broke into a gale of laughter. "Gabby, you and I both know they would never do such a thing. Imagine for a moment an ancient Greek scientist got his hands on a smartphone. Sure, he might never be able to figure out exactly how it worked, but that certainly wouldn't stop him from taking the thing apart."

Jack turned to Anna, whose android torso had been

deposited on a seat next to Rajesh. She glanced up in thought. "A dispassionate search for the truth should always be a scientist's prime objective. All other considerations are secondary. The question I have is why Dr. Bishop is so opposed to the idea."

"Spoken like a true robot," Gabby quipped, retaking her seat and crossing her arms without bothering to respond. As far as Jack was concerned, she didn't need to. Gabby's reaction made perfect sense. His co-chief was witnessing an expedition she'd spent years getting off the ground rapidly descend into a steep nosedive. The frustration on her face was clear to see—so too was the pain. But research often led scientists down alleys they never anticipated. Hell, if memory served him, Jack was pretty sure Viagra had originally been developed to lower blood pressure until doctors had noticed it was raising something else.

"There's no denying it," Billy said from the middle of the crowd. He was next to the other drilling engineers. "The government's in a real pickle. I'm with Dr. Holland on this one. They sure as hell can't blow it up and for the life of me I can't see how they could scoop something the size of Lower Manhattan out of the hole it's in."

"That's assuming we tell them it's down there," Jack said.

Gabby shook her head violently. He didn't need an interpreter to know which way she was leaning.

The mood in the room appeared evenly split between those who were frightened and felt it should be left alone and those who were excited by the possibilities.

"Anyone who wants to leave has my blessing," Jack told them. "Return to your bunks, gather your things and line up by the helipad. For everyone else, wait here." Jack began moving through the crowd toward the mess hall doors.

"Boss, where are you going?" Dag asked.

"To tell Admiral Stark some of us are staying whether he likes it or not."

Chapter 14

Needless to say, Jack wasn't going to pitch it to the rear admiral in exactly the harsh terms he had indicated earlier. It was persuasion he was after, not a game of chicken with a guy who commanded an aircraft carrier strike group.

Seconds later, he found Stark and his men waiting by the rig's busted drill. The rear admiral checked his watch.

"I gave you ten minutes," he said without smiling. "That was fifteen. Means you owe me five."

Jack made a mental note on the spot: *Remind me never to invite this guy to a party.*

"Your people are packing their gear, I assume?" Stark asked. "Once tensions in the area settle down, we'll allow the heavy choppers back in to remove the shipping containers and anything else left behind."

"That's what I wanted to talk to you about," Jack said, edging closer. "You remember those gamma rays you asked about? What if I told you we weren't the ones who caused it?"

That final drop of good humor on Stark's face melted away. "I'm not following you."

"I'm saying we are sitting on the greatest single discovery in the history of the human race."

Stark rolled back on his heels. "If I had a nickel every

time one of you science types gave me that line, I'd be a rich man."

"What if I told you we found a metallic structure five hundred meters beneath the ocean that would make a *Nimitz*-class carrier look like a tugboat?"

Stark paused and drew in a slow breath. "I would wonder what psychotropic substances you were on."

"You were the one who showed up talking about rays from space and binary codes, Admiral, not me."

"What kind of structure are we talking about?"

"That's what we were trying to figure out when you and your men showed up."

The glare in Stark's eye grew sharp, dangerous. "You better not be trying to yank my chain, 'cause…"

"I can prove it to you," Jack said. "But first, we need to discuss terms."

"Terms?" The admiral spoke the words as though they were in a foreign tongue. A man like Stark didn't negotiate. He took orders from his superiors and doled them out to those under him. Now Jack had the advantage.

"So far we've only seen it from the outside. There seems to be an opening of some sort, but getting inside may be a whole other kettle of fish. Some of the top scientific minds in the world are on this rig, just waiting to be unleashed. That's what we bring to the table."

"And what's our role in this?" Stark asked, amused.

"The Navy's deep-sea salvage units have the equipment we need to make it there and back in one piece."

"I'm not buying what you're selling, Jack."

Jack shook his head, his eyes turned to the heavens. "Oh, what a cynical world we live in."

He led Stark, Hart and Olsen to the ROV shipping container and the monitors they had used to oversee Zeus' recent dive. Jack accessed the log and replayed the most recent entry.

Stark and the SEALs leaned forward, squinting at the monitor, their hands on the edge of the desk. Jack sped up the footage, rolling past the descent, slowing it down once they'd cleared the fissure. Each of the men maintained a neutral expression as the silver tip of the pyramid came into view. But they were only humans after all, humans who lived in a world that was well-defined and often infuriatingly mundane. The unpredictable chaos of battle was one way some folks learned who they really were. Facing the incredible was another. After they were done, the three men remained quiet, their arms crossed over their chests, their faces ashen. Even Hart's flushed complexion had receded.

"Any second now, one of you is gonna ask me what the hell that thing is," Jack predicted. "And the answer is we don't know. What we *can* say with some certainty is that we didn't build it and we didn't put it there."

"By we you mean Americans?" Lieutenant Olsen asked, staring intently.

"By we, I mean humans."

Admiral Stark brought the back of his hand across his forehead, slick with sweat. "You know if this is real then we can't possibly honor any agreement."

"You can," Jack insisted, "and you will, because copies of all the data we've collected so far—seismic, GPS, video—have already been encrypted and sent to a safe place. I only need to say the word and all of it gets sent to every major news organization around the world. If I don't check in with a password within seventy-two hours, the same thing happens. And try not to forget, gentlemen, we're in Mexican waters right now. I'm sure if anyone has a rightful claim to this giant tin can, it's them. And you can bet your bottom dollar the Cubans and the Russians would put up one hell of a fight to get their hands on whatever's inside. So we can work together and get to the truth or you can watch this pissing contest in the Gulf spiral into a real war."

"Where did you find the time to send copies of the encrypted data off for safekeeping?"

Jack twisted the knife. "I used those extra five minutes you gave me."

Chapter 15

Mia's boots shuffled along a wide dirt road. On either side of her were rows of two-story homes with red-tiled roofs. The sun had set less than an hour ago, and a silence had descended over the street, broken only by the distant sound of a barking dog and the cell phone that kept ringing in her pocket.

Since fleeing from the hotel, she had slunk through back streets, attempting to evade both the people who wanted her dead and the police who wanted her for murder. When her cell phone vibrated in her pocket again, she checked it, having learned from her earlier mistake. The number flashing was one she didn't recognize. She let it go to voicemail.

She was still dressed in the same clothes she'd been wearing during the attack, her cargo pants and dark button-down shirt. On her feet were a pair of hiking boots and slung over her back was a knapsack filled with two extra shirts, underwear, socks as well as the journal and encrypted USB Alan had sent her. But not the voice recorder. That was back at the hotel resting in a sink filled with water.

Sweat from the evening heat beaded on her forehead and ran down her back. Mia wondered now whether destroying the recorder had been the right decision. The cops only had to listen to what was recorded to know she was telling the truth.

She kept playing the scene over in her traumatized mind. How her attacker had kicked the door in and lunged at her on the balcony. Mia let her hand fall to the assassin's pistol, now resting in her waistband. Why hadn't he shot her? He had even said he didn't want to hurt her. A killer with a heart of gold? Or maybe Alan's research wasn't the only thing he'd come to retrieve. The memory of his body hitting the ground ricocheted inside her head.

Grisly sights aside, the man's death had made one thing certain—she would never learn why he had tried to kill her. She wanted to believe the attack had been nothing more than a coincidence. Maybe it had nothing to do with Alan's research. Somehow the idea made her feel better, but she knew it couldn't be true. Had he simply intended to rob or even rape her, he would never have brought so much attention to himself by kicking down the door.

It wasn't long before the tail end of Mia's adrenaline began to wear off. And as it faded, the full impact of her mental and physical exhaustion began to hit home. Before long, the simple act of putting one leg in front of the other required a gargantuan effort. She needed to find a safe place where she could catch a few hours of sleep. Hotels, the most obvious solution, were a no-go. So too were hostels and bed-and-breakfasts. They would be the first places the cops would come looking for her. After that were the hospitals and maybe even the morgue.

An American embassy would've been nice, even a consulate. Heck, she wasn't picky. But either one was hundreds of miles away. Mia would need to rely on her own cunning to get to Manaus, where she could catch a flight back to the United States.

Lining the dirt road were a number of parked cars. If she could find one that was unlocked, she might be able to hunker down for a few hours.

The first few that she tried wouldn't open. Big surprise. Then she remembered something an old boyfriend had told her. Sean was his name. Large and muscular with a birthmark on his cheek in the shape of Idaho, he'd been a cop with the Richmond PD. For two years car thefts had been his beat. She recalled hearing him complain about how in older cars each door needed to be locked. It had meant that often folks walked away leaving three car doors wide open. So Mia began trying the handles in the back as well. She had worked her way down three quarters of the street when the rear door on a Honda Civic swung open. Breathing a much-needed sigh of relief, Mia crawled into the back seat. The car was stuffed with fast-food containers, empty wrappers and what looked like overdue bills. Under the circumstances, she wasn't going to be picky.

After removing the pistol from under her waistband, she nestled in among the trash. In a weird way, all that papery padding made for a comfortable bed, although the ghostly odor of fast food did nothing to settle the incessant grumbling in her belly. She hadn't eaten anything the entire day. And when she'd got back to the hotel…

Memories began to flood back in and Mia used what energy she had left to hold them at bay. Stabbing a hand into her pocket, she came out with her cell phone.

Fifteen more missed calls, most from foreign-looking numbers. Since escaping, she had fought against the overwhelming desire to call home, if only to hear her daughter's voice one last time. She knew Paul would object, maybe even lie that Zoey was sleeping. But then another, darker realization began to hit her. What if her family was also in danger? Since the people after her had failed, what was stopping them from going after the ones she loved? Cycling through her contacts, Mia pushed Paul's number and held her breath while it dialed. After four rings the voicemail picked up. Mia swore.

"Hi, this is Paul, please leave a message."

After the tone, she rattled off everything that had happened and told him to take Zoey and head somewhere safe. She disconnected, hoping she hadn't sounded like a complete nutcase. She then wrote him an email just to be sure the message got through loud and clear.

Yesterday, the news had been in a tizzy about the blinding flash experienced by a large swath of people in North and South America. Racking up what was undoubtedly going to be a monstrous data bill, Mia began searching the major news outlets. She hoped that a determined reporter might have gotten information on what had caused the flash and whether people outside of Brazil had also been affected. Twenty minutes of scrolling later she'd found nothing useful. Most of the articles talked about the event, but stopped short of explaining what had caused it.

While checking her local news in Richmond, Mia stumbled onto a link buried near the bottom of the website. The image showed firefighters dousing a flaming Cadillac XTS. The front was fine, but the rear of the vehicle was charred beyond recognition. She scanned the rest of the article with a growing sense of disbelief.

Authorities say the badly burned remains of a prominent scientist were found in the trunk of his car this morning. DNA testing has yet to confirm, but police are confident that the victim is Dr. Alan Salzburg. A leading geneticist, Salzburg pioneered a number of important advances, among them the human artificial chromosome and the rare genetic disorder which bears his name. Police are treating the death as a homicide.

The phone tumbled from Mia's hands, numb with shock. Now, with the terrifying news of Alan's death back in the States, one thing had become perfectly clear. Nowhere was safe.

* * *

Mia was awakened by a bang and a shudder as the owner of the car started the ignition and pulled away. It was nearly dawn, the darkened sky showing hints of grey. The driver flipped on the radio, blaring a Brazilian pop song, mouthing the words and bouncing to the rhythm. Peering out from the back seat, hidden amongst the trash, she could see he was both overweight and blessed with decent dance moves. His singing voice, however, left something to be desired. She reached carefully into the waistband of her cargo pants and felt a hot flush crawl up her face. The gun wasn't there. That was right—she had removed it when she climbed in, placing it on the floor next to her bag. Mia eyed the space without finding the gun. Had it sunk beneath the sea of wrappers?

The driver rifled through the debris on the passenger seat, looking for something. When he didn't find it right away, he swore and returned his attention to the road. Thankfully, the Civic was a stick shift, which required both his hands. After he shifted into third, he leaned back and jammed a hand into the back seat. For a moment, his eyes left the road, swinging toward the space between the front and back seats. A blaring horn cut that short and he jerked the car violently, rolling down his window to rattle off what Mia could only guess was an off-color expression about the driver's mother. Perhaps having learned his lesson, he stuck with the passenger seat and the floorboard. Then, with a victorious holler, he waved a gold-colored CD in the air, kissed its shiny surface and inserted it into the dashboard.

Even worse music ensued, but on the bright side it was loud and helped divert his attention away from her crouched form. Less than five minutes later, he arrived at his destination and pulled over. With a grunt, the driver got out and locked his door before moving away.

The morning light painted the sky with a palette of pastels, oranges and pinks. Tentatively, Mia raised her head and caught the driver waddling around the corner. This neighborhood, she noticed, was even more run-down than the last. She flicked away the trash and found the gun resting exactly where she'd hoped it would be. Shoving it down the front of her pants, she gathered the rest of her things and exited the vehicle. She locked each of the other three doors before fleeing.

Unlike the residential neighborhood last night, this street was populated with large, decrepit factories. In the distance she spotted what looked like a slum with shacks crammed one on top of another.

Mia went at a brisk pace, uncertain where she was or where she was heading. The news of Alan's death had thwarted her plan to rush back to Richmond. Not with his killer awaiting her return. It was the worst kind of 'damned if you do, damned if you don't' situation.

She could tell the local Brazilian police what had happened, but what proof did she have to back it up? Alan had left her as the custodian of what amounted to not only his life's work, but, assuming he was right about the coded message hidden in Salzburg syndrome, perhaps the most startling discovery in modern science.

Mia turned a corner and ran right into a man. She stumbled backwards. The man turned and so did the other three who were with him. They'd been sitting on wooden crates in loose-fitting clothes, smoking cigarettes and drinking from bottles of cachaça, an alcohol made from distilled sugar cane.

Mia waved an apology and quickly headed in the other direction. They catcalled and shouted after her in Portuguese. She missed almost everything apart from "come back," or had it been "get over here"? She glanced back and saw that her four new friends were following her. Their faces turned down in scowls, they had the expressions of men eager to make their first catch of the day.

Mia picked up the pace and so did they. She entered the slum. Along the dusty streets, a handful of people moved about, perhaps getting ready to go to work. She decided to move in amongst them. Surely the men following her weren't dumb enough to try anything in front of witnesses.

With every step Mia felt the pistol dig into her pelvis, a painful feeling, but also a reassuring one. She didn't want to pull the gun out just yet, not before she really needed it. If they were also armed, it could start a gun fight in the middle of the street.

Mia drew parallel with a small group of people. She began to cross the wide dirt road, intent on mixing in with the crowd. That was when she heard her assailants break into a run. Barely a few feet from the other side of the street, she pulled the pistol and spun around. The men skidded to a stop, two of them less than five feet away, the others not far behind.

"Take another step and I'll blow you away," she warned, hoping they couldn't see how much her hand was shaking.

The man closest to her took a step forward, testing her resolve. His features were surprisingly soft and kind, except for the scar that ran from his ear to the side of his mouth.

She tightened her grip on the pistol, her finger on the trigger. The only thing she knew about guns was you never put your finger on the trigger unless you were ready to shoot. Her uncle had taught her that. She was ready. "I'm not kidding."

Scarface took another step closer and Mia squeezed the trigger. Nothing happened. She squeezed again, then three more times in rapid succession, but the result was always the same. Her eyes widened with fear as the barrel of the gun sagged. The lead assailant narrowed his eyes and took one more step before a Toyota four-by-four struck both Scarface and his friend, launching them into the air.

The men landed with a thud and rolled, kicking up clouds of dust and screams from the locals. But they weren't the only ones hit. Right as the truck had clipped their legs, the side mirror had knocked the gun clean out of Mia's hand, spinning her in a circle. A few feet away, the vehicle skidded to a stop. A man leapt from the driver's seat and fired two shots into the air. Scarface's remaining friends took off running, leaving their wounded comrades moaning on the ground.

"What are you waiting for?" the man shouted with a heavy accent. "An invitation from the Queen? Let's go."

Never in a million years had Mia imagined being as excited to see Ollie's face as she was right now.

Chapter 16

The briefing room on board the USS *Grapple* was about as sparse and unattractive as Jack had assumed it would be. The walls were coated in a layer of lime-green paint while the floors were a darker shade, something closer to pond scum. Four rows of chairs lined the space. Up ahead was a podium and next to that a display screen. Above them was a mix of neon lighting fixtures and exposed air ducts.

After Jack and the rear admiral's little chat, Stark had called in the *Grapple*, a salvage ship at the time conducting an operation off Galveston, Texas. She was used for a variety of tasks and particularly well suited to deep-sea missions. Following their conversation, two things had become clear to Jack. The first was that his gumption had somehow impressed Stark. The second was that the Navy was now in charge of the operation.

Stark addressed them from the front of the briefing room. Grant, Dag, Gabby, Rajesh, and Anna were seated in rapt attention. At the back were Commander Hart and Lieutenant Olsen.

Not surprisingly, selling Gabby on this next phase of their research expedition had not been an easy task. Although stated in a dozen different ways, the gist of her argument against pushing any further was a good old-fashioned fear of the unknown, the same reasoning that might have kept us away from the depths of the ocean or the surface of the moon.

After Jack proceeded to knock down each one of her arguments, she had shifted tack and suggested they were no longer able to complete the research as outlined in their grant agreement. Jack countered by telling her the original mission hadn't changed. They had come to drill what was left of the meteorite suspected of killing the dinosaurs. Instead, they'd found what to Jack's mind was looking more and more like a spaceship. Of course, for all he knew, it might have landed in the crater afterward. But what if this had been what killed the dinosaurs? Any way you sliced it, finding answers required further investigation. After nearly an hour of a conversation that had ebbed and flowed from congenial to downright hostile, Gabby had finally thrown up her hands and surrendered.

It was nothing new for Jack and Gabby to butt heads. Hell, it was one of the reasons he loved working with her. Jack had a point-and-shoot style. She, on the other hand, had a keen ability to spot where he'd become myopic in his thinking. Put another way, he was the rifle while Gabby was the aiming reticule—precise, efficient, normally cool-headed. Now, they'd swapped roles and Jack was still trying to understand why.

After Gabby had thrown up the white flag, Jack's next mission was to speak with Rajesh, who had had some serious reservations about dealing with the military. During his time as an MIT grad student, men from DARPA had apparently showed up on campus, asking for a meeting. He had agreed and quickly discovered the focus of their questions revolved around A.N.N.A. version one point zero. In her they saw a tremendous potential to save lives on the battlefield. As Rajesh explained, their pitch had been to use her revolutionary self-learning neural network and algorithm in order to create a whole new generation of battlefield medics. It all sounded so wonderful until Rajesh asked them about the other military applications they had in mind, the kind that involved machines designed to kill. In spite of their assurances that would never happen, Rajesh wasn't an idiot. He knew the temptation would be too great and by then there would be no stopping them. If the military wanted to build an army of soulless killing machines, let them do it with their own code.

Jack fully understood Rajesh's objections. He promised that not only would Anna be safe, but if Rajesh, or even Anna, had a change of heart, they could leave the expedition at any time. For her part, Anna said she was eager to fill in humanity's knowledge gap in this area. It sounded nice, but Jack wasn't convinced she had any concept of the historical magnitude of what they were about to embark on. And maybe that wasn't such a big surprise. *Homo sapiens* had a long tradition of peering into the black recesses of space and wondering whether we were alone. Whatever Anna and her burgeoning intelligence represented, one could argue she was the first of her kind, a new species whose time spent on the earth could be counted in months rather than millennia. Anyone born into a world with flying cars and interstellar travel couldn't help but see them as terribly normal, even banal.

"Dr. Greer," Rear Admiral Stark said coolly. "I asked you a question."

Jack snapped back into reality. "Sorry, I was somewhere else."

Stark motioned toward the paused image on the monitor, which showed what looked like a space suit. "Have you ever used an exosuit on one of your geology expeditions?"

Jack leaned forward for a closer look and shook his

head. He was familiar with atmospheric diving suits. The shell was made from a hard aluminum alloy and featured rotating appendages outfitted with pincers for manipulating underwater objects. Stepping into of one of these five-hundred-and-thirty-pound beasts essentially transformed the wearer into a massive crab. Although expensive, the suits held several advantages over traditional scuba diving gear. The most striking was the pressurized interior. Much like a one-man submarine, the wearer could essentially bring earth's surface atmosphere with him several hundred meters under the sea. A scuba diver on the other hand was forced to breathe a dangerous cocktail of gases and spend hours in decompression chambers or risk the bends.

Stark pressed a button on a remote, switching the image to a live feed five hundred meters beneath them. On the screen were a number of Navy divers in exosuits securing a large circular habitat to the porthole of the USO (unidentified submerged object).

"Once in place," Stark explained, "the Orb will be your home for the next ninety-six hours."

"Ninety-six?" Jack said, shocked they weren't being given more time.

"It might very well be less," Stark told them. "Once agents from the ONI arrive, I got a feeling they're gonna want you and your people gone. So my advice is get in there and do as much as you can in the time you have."

The ONI stood for the Office of Naval Intelligence.

Jack bit his lip. Things might have been a lot worse. The Navy could very well have called his bluff and thrown them off the rig back to the US.

Stark zoomed out with the underwater camera, revealing just how tiny the Orb looked next to the alien structure.

"Let me bring in Captain Manuel Sanchez, commander of the USS *Grapple,* to explain a little more about your new home."

Sanchez strode to the front of the briefing room. A short Mexican American in Navy khakis, Sanchez was clean-cut with a slight deformity on his upper lip. He spoke slowly, struggling, it seemed, to keep his speech as clear as possible. "Hello, ladies and gentlemen, and, uh…" Captain Sanchez's gaze dropped to Anna, seated in a front row.

"Anna," Jack offered, knowing Rajesh would have looked on with delight as the captain struggled.

Sanchez's face became strained. Clearly Stark hadn't informed him a robot was on board. Recovering quickly, he carried on with his presentation.

"The Orb is a deep-sea research habitat capable of supporting a crew of ten members on five separate levels," he told them. He pulled up an image on screen. "It will also be your home for the next few days. As you can see, a narrow staircase provides access to each deck. Decks one and two are berthing quarters. Each of you will be assigned a bunk and a locker where you can store your personal items. The middle deck features a small mess with tables and chairs. Two microwaves will allow you to heat up the pre-prepared meals we will provide you with. The lower two decks will house a comms room and science lab.

"The Orb has two airlocks. The first is where the submersible will dock. The second leads to the structure. As we speak, Navy divers are beginning the process of pumping water from the porthole. A series of micro-ROVs sent into the structure have revealed a chamber no more than ten square feet. Within the hour, the last of the water should be pumped out and the Orb secured in place."

Jack spoke up. "What if we run into a problem and need to evacuate?"

"In the case of emergency," Sanchez informed them,

"the Orb can be manually released from the airlock connecting it to the USO. Compressed air will then fill a series of ballast tanks and bring you to the surface."

The captain then flicked to the image of a man in a baggy suit. "While on board the Orb, you may wear your regular clothing. However, specially designed biosuits must be worn within the target structure at all times. Failure to comply may result in cross-contamination or death."

Dag, his brain filled with endless knowledge on dinosaur bones, looked worried. "Cross-contamination?"

Grant, the biologist, jumped in. "It'll prevent us from leaving our microbes behind and mucking up any data we collect. The real question is, after millions of years on the bottom of the ocean, have any alien bacteria even survived?"

Gabby crossed her arms and held her elbows. "I'm starting to think this was what Stephen Hawking meant when he said we might not survive first contact. Didn't the Europeans wipe out millions of the native population with pathogen-carrying blankets?"

"What about the air?" Dag asked. "Once we're on board, will we be able to breathe?"

Rear Admiral Stark popped back up. "We're not sure yet, but your suits will be able to monitor air levels. Regardless, you're advised to keep your helmets on at all times." A cough from the back of the briefing room drew Stark's attention. "Oh, yes, there's one more member of the team I should introduce you to." Stark raised a hand and waved someone forward from the back of the room. All present shifted in their seats to see who it was. From out of the shadows, a thin man in his forties emerged, wearing a dark suit that was last in style sometime in the mid-nineties. His thinning hair was parted in the middle and combed flat on either side of his skull.

"This is Dr. Eugene Jarecki," Stark said, a note of reluctance in his voice. "A theoretical physicist sent to us compliments of Uncle Sam."

Uncle Sam was code for the government, which in turn was code for bureaucracy and red tape and meddling. At least that was Jack's reading of the pained expression on the rear admiral's face.

"Greetings," Eugene said, drawing his hand in an arc before him. "You can call me Gene or Doctor Gene, whichever you prefer." He was a soprano with blocked sinuses. "I'm here from the Office for Outer Space Affairs."

An air of bewilderment filled the room.

"That sounds made up," Dag blurted with typical Swedish bluntness.

Eugene's eyebrows flickered with resentment. "I can assure you the office is very real. We are located on Pennsylvania Avenue in Washington, D.C."

"Well, it certainly doesn't get more governmental than that, does it?" Grant said.

Scanning the room, Jack registered the mood before speaking. "I think we were all expecting the men in black. At the very least, a couple guys in dark suits with threats that if we spoke a word of what we saw we'd be made to disappear."

Before Eugene could respond, Gabby piped in. "Exactly how many people are in the OOSA?" she asked, saying the letters slowly to make sure she got the acronym right.

"Uh, only me," he said. "But you see, after Project Blue Book wrapped in sixty-nine, our government was pretty much done with the subject of aliens."

Jack shook his head in disbelief. He knew that Blue Book had been convened as a public relations gig designed to dampen the UFO hysteria rampant at the time. The major concern back then was that the lines of communication were being clogged with wild claims of UFO sightings and encounters, the same lines that needed to remain clear in case of impending Soviet attack. Could it really be that the US government thought so little about our chances of encountering an alien civilization that they had an office staffed by one person? Could the stories of secret cover-ups and captured spacecraft have been little more than an urban myth? Jack had never pretended to be particularly well-versed on the subject, although by the same token, he'd never considered everyone in the UFO community a complete nutjob. Many were, no doubt about it, but more than a few had seemed reputable. Jack had to admit he was rather disappointed. If nothing else, the sad state of the OOSA only reinforced the idea that in more ways than one, they truly were entering uncharted territory.

"All right, folks," Stark cut in. "Hate to break up the party, but the submersible dives in an hour, with or without you."

Chapter 17

As ordered, Jack and the others returned to the rig to assemble any gear and scientific instruments they would need for their time on the Orb. He had no sooner stepped off the helipad than a deckhand approached him.

"Doc, a call came in over the sat phone from a Gordon LeMay. Said it was urgent."

Jack sighed, feeling a cold dread settle over him. Something was wrong. In the five years they'd been working together, Gordon had never once called him in the field. Had there been an accident at the farm? Had the property been foreclosed on? Moving quickly, Jack made his way down the walkway and into the superstructure. Three stories up was his cabin. When he arrived, he dug in his pocket for the key, only to find the door unlocked and slightly ajar. That was strange. He never left his cabin open. Right away he dialed the general frequency on the rig to ask if anyone had been in his cabin. A few voices came back informing him they weren't aware of anyone doing so.

With growing concern, Jack pushed his way inside. There he found what looked like the aftermath of a category five hurricane. Picture frames and possessions had been thrown from every surface and sent crashing to the floor. His dresser drawers had been removed, the clothes dumped into small peaks and valleys at his feet. Even his mattress had been upended. Jack kicked at a pile of t-shirts by his feet and swore.

The toe of his boot struck something hard mixed in with his clothing. He reached down and scooped up his smartphone, the one he turned off whenever he was on an expedition. A moment later, he found his wallet, eighty bucks in crisp twenty-dollar bills still tucked inside along with bank and credit cards. Whoever did this hadn't been after money or electronics. Their motivation seemed clear enough. They wanted info on the alien object. But who? Admiral Stark was the first name that came to mind. Could this have been his navy goons, the VBSS (visit, board, search, and seizure) team that had stormed aboard earlier? A not-so-subtle attempt to get their hands on the digital packet Jack had said he'd sent off for safekeeping? Jack hadn't been in his cabin since the morning, which gave whoever had carried this out plenty of opportunity to rifle through his belongings.

The veins in his neck bulged with anger as he set the mattress back on his bed and dialed Gord on the sat phone.

The vet and caretaker answered on the first ring.

"I'm guessing you have more bad news for me?" Jack asked, removing his ball cap and rubbing his temples with his left hand.

"I thought you should know. There's a problem with the pigs," Gord said, cutting right to the chase.

Normally slicing off the fat was just the way Jack liked it, but given the situation, he could have used a gentler lead-in. "What do you mean? What's wrong with them?"

Gord grunted, his deep voice reverberating clearly over a bad line. "Not sure. I've quarantined Harold and a handful of others, just in case it's some sort of virus.

Problem is, their symptoms are all over the place."

Jack set his cap back on snugly. "I don't understand."

"Frankly, Jack, neither do I. See, I found Harold lying on the ground squealing like mad. Turns out he had fractures in both of his front trotters and three of his ribs. Figured that last bit must have happened when he fell over. But I can't make sense of what caused it. The flesh on two of the others, Betsy and Tommy, is all red and swollen. Looks to me like a nasty sunburn. Then this morning I found Jezebel walking straight into the fence post, over and over, like she intended to walk right through it."

Jezebel was a bright sow, maybe the smartest on the farm. She could understand about a hundred commands. "What about the horses and the llamas?"

"The other animals seem fine so far," Gord replied. "I been feeding and taking good care of 'em, like always. I'm sorry, Jack. I wish there was more I could tell you."

"I understand. Listen, I'd tell you to call a vet, but you were one of the best in the county. Keep an eye on them. I may be out of touch for a few days. Oh, did you find the money in the safe?"

"I did," Gord said. "And used it to fend off the bank and pay the farm hands. But we were still short. I just hope those two boys don't run off on me now. Not when I need them the most."

Jack felt the walls closing in on him. On the one hand, he was about to literally go where no man had gone before. On the other, he could only watch helplessly as his home and everything that gave his life meaning melted away.

'You still there, Jack?"

"I am, Gord."

"Believe me, I hate to burden you with all this bad news."

"It's not your fault," Jack assured him. "Soon as I get a chance, I'll send more money."

"You folks found that meteorite you were looking for?"

Jack smiled. "You could say that."

"That's no small feat. I'm sure your father, wherever he is, would be proud."

Looking down, Jack saw that he was rubbing his fingers again. The pads were growing red and tender. This was no time to relive the past and so Jack simply agreed with Gord and told his friend to take care.

•••

Jack tossed a few things into a bag, and then piled everything else onto his bunk. Ninety-six hours from now—as Stark had made clear—he would return and sort everything out. Jack returned to the helipad to find Billy Brenner, along with a handful of scientists and deckhands, loading up the Navy chopper. Much of the scientific instrumentation had been packed inside boxes labeled "Delicate" and "This Side Up". But they'd be spending the next few days in the cramped confines of a tiny habitat five hundred meters beneath the sea. Fancy as it was, a thermal cycler didn't keep your breath fresh or your armpits from stinking up the joint. When you were living in tight quarters, personal hygiene was vitally important. Ask any astronaut who spent time aboard the ISS (International Space Station).

As the resident astrophysicist, Gabby couldn't agree more. She saw the shaving kit under Jack's arm and motioned to her own. The two of them climbed on board. Both helicopter doors were open and when Jack glanced to his right he could see their next destination, bobbing less than a hundred yards away, the USS *Grapple*. Dag, Grant, Rajesh and Anna boarded next, settling into the seats that remained.

"I forgot how much you hate flying," Gabby

professed. "You look like a schoolboy waiting at the principal's office."

Jack tried to grin, but the muscles in his face weren't cooperating. He clenched his fists and let go, watching the blood pooling back into his palms.

"Is something else the matter?" she asked, worried.

In the cockpit, the pilots were running through a final round of checks.

Jack shook his head. He had no intention of talking about the break-in. That was squarely between him and Rear Admiral Stark. And as for the problems on the farm, discussing subjects for which there was no clear solution would only leave him feeling worse about the whole damn thing. Instead he decided to redirect the conversation.

"How's your mom?" Gabby's mother was nearly eighty and recently diagnosed with lung cancer. To the doctors, it hardly mattered that the woman had never smoked a day in her life.

The light in Gabby's eyes faded a little. "She's strong as ever. With a lot of arm-twisting and a touch of luck, we got her into a promising clinical trial over at Mount Sinai. We're hoping it'll buy her a few more years."

Gabby's mother was not only her parent, she was Gabby's whole life. After her father's death in a car accident thirty years earlier, Gabby had forfeited anything resembling a personal life in order to keep her mother company. They were more than mother and daughter, they were best friends, something Jack's own fractured past had never enabled him to fully understand.

"And what about you, Gabby? Maybe it's time you had a life of your own."

"I do have a life," she countered quickly. "Through my work and my hiking."

"I'm talking about a husband," Jack pushed.

Gabby scoffed. "I'm in my mid-fifties. You know

what the dating scene is like for a woman my age? We're looking for someone to spend time with while most men are hunting for a supermodel."

"You're not sad you never had kids?" he asked. It was a touchy personal question, but Jack was asking himself just as much as he was asking her.

She regarded him and then looked away. "It's funny how you can know someone for ten years only to realize you know so little about them."

She was talking about their decade-long friendship, but she might as well have been talking about Jack and the secrets he kept even from those he considered close friends.

"I grew up in a small town in Nebraska," Gabby said, apparently willing to share, "where you obeyed your parents and above all your God. The rules were quite simple, but for some reason, I had a real hard time following them. Met a boy in my senior year of high school and did something we had no business doing. There was no such thing as sex ed back then." She clasped her hands together. "Anyway, a few months later I realized I was pregnant and all hell broke loose. Imagine me at sixteen taking care of a little baby. Even back then I had dreams of becoming a scientist. Suddenly all that was gone."

"I never knew," Jack said, placing his hands over hers.

"How could you? I was sent away to Smith Falls for eight months. The plan was for me to have the kid and then give it up for adoption. There were other, more practical reasons for my disappearance though. My father didn't want the neighbors talking. My mother reluctantly went along. As much as I hated my father's reasoning, I knew there was really no other choice. So away I went, and seven months later I gave birth to a baby girl. Only got a brief glimpse before she was taken away. The weeks leading up to the birth, I wanted nothing more than for the baby to be out of me. But you see, all that changed when I saw her beautiful little face. Suddenly, all those bad feelings disappeared, just as the cramps and the pain had faded away."

"Did you ever try to find her?" Jack asked. "Reach out?"

The whine of the motor began, the rotors turning in a slow circle.

"Last year I started the process. It took months of research and mounds of red tape before I found out she lived somewhere on the West Coast and had a family of her own. But she declined to meet." Gabby's eyes glazed over. "Can't say I blame her. The choices we make."

She was lying to herself, but Jack let it go.

"Life is a series of choices," she said reflectively. "An endless array of yeses or noes. If I'd said yes to the baby, I probably wouldn't be here now, about to dive into something no human has ever seen before." The rotors kicked up a mighty racket as the individual blades disappeared from view. Gabby put her headset on and said one last thing. "What would you have done?" she asked him.

Jack lowered the mic to his lips. "Only someone who lived through it had the right to make that call."

The chopper pushed off the landing pad and began the short hop to the *Grapple*. Slowly, Jack's mind began to move away from the secret life Gabby had kept from him all these years. And further still from his own personal problems. His thoughts settled squarely on the metallic structure sitting in a pocket on the sea floor, an object which was sure to hold secrets of its own.

Chapter 18

The parking complex Mia and Ollie were hiding in was three stories high and in desperate need of repair. Sections of exposed rebar poked out from the crumbling concrete pillar he had pulled up next to in his Toyota four-by-four. He had brought her to the business district, a safe and more upscale part of Santarem, although safe was something of a misnomer. Slightly less dangerous was probably a more accurate way of putting it.

Mia glanced down at her phone. The ringer was off, but the number showing on the screen was the same one that had already called a million times since last night.

"Don't answer it," Ollie warned her.

"I won't. It's probably the police."

He leaned over, studying the number. "It's a local number, you may be right. Have you used your phone at all?" he asked, worried.

"A little."

"I suggest you turn it off completely unless you want them to find you."

Mia hesitated. She still hadn't spoken to Paul or Zoey to be sure they were safe.

He reached over, took the device in his right hand and held down the power button. The screen went black. "This isn't a game," he told her.

"I know that, Ollie. But you're asking me to cut myself off from the most important people in my life." Mia's voice wavered. Her clothes were wrinkled and smelled of fast food. "What if they try to call?"

"That's exactly how the authorities will find you. Most people still don't realize that this innocent-looking computer in our hands is nothing more than a tracking device."

Mia grew quiet. She hadn't asked for any of this. She couldn't help wondering how things might have turned out differently had she only refused Alan's package. Her mind traced through her flight from the hotel and the group of men who had tried to assault her. At last came the question that had been on the tip of her tongue for close to an hour.

"How'd you know where I was?" she asked, clutching her knapsack the way people clutched couch cushions while watching a scary movie.

"I didn't," he said. He scanned behind them for signs of danger before settling back on her. "I'd been driving around for hours. Your colleague, the Brit with the tea fetish, said you'd run off like a dingo into the night."

She gave him a look.

"All right, I added the dingo part, but he said you took the emergency stairs. So I told the police I'd help them find you and got in my truck."

Mia's body tensed. "Help them…"

"Oh, never mind that. I'm not paid enough to do their jobs for them. I just didn't want them thinking I was involved."

"I didn't mean to kill him," Mia pleaded, feeling that old reservoir of guilt firing up again.

"Just like you had no intention of shooting those idiots on the street?' He chuckled, rubbing his hand along the edge of the steering wheel. "Course, I have no interest in turning you in. Especially not to the buffoons in the Santarem PD. Any jerk with half a brain could see what that bloke did to your hotel room door."

The soft features of her face shifted into something like hope. "You think the police will believe me?"

"They might, although around here there are no guarantees," he said. "Depends on whether you're ready to pay a few bribes and then roll the dice. You'll be put on trial first, that's for sure. This isn't Texas or Florida or wherever the heck you can stand your ground and expect to be let off. First, you'll await your trial in a Brazilian jail and then hope to hell the prosecution isn't planning to make an example of you."

"Example?"

"Sure, a beautiful and educated American woman." The fingers of both hands gripped the wheel as Ollie let out a sardonic laugh.

Mia felt a smile creep over her face as her mind traced over the word 'beautiful,' before she snuffed it out.

"A sheila like you? Heck, it'll be just like that Amanda Knox, the way her sexually liberated attitude rattled those uptight Italian detectives and prosecutors. I can imagine the same thing will happen with you. But who can really say for sure?"

It didn't take more than a little common sense to understand Ollie was probably right. At least with the American legal system back home, imperfect as it was, she knew what she'd be up against. Over here, she'd be putting her faith in a judiciary that might be rigged against her for no other reason than she was a woman with an offending passport. Surely the situation in the Gulf wasn't helping things either. With Cuba standing up to what it perceived as American bullying, Brazil had fallen in line to support the communist country's cause. On top of the legal risks, Mia would almost certainly become a political pawn in a proxy war between the

United States and Latin America. She buried her face in her hands, overwhelmed by how badly the deck had been stacked against her.

A few seconds went by before she felt Ollie's hand on her back.

"Don't cry," he said, uneasy.

Mia lifted her head. Her cheeks were dry. "I cried all my tears a long time ago. I just don't know what to do."

"Why don't you start by telling me what happened?"

She studied the hard lines on his face, wondering if he could be trusted. "I'm not sure."

"Listen," he said, pointing to the camera gear in the back seat. "I've got a deadline of my own to meet. If I had any intention of turning you in, we'd be at police headquarters by now, not parked in this decrepit lot."

Mia knew she had to start trusting someone, or else the people after her would soon finish what they had started. Centering herself, she began by recounting the attack, ending right at the moment he arrived.

"You ever used a gun before?"

His question surprised her. "That's all you can say? After everything I just told you?"

"My friends always told me I liked to get straight to the point," he said, grinning.

"So you have friends?"

He let out a deep burst of laughter. "Hard to believe, I know." After a moment, he settled into something more serious. "About that gun, I sure didn't mean any disrespect. The way you told the story, it sounded to me like you might have had the safety on."

Her face dropped. "Oh, maybe I did." She smiled, embarrassed.

"Show me your pistol."

Mia raised her bruised wrist. "You knocked it out of my hand when you came charging in."

He gritted his teeth and rolled his bottom lip in a

silent apology. Ollie pulled out his own gun, a Beretta 9mm.

"I've been meaning to ask you," she said. "Where on earth did you get that?"

"When in Brazil," he said, "do as the Brazilians. If you think I'm dumb enough to drive around this country without some kind of protection, you're crazier than I thought."

He removed the magazine and racked the slide, popping the round out of the chamber. Before handing it to her, he showed her the safety, flicking it off and on with his thumb.

"It was the heat of the moment, Ollie," she said, her complexion still a little pale. "I hope you're not trying to rub it in."

He shook his head. "Absolutely not. The heat of the moment, as you say, is the difference between life and death. You never know when you'll need to pull the trigger for real."

Mia took the gun and fiddled with the safety, pointing it out in front of her. After a few more practice runs, she handed it back.

"You still haven't told me what you did to the Brazilian bloke who wanted you dead. You piss in his cornflakes or something?" Ollie's shit-eating grin was back in full force.

"It's complicated."

"You got something better to do than talk?"

"Get back home maybe."

He didn't seem convinced. "That'll depend on what this is about."

Ollie did have a point. And she couldn't deny he had risked his neck to save her when it seemed everyone else was trying to do the opposite. Mia drew in a deep breath and went even further back this time, going over everything she knew. She was taking a chance, but at this point in the game she had nothing else to lose. In a world filled with adversaries, she was thankful for at least one friend, even if only for a while.

She told him about Alan's work and their feud, skipping over the salacious details that were frankly none of his business. She told him about Alan's discovery of Salzburg a few years back and the disorder's emergence sometime in the nineties. She also told him about the encrypted data Alan had sent her and his belief he had located some sort of message in this new and mysterious human chromosome.

"But why you?" Ollie asked. "I don't mean any disrespect, but if I understood your story, the guy hated your guts."

She found herself about to relitigate her entire disagreement with Alan and bit her tongue. "It's complicated. But I do know that when I left, he considered me his protégée."

"Waiting for a bloke who's gone underground to contact you is liable to take months."

"He *has* gone underground," she corrected him. "But not in the way you're suggesting."

Understanding broke on Ollie's face. "He's dead?"

She nodded. "Maybe I'm better off throwing this stuff in the trash."

He considered this. "And if there's something in what that Alan fella discovered that could help those sick people, what then? I mean, didn't you say the emergency room at Santarem Municipal was suddenly filled with folks who had Slazburg?"

"Salzburg," she corrected him, considering his point.

"If someone is after you, do you really think they'll stop just because you threw the stuff away? It sounds to me like this Alan handed you a death sentence and the only way out is to figure out what he found and get it in the right hands."

"So what do you suggest?" she asked. The grip on her bag had slackened a little.

Ollie balled one hand into a fist and drummed his fingers against the space between his knuckles. He remained like this for several minutes, deep in thought. Then, "I got it. You mentioned something about an encrypted flash drive."

"Yeah, but I don't have the username or password."

"We might not need it. I did a story a couple years ago on computer hackers. I interviewed white hats, black hats and even a few blokes claiming to work for the Chinese and Russian governments. One of those white hat gents was a computer genius living in Argentina. Goes by the name Armoni. I can send him an email and see if he'd be willing to meet you."

She hesitated.

Ollie pulled out his phone. "What's wrong?"

"I just thought maybe you could…"

He glanced over at her, his chin sunken into his chest. "What? Go with you? Sorry. No. Can. Do. I got a deadline to meet."

"All right, fine," Mia said, biting her lip. "It was just a thought. I'm a grown woman, I can take care of myself."

"I have no doubt you can. Besides, I don't know a thing about genetics."

"Maybe not, but you know how to stay alive. I make one mistake and I'm done."

Ollie held her gaze before he returned to his phone, his fingers dancing over the tiny digital keys. Thirty seconds later he looked proud of himself and pushed his back against the seat. "That's done. First we wait for a response and then get you on a plane."

"But won't the cops be watching outgoing commercial flights?"

He winked at her. "Those aren't the ones I'm thinking of."

Chapter 19

Commander Hart met the scientists on the *Grapple*'s helipad. Toward the stern, a boom arm maneuvered in place over a large white submersible, the name *Trident* stenciled on the side in bold black letters.

Hart glanced back as Jack watched sailors attach the load hook to the sub. "That's our ride," Hart told him. "A real beauty, isn't she?" The SEAL smiled in a rare display of lightheartedness, the edges of his dense beard rising to meet eyes narrowed into half-slits.

"So long as she gets us there in one piece," Jack said, not ashamed of the uncertainty creeping into his bones. He wondered if his hatred for flying would be matched by the underwater equivalent.

"Leave your things on the chopper," Hart instructed them, brushing aside Jack's concerns in the process. "The sailors will load them on board after we're settled."

Hart led them down the walkway and toward the stern.

"Aren't we going inside for a final briefing?" Gabby asked, a note of desperation in her voice.

"No, ma'am. This bus is leaving."

Jack followed, noticing for the first time Commander Hart wasn't weighed down by body armor, ammo magazines or any visible weapons.

"No guns?" he asked, noticing the same thing.

"Doc, this is a scientific expedition. What would we need guns for?"

Jack glanced back, exchanging bewildered looks with the scientists.

Ahead of them, the sailors were rolling the metal staircase in place. Getting in and out of the *Trident* was accomplished through a sail hatch at the top of the submersible.

"I was hoping to have a final word with Rear Admiral Stark," Jack protested.

Commander Hart stopped, a look of annoyance spreading over his features. "What for?"

"The USO is a mile across and half a mile high. Ninety-six hours won't be nearly enough time to get what we need."

"The rear admiral was very clear about that in the briefing. You're here to find out what this thing is and why it's here with the time you have. Anything else you find is icing on the cake."

"And what's your role in all of this?" Jack asked, sweating now and not just from the stifling heat.

"Our first mission is to keep the lot of you out of trouble. Our second mission is to determine whether the beings who left this here intend to do us harm."

•••

Ten minutes later, the passengers and most of their gear were stored away. A seaman checked that all were accounted for before sealing the hatch. With a sudden jolt, the massive boom arm went to work, lifting the sub off the tarmac and slowly swinging it out over the water.

103

Jack found it hard to breathe. Inside, the craft was sweltering. A small mezzanine hung above them toward the bow where the cockpit was located. Below that was the forward airlock, in the center of that a tiny porthole window.

Rajesh sat clutching Anna in his lap. He had opted to forego bringing a suitcase in order to free up enough space for a few more of her processors.

"Ladies and gentlemen, travel time to the Orb will be thirty minutes," Hart announced over the loudspeaker. "The weather at our destination is a chilly twenty-three degrees. As we start our descent, please make sure your seat backs and tray tables are in their full upright position and make sure your seatbelt is securely fastened at all times. Thank you."

Dr. Eugene Jarecki glanced down, digging into the seat for a safety belt. By the looks of it, his growing panic at not finding one was the highlight of Lieutenant Olsen's day. If the SEALs could have gotten away with hanging the poor doctor on a locker by his underpants, surely they would have. But who knew, the day was still young.

The tiny portholes along the sides of the sub revealed a strange world bathed in shifting blues and emerald greens. Soon those colors began to darken before the sea became altogether black.

Grant's face was pressed against the porthole nearest him. "Hardly any light filters down further than two hundred meters."

The bizarre and rather frightening sensation of floating in space was now even more acute. Any concept of up, down, left or right was completely meaningless.

As if in response, the outside lights switched on, providing those inside a semblance of orientation.

Jack became aware that he was calm and clear-headed. Flying under the waves didn't send him into a panic the way it did in the air. The dangers were no less real, but his mind somehow drew a distinction he did not understand, but one he was thankful for nevertheless.

Before long, they entered the fissure, the gaping wound created by the blast wave. This was something Stark had asked him about privately on several occasions. More than intrigued, the admiral seemed positively obsessed with it. Was he evaluating how such an event might be weaponized? Surely not, since the power required to create the kind of gamma ray dispersion they had experienced was likely far beyond the means of modern science. Stark also wanted to know if it would happen again, as to which Jack was equally ignorant.

Despite their concerns, the Navy had gone ahead and secured the Orb to the USO's opening anyway. But given the limited amount of information he had, the only conclusion Jack had been able to draw was that when the drill bit had struck the outer hull it had set off some sort of defensive countermeasure, a theory which had led to the formation of an even more troubling thought. What else might it do if it felt attacked?

Chapter 20

A shimmering mirage soon began to materialize from out of the gloom. Gradually it grew, until finally it took on a distinctly rounded shape. They were seeing the Orb. Minutes later, both the bow and stern airlocks became visible, along with clustered rows of tiny portholes, a handful on each of the habitat's five levels. On land it might have been an impressive sight. They were told the habitat was the approximate height of a T-Rex, which was to say forty feet. But down here, next to the alien object, it looked far more like a pimple.

"Ten meters," the submersible pilot called out as they drew even with the rear airlock. This was by far the most dangerous part of the operation. Here, the slightest miscalculation, a nervous twitch, could send them thudding into the habitat and rupturing both hulls. At over five hundred meters down, their chances for survival were zilch.

"Five meters. Four. Three. Two. One. Contact."

The sub lurched forward, nearly pushing Gabby out of her seat. Jack swung an arm out to keep her in place. Then came a loud clang as the locking mechanism was engaged.

"Welcome to the Orb, folks," Hart said, hanging the mic on the nearest bulkhead.

One of the pilots climbed down from the cockpit and spun the airlock door. Air hissed out as the pressure equalized. Jack stepped onto the Orb. He turned to Grant, who was right behind him. "It's got that new-car smell."

It took close to an hour to unload all of their gear and equipment. Tight quarters didn't begin to describe what they encountered on the Orb. Jack's grandfather—step-grandfather, to be precise—had served aboard a sub during WWII. His grandfather had only spoken about it once and when he did he'd said the overall sensation was like riding inside a clown car with thirty other men.

Sure, the submersible was a confined space, but they weren't expected to live there. A spiral metal staircase led from floor to floor. The top two levels held a series of bunks, two high and shoulder-width apart. A six-foot length of foam wrapped in plastic served as a mattress. For a pillow they were given a chunk of foam covered in cotton fabric. No one complained. Nor should they have. With any luck, they would be so exhausted from studying whatever was inside the structure, they'd be able to fall asleep on a slab of concrete.

The middle deck was where the galley and mess were located. A small fridge and microwave stood at one end. A handful of tables and chairs were scattered about the rest of the space.

Over by the fridge was the inner airlock, which led to the USO. Jack crossed the room and peered through the porthole. Recessed neon lighting gave the chamber a sterile, forbidding feel. Red hazmat suits lined both walls. Beyond this airlock was one more and beyond that a world no human had seen with their own eyes.

Below the mess was where the comms equipment would be located. This was Olsen's world and he was busy checking that the fiberoptic link was working. It was from here that the Orb would keep in contact with

Rear Admiral Stark, who had decided to remain on board the USS *Grapple*. On the bottom deck was where most of the science would take place. Already, the bulk of the instruments had been set up.

The crew, as they were now known, was scattered about the Orb performing a variety of final sorting tasks as they hurried to put the place in order. Jack found Rajesh and Anna on the comms level. Rajesh was busy setting up the powerful computers used to maintain and expand Anna's impressive intellect. The fiberoptic cable would also allow her to access the servers on the rig.

"Hello, Dr. Greer," Anna said, turning her digital face to watch him descend the spiral staircase.

Jack spread out his hands, motioning to their surroundings. "So what do you think?" It was a question more designed to fill an awkward silence than a legitimate inquiry. As impressive as she was, he couldn't help feeling a little irked by the way her deep brown eyes were regarding him. She blinked twice before answering. The facial tics were a nice touch, Jack thought.

"The average human takes up three square feet when standing," Anna told him, her expression calm and jovial. "Four point five square feet while seated. I've calculated each level of the habitat to be five hundred square feet for a total of twenty-five hundred square feet. I then subtracted one fifth of that for furniture, scientific instrumentation and computer hardware. That leaves two thousand square feet to be shared among nine individuals. Given the circumstances, I think it's more than adequate."

Jack rolled his eyes. She still didn't quite get context, but there was something else she did get that Jack found interesting. When dividing up the Orb's square footage among its inhabitants, she'd included herself among those counted. On some level she seemed to understand the concept of inclusion, or at least felt—or maybe believed—that she was one of them. Jack's mother had always hated when people fed the family dog at the table. Said it confused the animal into thinking it was human. Maybe the same thing was happening with her?

Her head tilted slightly. "Penny for your thoughts, Dr. Greer?"

Rajesh was still fishing for a plug behind the table when Jack bent down and grabbed it for him. "Her spatial awareness and facial recognition are truly impressive." He didn't know fancy computer talk, but he was confident Rajesh understood what he was getting at.

"Dr. Greer?" Anna said, trying to get his attention.

Rajesh sat straight up, his face slightly distorted from the pooling blood. "Much of that has come from improving her optics."

"Dr. Greer?" Anna droned on again in a polite, monotone voice.

When she called Jack's name a third time, Rajesh got firm with her, pointing at Jack so Anna could see. "Do not be a nuisance. Dr. Greer and I are speaking." He leaned in closer to Jack. "When I told you she was like a ten-year-old child, I was not exaggerating."

Her expression became saddened. "My apologies. I was waiting for Dr. Greer to respond to my question."

"If someone does not respond to your inquiry," Rajesh informed her, "it either means they are busy or do not feel like answering."

"Or they did not hear the question." Anna looked at Jack and smiled.

"How long did it take your team to program her facial expressions?" Jack asked, feeling Anna watching him.

Rajesh stood and clapped the dust off his hands. "Program? No, sir, we did no such thing."

"Beg your pardon?"

"Anna developed those on her own, from observing

and interacting with humans. The rest she got from watching television."

Jack blinked. "TV?"

"Oh, yes." Rajesh turned to her, intent on illustrating his point. "What's your favorite program, Anna?"

"*Sesame Street...*" she began.

Rajesh beamed like a proud father and wiggled his head from side to side.

"And *Jersey Shore*," she continued.

The answer caught Jack off guard and he burst out laughing.

Rolling his eyes, Rajesh fell into a nearby chair. "Sometimes when we aren't paying her enough attention she sneaks onto the Web and watches videos on YouTube."

Jack shook his head in disbelief. A mind filled with *Sesame Street* and *Jersey Shore*. Now there was a scary thought.

After that, he left Rajesh to finish his work and headed up two levels to his bunk. There he found Grant, lying down. The nearly sixty-year-old biologist had the berth beneath Jack's.

As Jack came within a few feet, he noticed Grant's cheeks and forehead were bright red. In several places, the scientist's skin appeared to be blistering.

"You feeling all right?" he asked.

Grant glanced over without getting up. "Tip-top. Just a little hot under the collar is all. Perhaps I caught a touch of sun when I wasn't paying attention."

They were off the coast of Mexico, so that wasn't out of the question. In fact, on the rig, sunscreen was considered as mandatory as hard hats and lifejackets.

"I just wanna make sure you aren't sick," Jack said. "I'm gonna get a thermometer."

"Oh, for heaven's sake," Grant shot back, gearing up for a fight before quickly realizing it wasn't a battle he had any hope of winning. As promised, Jack returned a moment later, and inserted one of those new-fangled thermometers into Grant's ear.

When Jack checked the readings, he saw the biologist was telling the truth—his temperature was normal. But something about Grant's skin reminded Jack of the conversation he'd had with Gord. The caretaker had described burn marks on Betsy and Tommy, two piglets on his rescue farm. Of course it was silly to believe there was any kind of connection. But that was how Jack's mind worked. The world was a giant puzzle upended onto the floor—much like the clothes in his ransacked cabin—and he couldn't help but hold pieces out two or three at a time, looking for any that might fit together.

A voice over a PA system brought everyone to attention. It was Commander Hart.

"Time to suit up, folks. We're going in."

Chapter 21

It was an hour later that Ollie heard back from his hacker contact, Armoni.

"He's willing to meet, but he wants ten thousand dollars up front."

"Ten thousand?" Mia exclaimed, feeling the wind from yet another door slamming in her face.

"Armoni may be a white hat, but that doesn't mean he works for free."

"Perhaps, but I can't get anywhere near that much."

"Let me see what I can do," Ollie said and spent the next several minutes, emailing back and forth. "I got him down to two thousand, but he wants it wired first."

Mia crossed her arms tightly over her knapsack again. "What guarantee do I have he won't just take the money and blow me off? Tell him fifteen hundred and only when we meet."

Ollie grinned. "You're one tough biscuit," he said, returning to his phone to relay the message.

Mia giggled. "You mean cookie."

He glanced up. "Huh?"

"In America we say 'tough cookie'."

Ollie pulled out his best Bogart impression. "You're not in America anymore, sweetheart." A moment later his face lit up. "He agreed."

A sense of relief washed over her.

Ollie then showed her the email where Armoni included his address. He instructed her not to put it in her phone, but to memorize it. She stared intently at the email, committing the address to memory. She repeated it over and over.

They pulled out of the parking structure and headed for the airfield on the outskirts of Santarem. By the side of the road, a group of older men sat outside drinking beer and playing dominos. A scooter zipped by at high speeds, a family of five piled precariously on every available surface.

"I sent a text to someone else I know," Ollie said, weaving through traffic. "Bloke I met at a local watering hole. He's a bush pilot named Gustavo who said he'd bring you to Manaus. From there you can buy yourself a ticket to Argentina. Cash only." That last part he said extra slow, his Australian drawl on full display, as if to emphasize the importance of staying off the grid.

He swung into a bank parking lot moments later, instructing Mia to head alone to the ATM. It was better he not be caught on camera anywhere near her or the police might arrest him too.

Mia soon returned with a stack of bills. She had removed the maximum she could from her checking account and then borrowed against her credit cards. She leafed through the money, her lips moving in unison.

"Three thousand."

He laid a hand on it. "Good. Now put that away, would you, before someone carjacks us? And not all in the same pocket. Put some of it in your socks as insurance."

She did as he suggested, thankful for all of his helpful tips. As Ollie pulled out he saw that she was looking at him.

"Look, I didn't exactly grow up in a picturesque part

113

of Brisbane," he told her. "My father was unemployed and drank to numb the sting of a life he felt he didn't deserve. There was often little food and plenty of discipline. For breakfast we were given a slice of plain white bread. For dinner we got a beating. Sometimes when I was lucky I got a beating and a bowl of cold soup. Trust me, you spend your childhood living with an old man who hates you for no good reason, and then your adolescence running with the wrong crowd to escape your crappy home life, you tend to pick up a few survival secrets the average bloke doesn't need to worry about."

Mia's eyes traced down to his hands as they worked the steering wheel, taking note of the nicks and scars. These were clearly places where a difficult life had left its mark. And those were only the scars she could see.

Ten minutes later, they were at the airfield. Ollie's friend flew a green-striped four-seat Cessna he kept at the far end of a grassy field. To their left was a long line of small aircraft parked on the apron, most of them two- and four-seaters. To their right was a row of hangars with open doors where mechanics were busy performing maintenance.

"There he is," Ollie said, motioning ahead. "If there's one thing I can say about Gustavo, he seems very dependable."

"Seems?" Mia repeated with alarm. "I thought you knew this guy?"

"We've shared a few cocktails here and there." Ollie sounded defensive. "Don't forget, lass, I've only been in this Godforsaken country a few weeks. The accent may be deceiving, but I'm not exactly a native."

They pulled up to the plane and jumped out. Everything Mia owned at the moment was contained within the little red knapsack now slung over both of her shoulders. Gustavo was wiping down the ivory-colored wing of his plane with a rag.

"Thank you for doing this, mate," Ollie said, gripping Gustavo's hand in a long shake. "I know it was last-minute, but once you bring my friend here to Manaus you can consider your debt to me paid in full."

Gustavo broke into an awkward smile. Mia noticed the slow change in Ollie's face. The two men continued shaking while an intense nonverbal conversation passed between them.

"Get in the plane," Ollie hollered as the sound of vehicles cutting around the distant hangar caught Mia's ear. She turned to see a convoy of police cars heading toward them.

"You double-crossing son of a bitch, Gustavo," Ollie shouted as he pulled the pistol and aimed it at him.

"Don't kill him," Mia pleaded. She'd seen more than enough death in the last twenty-four hours.

"Why would I kill him when he's the only one who can fly us outta here?" Ollie grabbed Gustavo by the collar and shoved him into the pilot's seat. "That's not to say I won't wound him a little." Ollie went around to the other side while Mia climbed in the back.

The propeller started to spin as Gustavo fiddled nervously with the controls.

"You keep stalling and I'll blow your kneecaps off," Ollie growled. "Now get us in the air."

Mia looked back, butterflies fluttering in her chest. The convoy of cops was getting closer. "Oh, God, hurry up."

Ollie pressed the barrel of the gun to Gustavo's knee and pulled back the hammer. "Your choice, mate."

Gustavo whimpered and threw the throttle, lurching the plane forward. Behind them the cops had reached the last hangar.

"Go, go, go!" Ollie bellowed.

Gustavo put on his headset and said a few words in

Portuguese. The plane straightened out.

"What are you doing?" Ollie demanded.

"Waiting for permission from the tower to—"

"Permission granted." Ollie forced the throttle all the way, throwing them back in their seats.

Police cars raced out onto the grassy runway and pulled alongside them, their weapons drawn.

"Hold on, everyone," Gustavo said, closing his eyes and pulling back on the yoke.

Mia felt gravity pushing down on every part of her body as the Cessna climbed into the air.

"Where are we going?" Gustavo asked, his frantic eyes falling to Ollie's pistol, still trained on him.

"Originally Manaus," Ollie replied. "But thanks to that little stunt you pulled, you're gonna have to take us all the way to Buenos Aires."

Gustavo's darkened complexion turned ashen. "We don't have enough fuel."

Ollie pulled out a map and spread it over his lap. "One stop in the state of Matto Grosso and another in Paraguay should do just fine." He turned back to Mia. "Oh, and you're really gonna love the in-flight movie. It's about this guy and girl from opposite sides of the world who get thrown together as they try to stay one step ahead of the authorities."

Chapter 22

Jack pulled his helmet on. As he clicked it in place, a cool rush of air caressed his cheeks. Each of the team members was nestled into a tight-fitting white biosuit made from organic polymers woven into a three-dimensional framework. Far from the unwieldy spacesuit or a bulky hazmat, the biosuit was light, flexible and filled with an array of biometric and toxicity sensors monitored by mission control. In this case, mission control was Lieutenant Olsen, who in turn would update Admiral Stark on their progress at the top of every hour.

Modular sockets on their backs allowed for a hydration bladder and a closed-circuit rebreather. But the pièce de resistance was the fancy-looking glasses they were all given, something Hart referred to as an OHMD (optical head-mounted display). A tiny digital recorder embedded into the right end piece enabled point-of-view video recording. On the left was a holographic display which could project images onto one of the lenses or into the empty space before them. Hand movements could then be used to scroll through maps or to flip through pages of data. Additionally, the glasses were networked, allowing all members to communicate as well as send information to one another.

Each suit also had a built-in LED light—two

thousand lumens strong—secured to the top of their helmet.

Gabby and Dag headed into the airlock, carrying cases with scientific instruments. Behind them was Anna's upper torso, which had been rigged to a rover platform with variable drive wheels. Jack watched as she navigated the airlock door's lower lip and maneuvered herself inside.

"She driving all on her own?" he asked Rajesh, over the radio.

The computer engineer wore the expression of a proud father watching his child take her first steps.

A few feet away, Hart was helping Eugene get his helmet secured.

"I can't turn my light on," the theoretical physicist said in a panic.

"Blink your left eye three times," Hart told him.

Eugene's mouth popped open in a thoroughly unattractive look as he pumped his left eye open and closed. "It's not wor…"

A burst of light shot out from Eugene's head lamp. Blinded, Jack spun away.

"Oh, there we go," Eugene cried. "Let's do this." A second ago he was about to cry, now he was the Terminator.

Once they were all assembled, Hart spoke over channel one, the main frequency. "Closing inner airlock door," he said, shuffling past the others, who pressed themselves and their gear up against the curved walls to make room. "Opening outer airlock door." A swoosh of condensed air flowed into the chamber.

Jack's heart thumped wildly.

"Jack, your vitals are a little elevated," Olsen said, from the Orb's command center.

Jack laughed. "I hear it's common when entering alien structures for the first time."

Gabby turned back and threw him a half-smile. The unglorified truth was, they were all pretty much crapping themselves. Except for Eugene, perhaps, who kept clapping his hands together like an infielder waiting for a ground ball. If Jack didn't know any better, he would say the theoretical physicist seemed on the verge of pushing past everyone so he could be the first one inside.

First one in and first to die.

Jack swiped the dark thought from his mind.

Regardless of Eugene's enthusiasm, Hart took the lead, disappearing into a puff of mist. They followed, lumbering along behind him in single file. Less than five feet in, they came to a hole where the engineers had installed a metal ladder. At the top of the hole was a small crane arm. This was how they would get Anna up and down. Not the most elegant solution, but certainly a limitation of having a team member without any legs.

This small chamber must have been the section that was flooded. Bits of slag and the distorted shape of the opening near the crane gave evidence that once the water had been pumped out, other Navy personnel had cut an opening into the structure.

Rajesh and Jack manned the crane, while Hart and Dag climbed below to help set Anna down. Jack closed the outer airlock and then climbed down as well. From there, an oval archway led from the stairs into a vast and darkened structure. Dust motes floated through the beam cast by his LED light as he stood fixed in wonder at the immensity of the area before him. His pulse quickened. The moisture in his mouth dried up with the dizzying array of thoughts coursing through his mind. They were venturing into an eerie world undisturbed for millions of years.

They were on some kind of open platform, with edges that vanished into darkness. The walls had what looked like piping or ducts running in several directions.

A central column ran through the center of the structure, all the way to the top. Jack wondered if it was some kind of lift. Like the spokes on a wagon wheel, a series of walkways connected the central column to the rest of the level.

Atmospheric readings appeared on Jack's OHMD glasses. "Keep your helmets on, folks," he told them. "The air down here is close to ninety percent nitrogen and nine percent oxygen." Such a mixture would leave them dead in seconds. By contrast, the Earth's atmosphere was seventy-eight percent nitrogen, twenty-one percent oxygen and one percent argon.

Swiveling around, Jack spotted what looked like railings fifty feet away. He had wondered whether the structure was right side up or upside down, but now he had his answer. He headed toward the railing and aimed his lights up into the ever-narrowing angle of the USO's roof. Once again the beams were eaten up by blackness. They had entered near the top of the structure. If there was still that much space left above them, he could only imagine what vastness lay below.

Jack's boots clanked on a metal surface. Glancing down, he studied the slate-gray floor. After touching the surface with the tips of his gloved fingers, Jack opened the sample case tied around his waist and removed a scraper and a plastic collection tube. The metal was hard, but he managed to peel off a few flecks and push them into the tube. Once it was sealed, he snapped it back into place next to dozens of empty tubes.

It was hard to regard even a simple metal surface without wondering what alien hands had been responsible for manufacturing and then putting it in place.

"Everyone, gather around," Hart called out over channel one.

Jack watched beams of light from each member

spear the murky darkness in every direction as they came together.

"Given the enormous size," Hart told them, "it's obvious we won't be able to cover enough ground if we're clumped together like a busload of tourists snapping shots of the Eiffel Tower. I think it's best we break into groups of two or three and maintain constant radio contact. You see anything that looks noteworthy, you call out before you go touching anything."

"I'll head in this direction with Gabby and Anna," Jack said, pointing ahead of him. He turned to Rajesh, who looked uneasy. "Don't worry, bud, I'll take good care of her."

The computer engineer hesitated, looking to Anna, who smiled reassuringly.

"I'm excited to be exploring on my own," she told Rajesh, who relented.

Grant nodded. "In that case, Dag, Rajesh and I will look for a way down to the lower levels."

Hart glanced over at Eugene, who had his hands on his hips like an Apollo astronaut. "I guess Buzz Lightyear and I will head to the upper decks and see what we can find."

"Buzz Lightyear?" Eugene repeated, bewildered. "That's a compliment, right?"

The others laughed.

"Have fun," Jack said, as he and Gabby set off.

"Wait for me, Dr. Greer," Anna pleaded, rolling after them, her illuminated face standing out against the darkness.

They continued for several minutes on the same level, until their lights caught the curved edges of what appeared to be an opening. Jack's initial estimate put it at twenty feet wide and just as high. The closer they got, the more it took on the distinct shape of a chamber. Over the radio, they could hear the other groups talking excitedly amongst themselves. Eugene was peppering Hart with questions about his SEAL training and whether he'd ever killed a man.

"Switch to frequency two," Jack told Gabby and Anna, which they did. "If I had to listen to another second of that, I think I'd throw myself over that railing." He was talking about the one circling the central pillar. Although the very thought of falling through nearly a mile of pitch blackness sent tingles up his vertebrae.

They stood at the mouth of the chamber, spearing rows of containers with their lights, some stacked one on top of another, others toppled over, lying on their sides, lids ajar.

"What do you make of it?" Jack asked, to no one in particular.

"Insufficient data," Anna said, rolling ahead as she scanned the unusual scene.

A voice with a British accent came onto channel two. "Jack, are you there?" It was Grant.

"We are. You find something?"

"You were right. The central shaft appears to be some sort of lift, although we haven't the slightest clue how it works."

"It may not have—" Jack had been about to say 'power' when soft red lighting illuminated the chamber. Anna stopped, craning her head upwards.

"Hold on," he told them. "Did we trip some kind of motion sensor?" he asked Gabby.

"I don't think so," Gabby replied. She was standing next to him, her breathing growing louder. "Anna was the first one in and nothing happened until you and I entered."

Jack grew pensive.

"What do you think it means?"

"It must have been activated by our biosignature," he

said, the implications rolling out before him like a long black carpet.

"And that's a bad thing?"

This time it was Anna who spoke. "Dr. Bishop, I believe it means that biological life forms once inhabited this structure."

A rogue thought occurred to Jack, one he kept to himself.

Perhaps they still do.

Chapter 23

It took three refueling stops before Ollie and Mia reached their destination. The final one occurred in Posadas, a city of close to three hundred thousand in northern Argentina. A three-hour flight followed, after which they landed at La Plata airfield, three miles southeast of Buenos Aires. The morning air was more than cool, it was downright frigid. For a brief moment Mia wondered how it could be so darn cold in August, until she remembered once you crossed south of the equator the seasons were reversed.

They had paid for the fuel with Mia's money. Now Ollie reached into his wallet and pulled out three American hundred-dollar bills and handed them to Gustavo. "This should get you home and then some."

Gustavo, resigned to his fate, took the money just as he had taken money from the police to rat them out. It was the way business was done among a certain shadier segment of the world's population. As it turned out, the old cliché that there was no honor among thieves bore more than a little truth.

On legs still stiff from the long flight, Ollie and Mia began a brisk walk in search of a taxi.

"I can't believe you gave him money after he tried to turn us into the police."

Ollie wiggled his index finger at her. "Technically, the only one he tried to turn in was you. My arrest would have merely been guilt by association."

Mia frowned. "Fine, but I still don't understand."

"It was hush money. A guy like Gustavo is what the Brazilians call 'un rato'." He scrunched up his face and scratched at her with clawed hands.

"Yeah, a rat, I get the picture."

"Inevitably, he'll spill the beans about us to anyone willing to pay. With any luck, that three hundred bucks just bought us a decent head start."

A string of taxis were lined up outside of the tiny airfield terminal. They got into the first waiting car.

"I hope your Spanish is better than your Portuguese," he said.

She recited the hacker's address from memory in fluent Spanish.

Ollie gave her an impressed look. The driver, on the other hand, was far from pleased. He began waving his hands in the air, speaking rapidly.

"What's the problem?" Ollie asked, looking annoyed.

"He's saying that the area is very bad. That we shouldn't be going there."

Ollie waved a fifty in front of the driver. "You heard the lady, now let's get moving."

The driver's eyes flitted from the fifty to Ollie and back again. He made the sign of the cross, snatched the bill and started driving.

They headed down Perito Moreno Avenue, a wide and bustling street which featured a large park and football stadium on one side and a shanty town on the other. The taxi turned into a neighborhood lined with three-story red-brick shacks. It made Santarem look like Beverly Hills. Scanning around, Mia was beginning to understand the driver's hesitation in bringing them here.

"Tell me you still have it," she said to Ollie, referring

125

to the pistol he'd kept trained on Gustavo for a big chunk of the flight.

He patted his hip with a metallic clank and gave her a wink.

Turned out they were in Bojo Flores, one of the toughest neighborhoods in Buenos Aires. Even worse, they had entered an area of Flores called Villa 1-11-14, the sort of place cops didn't enter unless riding in an armored car. And yet, for all of its grit, Flores had gained some notoriety recently as the birthplace and stomping ground for Jorge Mario Bergoglio, a man who in 2013 became Pope Francis.

But clearly not all of the country's residents were so benign. Both before and after World War II, Argentina had had the dubious honor of harboring Nazis in particular and fascists in general. As a result, a large segment of the population spoke German, Italian and in some cases both. After the war, rumors began to circulate that Adolf Hitler had escaped to Argentina. To that end, through the late forties and into the fifties US intelligence agencies—the FBI as well as the CIA—had dispatched agents to South America to investigate the claims. In spite of a lack of evidence, to this day, some continued to believe the Führer had died of old age in an Argentine villa rather than from a bullet to the temple in his Berlin bunker.

Mia and Ollie stepped out of the taxi and into a chilly wind. Her boots scuffed against faded asphalt. At least the streets were paved, a step in the right direction. She scanned the house numbers as the taxi tore off at a high rate of speed.

"Run, rabbit, run," Ollie said under his breath as he appeared next to her. He pointed. "This must be the one."

Mia scanned the run-down three-storey building before them. On the roof the tail end of a clothesline

126

was visible and below that a balcony with a set of a grey plastic table and chairs. On the street level, the entrance was flanked with dark passageways, no wider than a few feet. Ahead stood an imposing iron gate and a box on the wall with names and numbers next to it. Above the box was a camera. All of the name plates were empty except for one: Armoni.

"Moment of truth," Mia said, pushing the button.

They waited for nearly a minute without a response.

"You think maybe he didn't hear?" Mia wondered.

Ollie stepped in and tried his luck, this time holding the buzzer a few extra seconds.

Still nothing.

Neither of them dared turn on their phones to call or email, since that would risk giving away their location to the authorities.

Ollie cursed and threw up his hands, waving at the camera. "Open up, mate. We're freezing our balls off out here." He glanced over at Mia, who didn't look impressed.

They'd already started to walk away when the intercom sounded.

"Do you have the money?" a distorted voice asked. It was obvious English wasn't their first language, making it difficult to detect what was.

They headed back. "Yes," Mia said, reaching into her pocket before Ollie stopped her.

"All three thousand in American currency?"

She looked over at Ollie, confused.

"Uh, mate, we agreed on fifteen hundred. Remember?"

"Three thousand," the voice replied.

"Oh, come on, Armoni," Ollie barked. "We just flew four thousand bloody miles to see you. The police were chasing our plane. Don't do this."

"Three thousand or it's off."

Mia's spirits fell. After paying for the fuel, she only had twenty-five hundred left and Ollie had given Gustavo everything in his wallet.

"Would you watch my back while I show Armoni the money?" she whispered to Ollie.

His eyebrow went up.

"Just do it."

Ollie spun around and scanned the long, narrow street. "You're clear."

Mia drew closer to the camera and pulled out the amount they had agreed on. "I'm afraid fifteen hundred is the best we can do." She pouted, nudging her chest as close to the lens as she could. Using sex to get what she wanted wasn't Mia's style, but then again, neither was freezing her butt off. Three seconds later, the buzzer on the door sounded.

She pulled open the gate and shoved the money back into her pocket before waving Ollie in. "After you." Now it was Mia who wore the shit-eating grin.

Chapter 24

Jack knelt down beside one of the overturned containers, studying the translucent pouches that appeared to have spilled onto the floor. He reached out to pick one of them up with his gloved hands.

"Do you think we should wait?" Gabby asked, eyeing the strange hieroglyphs etched into each box.

"We can't very well call them in every time we stumble on something. Grab a scalpel and a sample bottle, would you?"

Gabby did so, while Anna pushed further into the chamber. It seemed to go on another fifty meters before tapering off along the structure's eastern bulkhead.

How could they be expected to get any answers to their questions if they weren't allowed to touch anything? Chief among those questions was whether millions of years ago this city-sized behemoth had flown here on its own, or whether it had been built inside the hollowed shell of the Chicxulub crater.

Jack studied the pouch, reflecting on how much it resembled a blood bag one might find at a hospital or emergency room. Along the top were a series of images strung out in a straight line. If they could speak alien, they would know right away what they were looking at. He squeezed the contents, feeling it crumble beneath his fingers. The stuff inside was dry, holding the consistency of a powder or spice. Jack used the scalpel to slice through the membrane, scooped out a few grams of the dusty substance and deposited it into one of the sample tubes.

Just then Anna returned from inspecting the rest of the chamber. She rolled over at once and picked up one of the pouches, examining it intently. "Dr. Greer, I have counted five hundred and thirty-two containers. I have also recorded similar sets of symbols on every case."

"Similar?" Gabby asked. "They aren't identical?"

Anna's wheels squealed as she turned to face Gabby, her head tilted slightly to one side. "No, they are not identical, Dr. Bishop. It might indicate a variation in the cargo held by each container."

Gabby turned to Jack. "Any ideas on what this stuff was used for?"

He shook the question away. "Too early to say," Jack replied, storing the tube back in the kit on his waist. "But whatever this was, they had a hell of a lot of it."

Commander Hart's voice sounded over the comms line. "I'm up near the top of the pyramid and there's something I think you folks should see."

•••

Jack and the others scaled a series of ramps along the outer bulkhead. They went up four levels before they passed through a high doorway and into what appeared to be the bridge of a ship. The light from Hart's and Eugene's suits fused with the soft greenish glow from panels recessed into the walls. Bolted into the floor before each panel stood something that looked like a cross between a bench and a chair.

Up from the center of the bridge rose the elevator shaft. Like the rest of it, the lift was a closed unit with a single entrance and exit. The remainder of the bridge was illuminated by flickering control panels and holographic displays.

Hart was over by the floating green hologram of a diamond. Upon approach, more and more details began to fill in.

"Well, I guess we can put one question to rest," Dag said, the bottom of his red beard folded inside his helmet.

"This is no building," Grant said, finishing Dag's thought. "It's a ship. Which leads us to what you might say is the elephant in the room, or at least one of them."

Ever the protective father, Rajesh was bent over Anna, running a quick diagnostic. "Which elephant is that?" he asked.

Grant pushed his gloves on tighter. "The Yucatán asteroid impact sixty-five million years ago has long been regarded as the prime suspect in the demise of the dinosaurs and many other species. I think it's rather obvious at this point that that theory is in dire need of retooling."

Eugene slid back into one of the unusually-shaped console seats. "You're suggesting that this ship and not an asteroid was what crashed, devastating the planet?"

"As difficult as it may be to accept, I await a more plausible explanation."

"Do you know the kind of forces such an impact would generate?" Gabby said, her mind working out the math.

Ever the good student, Anna raised an arm. "The approximate forces generated by this structure impacting the earth at twelve miles per second would equal one hundred million Hiroshima bombs."

Jack's forehead furrowed. "That's strange. Prior calculations had estimated the asteroid was nine miles wide and generated a destructive force equivalent to a billion Hiroshimas."

"But this thing isn't nine miles wide," Dag said,

scratching his helmet.

"In that case," Jack said, "could it have been coming in a lot faster than we thought?"

"Which still begs the question," Eugene said emphatically. "Why didn't it simply disintegrate? I mean, meteorites that impact the earth are almost always pulverized and thrown up into the atmosphere. It's the reason we only tend to find little chunks of them spread all over."

Jack turned to Commander Hart. "Those Navy divers in the atmosphere suits, the ones who set up the Orb. Can you have them attempt to get samples from the hull and the sediment around the base of the ship?"

"I'm sure I can," Hart said. "What are you thinking?"

"What are the chances the Navy's in the market for a nearly impenetrable metal alloy?"

"I see what you mean," he replied. "But they aren't dumb. You can rest assured if a sample's been taken, it's already being analyzed."

"See what you can find out then," Jack said. He drew in a deep breath and turned to the rest of the group. "If this ship was a speeding bullet, impacting the earth and initiating a mass extinction, the question is why? Was it an accident?"

"You mean like the *Exxon Valdez*?" Dag asked. No one reacted. "You know, the captain downed a few too many and then blammo. They struck Prince William Sound's Bligh Reef. Millions of gallons of oil came pouring out, destroying the ecosystem."

"Drunk aliens," Gabby said, summing up Dag's theory rather succinctly. "I like the way you think. Where'd you get your degree again?"

Grant slapped a hand on Dag's shoulder. "Wasn't it a box of Lucky Charms?"

"I can see his diploma now," Eugene said, jumping in and hardly able to contain himself. "Across the top in big yellow letters…" He broke down, howling laughter, struggling to get the words out. "'M-magically delicious.'"

"No joke," Dag admitted. "I'd do anything right now for a bowl of Lucky Charms."

"Both of you need to get out more," Gabby said, moving over to one of the consoles, staring at it.

Jack followed, giving her a sign to switch to another channel. "What is it you see?"

"You asked before if some sort of accident had caused the ship to crash."

As she spoke, he couldn't help thinking about the toppled containers they'd found earlier. "What about it?"

"Well, maybe there's something in the system that maintains the ship that could tell us. It's been running, albeit in some sort of sleep mode, for millions of years. Surely the answers are in here."

"You may be right," Jack admitted. "But I gotta say, my knowledge of alien languages and computer systems is a little thin."

"Mine too," she said, her eyes tracing over to Anna, who was busy running her robotic hand along a seat on the other side of the bridge. "What about her?"

Rajesh moved in. "I'm very sorry to admit, Dr. Greer, but I was eavesdropping on your conversation."

"Well, do you think it's possible then?" Jack asked.

"An alien language holds a nearly infinite range of possibility. When the Allies were decoding German messages in World War II, for example, they were doing so with a working knowledge of the German alphabet."

Gabby nodded. "Yes, this would be closer to deciphering Aztec hieroglyphics."

"To a degree," Rajesh said. "But even then, much of language is about context. We search for repeating patterns in the text. Patterns describing elements of a shared experience. For example, tree, river, bird, food, war. Of course, these are only the tip of the iceberg when it comes to what two earthly cultures might share. But go ahead and remove those common experiences and all at once you find yourself lacking a common framework, or even a starting point."

"So it's doable," Jack said, brushing aside the difficulty of the task.

Rajesh wiggled his head, an enigmatic Indian way of saying yes, no and maybe all at the same time.

"Good." Jack left and went over to Anna.

As he approached, the robot's face brightened and her lips moved. Jack held up two fingers. A second later, there she was on channel two. *Smart bugger*, he thought. "Dr. Greer, I have been analyzing the seats on the bridge and they are most enlightening."

"Oh, really? How so?"

She dipped the pads of her fingers into a groove along the seat back. "If you look closely, you will see a rather specific indentation."

Jack moved closer and reached in with his gloved hands. Anna was right. There was a series of raised lines and deep depressions. Looking closely, you could just make out the distinct shape of what might have fit inside the space, much the same way that one might guess the dimensions of a human foot by studying a shoe.

The indentation resembled a pair of wings.

A call from Lieutenant Olsen sounded over all available channels. "Admiral Stark wants you all back on the Orb ASAP."

"What's the problem?" Jack asked, no doubt expressing a concern shared among all of them.

"He's mighty pissed," Olsen explained, not mincing his words. "Apparently, one of you leaked to the media and he's threatening to pull the plug."

Chapter 25

Mia and Ollie climbed a narrow stairway that led to Armoni's flat. At the top and to the left stood a blue metal door. A jailer's slit snapped open, revealing a pair of eyes that glared down at them. They banked to the right, as if to make sure no one else had snuck in behind them. The slit slammed shut. A large bolt turned and the door swung open. Inside was a space far nicer than Mia had expected—by no means opulent, or even luxurious, but it appeared to have four solid walls and a roof that didn't leak. Energy-saving bulbs hung from the ceilings, casting a hazy mist about the corridor. A figure wearing black jeans and a hoodie stomped down the hall before disappearing around a corner.

"Leave the money in the wooden box on the wall and close the door behind you."

Ollie and Mia exchanged a look and did as they were told. The box was just large enough for a stack of bills two inches deep.

Tentatively, they made their way down the corridor and into an open kitchen and living room.

A young woman was by the fridge pulling out a bottle of cacao-flavored Soylent meal replacement. She tossed one to Mia and one to Ollie. Both of them studied the label.

"It tastes like pancake batter," she said, "but you get used to it."

"We're here to see Armoni," Ollie said, his impatience bleeding through. "Where is he?"

The girl stopped in mid-sip. "Depends. What do you need him for?"

"We have an encrypted USB we need him to crack," Mia said. "And maybe more. Is he here or not?"

The girl finished her drink and raised her hands, palms flat and angled inward—a sign even Mia understood to mean, *You're looking at him.*

"I thought you said Armoni was a guy?" Mia asked Ollie.

"We've only ever communicated online," Ollie explained, just as surprised.

"Uh-huh, the famous *Nat Geo* interview," she said, staring at him accusingly.

He shrugged. "What can I tell you? We had budgetary constraints. Email is free. Plane tickets are not."

Armoni watched the back-and-forth with something resembling amusement. She was five feet, maybe a touch more, with short stringy hair that was angled in every direction at once. Her facial features were strangely androgynous. Perhaps in darker light she might have passed for a guy somewhere in his twenties, an illusion that was dispelled by the unmistakable bumps beneath her hoodie and her wide female hips.

"You're less endowed than you looked at the front door," Armoni observed, eyeing Mia's cleavage.

Her cheeks flushed. "They say the camera adds ten pounds."

Armoni let out a genuine laugh, her hand covering her mouth, the first girly thing she'd done so far. "So where's this unbreakable USB key?"

Mia fished in her backpack. "Unbreakable for us at

least." She looked at it for a moment and hesitated before tossing it over.

Armoni led them into a darkened room lit by the glow of half a dozen computer monitors. Pushed up against the walls was a disparate array of office furniture: a stainless-steel filing cabinet, a coffee maker, and a rack of servers, each connected by a length of black wires that snaked up to the walls and along the ceiling like water pipes on a submarine. In the center of her little Batcave were two semi-circular desks dotted with monitors. Each was set end to end, creating a three-hundred-and-sixty-degree hacking interface. Just the thought of climbing inside gave Mia a migraine.

Since she had guests, Armoni cracked open her circular workspace and settled into a plush leather chair. She inserted the USB and then proceeded to crack her knuckles. "A little ritual," she told them. Straight away, the window popped up asking for a name and password. Armoni ignored that and clicked on a program called Pass-Sniffer. A progress bar appeared as the program went to work. Within no time it had climbed from thirty percent to ninety and then to an error.

Armoni sat up in her seat. Clearly the USB wasn't nearly the pushover she had expected. Seemed things were about to get interesting. "Looks like we got a FIPS 140-2 on our hands."

Mia and Ollie looked at one another, equally lost.

"It's an encryption protocol. A real pain. Usually reserved for government stuff." She drew in an excited breath and tried another program called FIPS-MD. "Don't you just love the smell of smoking CPUs in the morning?" she said, presumably loading up an array of movie quotes. The progress bar on FIPS-MD started at one percent and stayed there for several minutes. Armoni drummed the fingers of her left hand on the desk, her gleeful features bathed with harsh light from the monitors before her.

She then clicked a program called Dragon Slayer.

"What will that one do?" Mia asked, feeling she was slowly getting the hang of this.

Armoni chuckled. "It's an MMO." Then, after Mia wasn't getting it, she explained, "Massively Multiplayer Online."

Mia turned to Ollie for guidance.

"I think it's a video game," he said.

"Oh."

"Anyway, this is gonna take a while. Feel free to grab a seat somewhere and make yourselves comfortable." That subtle hint at an accent returned with the word 'comfortable,' making it come out sounding like 'come four table.'

"I think I'll go freshen up," Mia said, painfully aware of the heat emanating from her armpits.

Chapter 26

Mia returned a few minutes later to find Ollie in the living room, leaning back on a dingy-looking futon. He stared at a muted television on the far wall, his expression blank.

A shout from Armoni's hacker den startled them. She was asking for someone to buff her.

"Back in my day," Ollie said, taking a sip from a warm bottle of Soylent, "a nerd was a wanker with thick glasses and jacked-up pants."

Mia chuckled. "How things have changed." And almost on cue, a shout erupted from the other room.

"Heal the tank, dammit!"

"I have no clue what's going on in there," Mia continued, the remnants of a grin still on her face. "I just hope this won't take much longer."

"Why the rush? I mean, it's probably still not safe to head home."

"I have a daughter," Mia explained, her tone growing sullen. "I need to make sure she's okay." Her eyes traced down to the phone in her pocket.

"Don't," he warned, putting his hand on hers. "When Armoni's done killing goblins, I'm sure she'll be able to route an untraceable call for you via the internet. Tell me about your husband," Ollie said, his eyes

139

unwavering.

She looked away and shook her head. "No husband. Not anymore."

"He cheated on you, the bastard."

"It's more complicated than that."

Ollie's eyes grew wide before settling back to their normal size. "You were the unfaithful one?"

That faraway look again. "Like I said… What about you?" she asked, trying desperately to change the subject.

"If you're asking if I'm married…"

"No." She cut him off. "I can't imagine any woman who would wait at home while you go galloping around the world."

"For your information, I do far more trotting than galloping. But you may very well be right. I've had more short-term relationships than I can remember. At some point, it always seemed like someone would pull a switch and everything would fall apart." He looked down at his hands, as though he could see sand pouring between his fingers.

"And when you arrive back home between gigs? Is that when they're usually gone?"

He looked up at her. "I suppose I won't be winning Husband of the Year anytime soon."

She shook her head. "I'd say it's more of an occupational hazard."

"Doesn't help when the occupant is damaged goods."

She let out a laugh that didn't have an ounce of humor in it. "Aren't we all? Life starts beating the crap out of us from the moment the doctor slaps us on the ass and rarely takes a day off." She studied the lines on his face. "Did you serve in the military? Is that what did it?"

"In a manner of speaking."

"I don't understand."

"My first assignment for *National Geographic*, I was sent to Afghanistan and embedded with the 173rd Airborne Brigade. Summer of 2008. They were a platoon, no more than fifty soldiers, many of them kids, who were struggling to establish a remote outpost in the Waygal District.

"The first sign things weren't okay? The chopper I flew in on took sporadic fire the whole way there. Then I arrived and saw that the outpost was positioned at the bottom of a deep valley. A first lieutenant, young man by the name of Bows, let me know in no uncertain terms he'd been expecting reinforcements and resupply, not a damn photojournalist. These guys were low on water and equipment, left to fill sandbags by hand.

"Sure didn't help that the local Afghans were acting strange. Men of fighting age sat around watching the preparations intently. Some were even observed counting off paces around the perimeter. Go shoot 'em, right?" Ollie laughed. "I asked the same thing. But Lieutenant Bows made it clear relations with the locals were already frayed.

"On my end, I kept snapping pictures and asking questions until Bows grabbed a rifle and pushed it into my chest. Said if I wasn't prepared to pitch in if and when the shit hit the fan, he could arrange my immediate transport out. He was challenging me, throwing down a gauntlet, so I did what anyone would do."

Mia frowned. "You accepted."

"Damn right I accepted. But it wasn't just my ego talking. I figured it might help ingratiate me and break down the wall they'd put up to keep me out. Bows showed me the ins and outs of an M4, how to reload, clear a jam. All the while, I got to keep asking my questions and snapping some great shots.

"Then two nights later, the Taliban swept down from the mountains." Ollie's hands surfed along an imaginary current of air. "Must have been hundreds of them, pouring out of the hills like a spring thaw. Bullets buzzing all around us. That was when the incoming artillery started. Mortars shook the ground. Rocket-propelled grenades sizzling past your nose before crashing into half-filled Hesco barriers.

"If there is such a thing as hell on earth, let me tell you, that was it. The air was thick with bullets and the screams of the wounded on both sides. Lieutenant Bows and I were on a small mound of earth with six other men, pinned down by fire from every direction. The soldiers had erected razor wire around our position, but the Taliban came right up, unloading their weapons. I can still see their faces, that look of hatred and determination." Ollie was staring off into the distance, as though he were watching a movie play out inside his head. "It was soon after that Bows was shot and killed. That's when I swapped the camera for the rifle. I felt like General Custer at Little Bighorn. A head wrapped in a dark cloth appeared in the window of a nearby hut and I riddled it with bullets. Then ten feet away another fighter charged the razor wire with a hand grenade." Ollie's right hand rose into the air. "I shot him too, but not before he tossed it inside our perimeter. Time slowed to a crawl. I remember looking back in panic, trying to see where it had landed. I'd watched enough movies to know if you were quick you could toss them back. What I didn't know was that this particular Taliban fighter had let the grenade cook off for a couple of seconds before he threw it. I just remember an ear-shattering boom before I blacked out." Ollie grew quiet, the fingers of his right hand shaking. Mia took his quivering hand and cupped it in her own. He remained silent for another few minutes before he said, "So when you ask if I've ever served, the answer is no, but I guess like everything else in life, the truth is never so clear-cut."

Ollie went on to tell her he still had pieces of shrapnel lodged in his body. These were the scars Mia had caught glimpses of. She was still comforting him when her eyes happened upon the television. A small picture next to the newscaster's head looked like the radar image of an object underground. Then it cut to footage of a strange metallic structure from an underwater ROV. Although it was in Spanish, Mia could still make out the headline.

Scientists discover proof of alien life beneath the waves.

The remote was on the coffee table, nestled amongst discarded bottles of Soylent and empty pizza boxes. Mia grabbed it and flipped though the channels, searching for one of the twenty-four-hour cable news networks in English.

When she finally found one, they were showing the same images. A moment later, they cut to an anchor seated against a backdrop of the White House.

"There is still no confirmation of the discovery's precise location, but sources close to the story tell us the US military is currently involved with investigating as well as examining the object. If you're just joining us, the information coming in is sketchy at best, although initial reports suggest a massive unidentified object has been found deep underwater. We've reached out to each branch of the military and have yet to hear back. All of this is in the midst of perhaps the greatest international incident the United States has faced since the Cuban Missile Crisis brought the country to the brink of war some fifty years ago."

The cable news show's next guest was an eccentric white-haired theoretical physicist named Kenichi Sato, who came on to explain the Kardashev scale. Proposed by Soviet astronomer named Nikolai Kardashev in 1964, the scale was intended to classify alien civilizations according to their level of energy utilization. A Type One civilization was so-called because of its ability to harness all of the energy that fell on the planet from its parent star. In our case, humans currently consumed less than twenty terawatts of power, one-one thousandth of the energy that reached our planet. And yet the sun's total output was much greater, closer to four hundred billion terawatts.

A Type Two civilization, Sato went on, was able to gather the entire radiation output from its parent star by using a Dyson Sphere, a massive theoretical enclosure built around the sun and designed to absorb every last drop of energy.

Third on the Kardashev scale was a Type Three civilization, one which could control and consume the energy of an entire galaxy.

According to this hypothetical template, humanity ranked somewhere shy of a Type One. But Sato refused to speculate how advanced a civilization might need to be in order to reach our solar system and build the kind of structure discovered underwater. "We could be talking about hundreds of years more advanced than us, maybe even thousands."

Still reeling, Mia's mind turned to the package Alan had sent her and his claim of having found some kind of message hidden in the Salzburg chromosome's DNA. She wondered whether those two things could somehow be related.

Just then Armoni popped out of her gloomy computer cave. The smile on her face faded. "Did a war break out?"

"Not yet," Ollie said, ominously.

"Then you'll be happy to hear my guild cleared Ashglenn dungeon."

Mia did not look impressed.

Armoni turned to head back to her computers and stopped. "Oh, and I cracked your USB."

Chapter 27

Stark glowered down from the monitor that hung in the Orb's mess. "Which one of you did it?" he barked, his accusation hanging in the air like a heavy mist.

None of them said a word. Most had already removed and hung up their biosuits, except for Dag, who'd opted to lose the helmet, but keep the glasses and the fitted polymer body stocking.

The group glanced from one to another, their expressions ranging from guilt to utter bewilderment. Jack knew he was innocent, although he was just as certain he was at the top of Admiral Stark's suspect list. And why wouldn't he be? Jack had threatened to notify the media to prevent Stark from kicking them off their own scientific expedition. It was a game of high-stakes poker and Jack had thrown in with nothing but a three and an eight, which was to say he'd been bluffing his ass off. Of course he'd never sent Gord a backup of the USO data. Even if he had, Gord would not have had the foggiest idea what to do with it.

"What makes you so certain it was one of us?" Jack asked, stating what others in the room were probably also wondering. "We've been down here for a while now."

"Yes," Stark said. "But that fat fiberoptic cable running down to the Orb gives you access to the outside world. Someone sent out ten emails with nearly the exact same picture and video files attached to each one. They did everything but lay a trail of breadcrumbs to the structure."

"Ship," Grant corrected him.

"Excuse me?" Stark snapped.

"We've discovered that it's a ship," he went on, folding his sunburnt hands under his armpits. The flesh on his face was peeling, giving him the distinct appearance of a charbroiled chicken. "Landed here approx—"

"Crashed," Dag corrected him.

"Yes, of course." Grant leaned forward. "It crashed quite a while ago, ending life for a good seventy-five percent of the species on earth."

"So they attacked us?" Stark asked, his jaw tightening.

"Hmm, not exactly." Jack jumped in, rocking forward in his chair. "*Homo sapiens*, heck, *homo* anything, wasn't around sixty-five million years ago. So they weren't exactly attacking us."

"So what are we looking at here?" Stark asked. "A joy ride through space?"

Jack smiled and planted his feet. "That's what we're trying to figure out. I have a feeling if we can decrypt their language we might answer that question."

"Well, that little stunt you people pulled will likely spell the end of this research project. I just got off the phone with the president. Due to its sensitive nature, Secretary of Defense Myers is being flown in to oversee

146

the operation. Not to mention Naval Intelligence has plans to deploy sooner than expected. And let me assure you, when they arrive, their only mission will be to extract as much foreign technology as they can get their hands on. So whatever you need to do, do it quickly."

The screen went black.

"From now on," Olsen informed them, "all digital access to topside is restricted."

Rajesh raised his hand. "What about Anna's servers on the rig? She must be able to access them."

Olsen didn't look hopeful. "I'll see what I can do, but to everyone else it's off limits." He flicked through screens on his tablet and floated them over to the big screen. "It isn't all bad news, thank goodness. Information on the hull composition has just come in. It appears to be eighty-six percent magnesium and fourteen percent silicon carbide particles. The technicians up top are calling it a nanocomposite metal and say whoever manufactured it needed to disperse and stabilize nanoparticles in molten metals, a process they suspect was performed in a zero-G environment." Olsen raised his eyebrows. "That mean anything to you?"

"Sure does," Gabby said, rubbing her neck.

"Humans have only just become aware of this sort of thing," Grant said.

"What he's saying is that whoever crashed that ship into the Yucatán Peninsula was only a few hundred years more advanced than we are today."

"At least a few hundred years," Eugene added. "But no more than a thousand. And who knows where they are now, sixty-five million years after the fact."

"For all we know," Jack said, "they've blown themselves to smithereens."

147

Gabby grimaced. "The more we get to know them, the more they sound just like us."

Chapter 28

Mia and Ollie stood hunched over Armoni's shoulder as she opened the now-decrypted USB.

"Whoever scrambled this thing really didn't want anyone getting inside," the hacker said, enlarging the window.

Frowning, Mia remarked, "Alan was always ultra-protective of his work." She recalled how scientists working in the lab were prohibited from bringing home research data they'd collected. Banning samples and biological material made perfect sense, but even laptops had to stay behind. That meant long hours at the lab. Back then, Mia had assumed this was Alan's twisted way of keeping her close to him.

"Uptight about security," Armoni replied. "There's an understatement if ever I heard one. You wouldn't believe the hoops I had to jump through to crack this little sucker. I've only ever seen anything like this once before."

The thought crossed Mia's mind that Armoni's supposed hardships could very well be part of a ploy to extract more money from them.

With the window now enlarged, three folders became visible: BreakerAlt, GenMark and SS Genome.

"Click on 'SS Genome,'" Mia suggested, rushing

149

back to grab Alan's notebook from her red knapsack. Much of what he'd written there was a jumble of ideas that had occurred to him throughout his research on Salzburg.

Armoni did so. "It's asking to install a program called GeneMark-ET v.4.29," she said a moment later when a window popped up requiring her confirmation.

"Do it," Mia said. "I can't imagine Alan would have entrusted this to me only so he could infect your system with a virus."

Armoni ran a protective scan on the program anyway. When it turned up negative for viruses or malicious software, she unpacked and installed it. Once finished, GeneMark opened up, filling the majority of the program window with a series of letters. GATC. Scrolling down with her mouse, Armoni whistled. "There sure is a lot of this stuff."

They were looking at pages and pages of genetic information containing the Salzburg genome.

Ollie snickered. "What do you call half a chromosome again?"

"A chromatid," Mia replied. "That is, one side of it, but holding all the DNA information for that chromosome."

"Yeah, that's right. Who woulda thought such a small chromatid could pack so much punch?"

What neither Ollie nor Armoni realized was that some ninety-seven percent of what made up Salzburg contained non-coding DNA, a number that was also true for the other twenty-three chromosomes in the human body. Some liked to call it junk DNA, since it was part of the genome not related to a specific gene, or, put another way, sections of DNA that did not code for proteins. But recent discoveries had demonstrated that the disparaging nickname was far from accurate. Instead of being useless, scientists were only beginning to understand that non-coding DNA helped to regulate how our genes expressed themselves. And that was just the tip of the iceberg. Mia was confident that in the coming years we would begin to truly appreciate the full role non-coding DNA played in our daily lives as well as our genetic evolution.

Mia leafed through Alan's notebook, searching for clues about how he had discovered any kind of message in all this. Technical terms jumped out at her from every page. Information theory, cryptography, statistical analysis. Ten pages in, she found 'Breaker1' underlined three times. They had a folder named 'BreakerAlt'. She knew about Breaker1 from her work as a researcher. It was an algorithm designed to help locate genes by signaling their most likely location in a genetic sequence. But Mia had never heard of BreakerAlt before. She suggested they start there.

Armoni ran the BreakerAlt algorithm on the genetic material for Salzburg. The process took close to half an hour and Mia's legs were starting to buckle. Ollie fetched a plastic folding chair from the kitchen and offered it to her.

Smiling, she thanked him, and then returned her attention to the screen. After the algorithm had run its course, a new stream of data emerged. It had somehow taken the four letters of the genetic code and simply jumbled them further.

Mia sighed, tapping her pant leg to an invisible beat. "We're missing something." She went back to the notebook for any other clues.

"If you ask me," Ollie offered, growing more annoyed by the second, "this Alan guy was batshit crazy."

"I'll be the first to attest that Alan was a lot of things," Mia admitted, shocked to be defending him. "But crazy he was not."

151

Armoni swiveled in her chair. "Looking at all these letters gives me a headache." Her eyes turned to the heavens, her arms splayed, bellyaching to God or whatever deity she happened to believe in. "Oh, great Creator, what on earth was wrong with using zeros and ones? I'll take binary any day of the week."

Mia smiled and was about to turn back to the notebook when something struck her. "What did you just say?" she asked Armoni.

The hacker regarded her with a look of uncertainty. "Uh, these letters give me a headache?"

"No, after that," Mia said with renewed intensity.

"I'll take binary…"

"That may be why this isn't working," she shouted.

"Ladies, for the record, I have no idea what you're on about," Ollie interjected. "How about I put some coffee on?"

"Hold the coffee," Mia said, staring at the jumble of letters on the screen. "The genetic code consists of two base pairs formed from the letters GATC—guanine, adenine, thymine and cytosine. The structure of DNA forms a double helix—uh, think of a long winding ladder with each rung representing a base pair. In simple terms, that means that on a given rung of our imaginary ladder A is always paired with T and G is always paired with C. And it doesn't matter what order they're in. You can have AT or TA. The next rung might show GC or CG. But here's the important part, A never goes with C or G, only with T."

"So you're saying I shouldn't have dropped out of school," Ollie quipped.

Mia, took Armoni by the hands. "I'm saying, just like computer code, DNA is also written in a binary format. If the message is in there, that's how we'll find it."

Chapter 29

After Admiral Stark's scathing rebuke and assessment that time was running out—and fast—the scientists agreed it was best to head back into the ship as soon as possible. Before donning his biosuit, Jack descended to the lab, where he found Grant running some last-minute tests on the substance from the translucent pouches. The mass spectrometer was nearly finished. It operated by creating a beam of ionized atoms from the sample. A magnetic field then diverted those atoms into sensors, called Faraday cups, that measured the isotopic signature and helped to identify the sample.

A shrill beep sounded as a trio of pages emerged from the nearby printer. Grant went over and picked them up. Surprise emanated from the back of his throat.

"Feel like sharing?" Jack asked, stepping closer to peek at the results.

Grant cleared his throat. "Yes, of course. Um, hexadecanoic acid ethyl ester. Gallocatechin. Beta-tocopherol—"

"You're losing me," Jack said, frowning.

"It's a consumable," Grant replied, taking a final look before he let the paper drop to his side.

"Food?"

Grant nodded enthusiastically.

"Can you tell what kind?"

Grant glanced at the paper again. "My best guess is some sort of fruit. Something with compounds similar to a banana peel."

"Hmm, crates of banana peel mush," Jack said, as though relishing the idea. "Doesn't exactly sound appetizing. Most of the stuff we found was little more than a coarse powder."

"But it tells us this was a manned mission with a crew that was expecting to stick around for a while."

Jack swallowed down the taste of banana in his mouth. "So where did they go?"

•••

Thirty minutes later, they were back on the ship. Anna headed to the bridge where she would attempt to decipher the alien language. It was a long shot, but Jack had seen mysterious hieroglyphs cycling across the display screens. It wasn't much, but at least it was a start. Perhaps if they found a library somewhere on board, they could redeploy her.

This time, Jack teamed up with Grant and Dag to form team one, while Hart, Gabby and Eugene would stick together to form team two. Team one's mission was to see if they could reach the bottom floor. Perhaps there they might get a glimpse of the ship's propulsion and any damage that might have been caused by the impact. Meanwhile, team two would descend one level at a time, taking care to investigate any notable rooms or areas of interest.

The three men maneuvered down the ramp, chasing away the darkness with their powerful lights.

"I should be used to this," Grant said, his reddened face a mask of nostalgia. "My father worked as a coal miner all his life. Left at dawn, came home after dark. He went days on end without seeing a single ray of sunlight. My overriding memory of the man was his skin stained with coal dust and his bulging eyes. Once he took me along, deep into the guts of the earth. The smell, the chill in the air. I'll never forget it."

"Sounds like he wasn't around much," Dag said, adjusting the light on his helmet, which was flickering on and off.

"What child ever sees their parents enough?" Grant threw back. "Maybe nowadays things are somewhat different with fathers staying home. But back in my day, you were grateful for what little time you got. I loved the old man and looked up to him. Wanted to be a coal miner myself, until I realized I'd never really gotten over my fear of the dark."

Jack caught his eye and motioned to the inky blackness before them. "I suppose this time, the coal mine found you."

The other two laughed.

"Don't worry, Jack. I won't go and wet myself. My antipathy for the dark is nowhere near your fear of flying."

"That may be so, but I still fly when I need to," Jack replied, challenging the biologist. "Sure, I grit my teeth and knock back a drink or two when I can, but I fly."

Dag piped in. "I heard about your fear of flying the first time we worked together."

"The Popigai diamond mine," Jack said.

"Yes, quite a find," Dag said. "Helped to cement your reputation as the diamond whisperer. And it was only on the next job we worked that I found out you ran a zoo."

Jack flashed his teeth in a hearty laugh. "It's a rescue farm."

"Oh, that's right. So what fun fact will I learn about the great Jack Greer this time around?"

"Maybe that I'm no good at giving interviews."

Dag's eyes narrowed in amusement. "I doubt that

very much. Your pitch to DiCore seemed to do the trick, although I'm sure they're beginning to realize finding any lucrative gems at the impact site isn't gonna happen."

Jack agreed. "Well, at least they can take some solace knowing their company name will forever be attached to the story of man's greatest discovery, namely that we are not alone in the universe. But to answer your question, you've probably heard everything about me worth knowing."

They reached another ramp and continued even deeper.

"There is that rumor about your father," Grant said. "Although I understand if you don't feel like discussing it."

Jack felt his teeth click shut. "What's to say? Your dad was a coal miner, mine was... well, something else."

"I heard he was a famous geologist at NASA," Dag replied in awe. "That he studied the moon rocks and died in a plane crash at twenty-three. Of course, that would have made you—"

"Six months old," Jack said, not sure he was interested in heading down memory lane. It was a path filled with webs of shadows and lies, a little like the journey they were on right now. "I distinctly remember hearing the name Kip Greer a half dozen times a day growing up. My mother seemed determined to keep his memory alive any way she could.

"It was true, my old man was a scientist and, growing up in Houston, something of a local hero. I guess it's one of the reasons I eventually became a geophysicist. But the road I took to get there wasn't a straight one. I'd just become a teenager when my mother met a man named Roy Bradley. An insurance salesman. He was a moose of a man with a booming voice and a fondness for hard liquor. The sorta guy who made you feel like you were his bud. Unless, that is, you didn't quite see the world the way he did. Then all that charm melted away like ice on a hot summer's day.

"For some reason, Roy was determined to prove he was better than me. Quite frankly, I'm not sure why, but by my senior year of high school I'd had enough and ran away. Worked on oil rigs in the Gulf for a while before I found my way back to school and to a degree. By then, Roy had drunk himself into a coffin from cirrhosis. My mother soon followed.

"All I had left was a father I'd never known, Kip Greer. So I did what any son should have a long time ago. Once a month I started visiting the cemetery, laying a bouquet of flowers by his grave. But I wasn't the only one. Seemed like whenever I showed up, I found a bundle of white tulips resting up against his headstone.

"It got me curious. I mean, was NASA laying these down for my dad on account of him being a hero struck down in his prime? Slowly that kernel of curiosity grew into a full-blown obsession and I began staking out his grave. I needed to know who it was who kept showing up."

Jack stopped at the base of the ramp. "Then one day I see her. A tall woman in a trenchcoat. She's attractive, about my age. I get out of the car and go up and ask her if she knew my father and her face goes as white as the bouquet of tulips in her hand. She tells me Kip was her uncle. That he never married and, as far as she knew, never had any children. You can imagine I had to stabilize myself. Here we were, two strangers standing eye to eye and both of us just about ready to topple over. I wasn't sure what to believe and didn't have anyone left alive who could clear things up.

"When I got home I went through my mother's possessions and that's when I found it. An article she'd clipped from the *Houston Chronicle* announcing the plane crash that killed a young NASA scientist named Kip

Greer. I dug a little longer before I came upon a visitor's pass in her name to the Texas State Penitentiary. She'd gone to meet a prisoner there by the name of Ike Greer. A guy in prison for petty larceny and insurance fraud. Guess my mom had a fetish for insurance men.

"Anyway, wasn't long before I found a diary she kept and pieced it all together. Turns out she met Ike at a state fair and the two had something of a whirlwind romance that night in the back of his Buick. But Ike wasn't a nine-to-fiver. He was an impatient man, eager to make a buck the fast way, the easy way. That his business plans were distinctly illegal didn't matter much to him. By the time my mother realized the future with Ike was bound to be a bleak one, she was already six months pregnant. And in those days, unwed mothers weren't nearly as fashionable as they are today. Not long after I was born, she happened upon the article about Kip Greer's death. The last name was the same and the space race was well underway. In her mind, she had finally found the perfect role model for her little Jack, even if it was all built on a foundation of BS."

Grant and Dag stood in stunned silence.

Jack stared back. "You wanted the truth, didn't you?"

They both nodded, digesting everything he'd said.

"Is Ike still alive?" Dag asked, uncertain whether he should.

"Unfortunately, he is."

"Any plans to visit him?"

"Probably not," Jack replied. "What for? To find out how to cheat insurance companies? No, thanks."

The three men continued in silence, hugging the outer bulkhead, descending yet another level.

"Dr. Greer," a female voice said, chiming into their private radio channel.

"What is it, Anna?"

"I thought you should be made aware. I was in the

process of cataloguing the extraterrestrial symbology here on the bridge when a new string of images appeared."

"Can you show me?" he asked.

"Please hold."

A moment later, Anna patched a video feed from the bridge into each of their OHMD glasses. The visual showed a console with a short row of constantly shifting holographic symbols.

"I don't recall seeing that earlier," Grant admitted.

Dag agreed. "Maybe Anna touched something."

"I can assure you I did no such thing," the robot replied with a touch of sass.

"At this time I suggest you continue your cataloguing procedures," Jack advised her. "Unless you have an idea what they're saying."

"Unlike the others I have seen on the bridge, these new symbols are alternating at a predictable rate. I have observed the changes over the last sixty-four minutes and thirty-five seconds. Based on that limited sample, I am prepared to offer an initial hypothesis."

"It's called a guess," Jack offered. "Go ahead, I'm all ears."

There was silence on the other end. Then, "It appears to be a timer," Anna said.

The three men exchanged glances. "Can you tell whether it's counting up or down?" Jack asked.

"Not with complete certainty. Although I could… guess."

"Go ahead."

"The clock is counting down."

Jack felt the temperature of the blood in his veins drop by ten degrees. Scanning from Grant to Dag, he could see the same question on all of their lips.

What would happen when the clock reached zero?

As if in response, Jack felt a low vibration, followed

by a rumbling. The platform beneath his feet began to shudder.

Grant's eyes flashed a look of intense fear.

The hell's going on? those eyes were asking. But Jack didn't know any more than he did.

The trembling grew more intense and with it came an electrical hum that pounded against his eardrums in successive blows. It seemed to continue for a minute, maybe more. Then all at once it was over.

Dag clung to a horizontal duct running along the bulkhead. Grant struggled to catch his breath.

Jack flipped to channel one and ordered a roll call. A rather frazzled Gabby, Eugene and Hart replied at once.

"The countdown?" he asked Anna. "Is it still up?"

"Negative, Dr. Greer."

Chapter 30

After Armoni inputted the new binary parameters into the BreakerAlt algorithm, she ran it again. Up came the progress bar as the computer began crunching through the data.

Ollie yawned. "Coffee, anyone?"

"I'll take you up on that offer," Mia said.

He looked at Armoni.

"Grab me a Soylent, would you?" Armoni asked.

Ollie shook his head. "Is that all you ever have? I've known you for a few hours and I'm already worried about your health."

"Thanks, Dad," Armoni joked, turning back to the safety of her computer screens.

"So what's your deal?" Mia asked as soon as Ollie left the room.

The hacker shrugged her shoulders. Never one to be brushed off, Mia pressed her again.

"Look, Mia, you're nice and all, but I'm not exactly looking to make new friends."

"I can respect that. But what *are* you interested in? I mean, how does a runaway become a world-famous hacker?"

"I never said I was a runaway."

"You didn't need to."

Armoni fiddled with the mouse, minimizing the GeneMark program and pretending to sort through open folders. "I did what I needed to survive."

"How's that?"

"Your old man ever sneak into your room at night and when you tell your mom she accuses you of lying?" Armoni asked, pain and anger flaring in her eyes. Her lips had become a thin line of tension.

Mia felt the emotion in Armoni's voice surge through her. "No, I can't say that they did. My parents hated one another, but there was no abuse, not of the physical variety at least. They did what was expected in those days—they stayed together. They didn't want to set a bad example for me and my sister. Till death do us part. That's what they believed."

"So I take it you're married then?"

Mia let out a humorless little laugh. "I was once." She tried shooing away the pain. She had hoped that working for the WHO would put her on a track toward stability and a life that included Zoey once again. But ever since leaving the States, things had only gone from bad to worse. She came back to the little girl trapped inside of her. "I suppose after watching my parents verbally peck away at each other all those years, the lesson I took away had nothing to do with commitment or thick and thin. The real lesson I learned was that marriages aren't supposed to be happy."

Armoni's expression didn't change. "That sounds rather hopeless, don't you think?" the hacker asked her in a soft voice.

"I'm not saying that's what I consciously believe. If I took a psych test I'm sure you'd find I'm as optimistic as the next person. But then take a look at the men in my life and you'll find something far different."

"I guess on some level we're all a little messed in the head."

"The human mind is a tremendous learning machine, unmatched by any computer we've ever made or ever will make. What we try to teach people, however, and what they come away with are often two different things."

Ollie returned juggling two steaming mugs of coffee and a bottle of Soylent. He set them down right as the computer let out a loud beep.

"Perfect timing," he said, clearly proud of himself.

Armoni pulled up the results. The DNA letters from the genetic code had now been replaced with reams of zeroes and ones. "Well, at least it's in binary this time."

"So how do we make sense of it?" Mia asked, feeling suddenly out of her depth.

But Armoni was already ahead of her, whizzing across the screen. "First things first, we need to convert it to ASCII."

"Pardon me?" Mia asked.

Ollie sipped at his coffee and said, "I think she's speaking Mandarin."

ASCII stood for American Standard Code for Information Interchange, by far the most ubiquitous format used for text files and web pages. Each letter, number or special character was often represented by a string of eight zeroes and ones (a byte). Therefore, the letter A was represented by the following binary string: 01000001.

A few minutes later, as the progress bar reached one hundred percent, the digits on the screen were replaced by letters. Even with the eight-to-one reduction, the amount of information was massive. All three of them took a closer look. They had pages and pages of random letters, numbers and symbols arranged into walls of solid text. How would they ever sort through all of this? It was worse than looking for a needle in a haystack. It was like looking for a needle in a field of haystacks.

"I've got one more trick up my sleeve to separate the wheat from the chaff," Armoni said.

"Oh, thank goodness," Mia replied, feeling a momentary burst of optimism. "I was afraid if I looked through all those pages my eyes would pop out of my skull."

Armoni brought up another program and imported the millions of characters from GeneMark. ASCII consisted of one hundred and twenty-eight characters, many of which were commands and symbols. She told them this new program would remove everything except for the twenty-six letters from the English alphabet and cut the number of pages they needed to search through by four-fifths. In only a matter of minutes, it was done. Once again, the process had cut down the pages of text. Now instead of nearly a thousand pages, they were left with one hundred and fifty.

"Let's get this printed out," Mia suggested. "Then each of us can scan through a stack of pages and see what we find."

Just then, a blinding flash struck each of them. Mia blinked and rubbed at her eyes. This wasn't like the first time it had happened. It was stronger.

Chapter 31

"Olsen, are you there?" Jack called out over the radio. Ever since the event, mission control on the Orb had been silent.

Hart came on. "I'm already on my way to check on him. It might be his radio is out."

Jack hoped the commander was right, since their attempts to reach topside had also failed.

"Gabby and Eugene?" Jack asked. "What's your status?"

"We'll be staying here," she answered for both of them. "We seem to be in some kind of repair shop. You should see this stuff."

"Show us," Jack said, delicately reminding her about the glasses she was wearing.

She giggled. "Duh. Okay, here it comes."

The feed from Gabby's camera was relayed to their visors. The frame shifted from a series of wide tables where strange-looking tools were laid out. Next to them was a metallic cone of some kind. It measured three feet wide and three feet high, with what looked like fiberoptic cables running out the bottom edges.

"I dare say that almost looks like the tip of a missile," Grant exclaimed. He was joking, of course. What need would an advanced race have for such primitive weapons?

Gabby tracked the camera across the room.

"Whoa," Jack called out. "Scroll back to the left, would you?"

She did so, revealing a large prolate spheroid, which was to say a machine of some sort shaped like a three-meter-high football.

"Back up a few paces."

The image came into focus. The object bore a transparent membrane—either glass or an epoxy resin. Behind the membrane was an interior chamber.

"Looks to me like a probe of some kind," Dag wondered out loud.

Jack stared intently. "Or something else."

"Like an escape pod," Grant added.

Hart came through a moment later. "Hey, Doc, I've reached the Orb and I found Olsen."

Jack felt a lump rise in his throat. "Found? Is he all right?"

"He's alive, but he must have gotten knocked out during the blast. Spotted him on the floor next to the communications equipment. He's laid out now on a mattress I grabbed from Eugene's bunk."

A half-hearted protest rose up from the theoretical physicist.

"Yeah, well, you can bite me," Hart fired back. "Anyway, it was a bitch and a half trying to lug that thing down two flights of narrow stairs. The Orb sure isn't as spacious as the ship. Anyway, for now I'll stay here and take over his duties."

"Any word from topside?" Gabby asked.

"I'm trying them now," he said, static hissing in the background as if to underscore his point.

Jack spun to find Grant sitting on the metal floor.

"You know, in spite of its size, there isn't an ounce of comfort in this place," Grant observed. "Have you noticed that?"

Jack had. It was difficult to miss. Everything about this ship was cold, industrial and rather pragmatic. If you were to tour an aircraft carrier or even the International Space Station, you would be hard-pressed not to find a few hints at missed loved ones or pictures of gorgeous natural vistas taped to the walls. Either the beings who operated this craft were consummate professionals, or they were a bunch of cold-hearted S.O.B.s. Of course, it was easy to project human feelings onto a thoroughly non-human entity. But apart from the biologist's keen observations, there was something else Jack had noticed about the man. Since the most recent blast wave, Grant's peeling skin had gotten a lot worse.

"You don't look so great, my friend," Jack told him. "I think you should consider heading back to the Orb."

Grant scoffed at the idea. "And miss out on the opportunity of a lifetime? Are you mad?" He raised his hand and Dag helped him to his feet. "I'll have plenty of time to rest when I'm dead."

A terrible thought formed in Jack's mind:

Death might come sooner than you think.

He quickly waved it away.

A burst of static through their earpieces made them wince.

"My apologies," Admiral Stark said. "But we've been having a hell of a time up here. Commander Hart has apprised me of your situation and I felt I should let you know about our own. Since the most recent blast wave, thirty percent of our sailors have been put out of action. Not to mention we nearly lost the USS *Grapple* when a vortex tried to swallow it whole. We are repositioning her at this time. But in the process, several of our sailors have suffered bumps and bruises while others are displaying a range of symptoms, the kind that have become all too common these last few days. I'm not here to give you a sob story. I'm here to inform you that the mouth of the fissure has opened considerably. In fact, a chunk of rock the size of the USS *Eisenhower* broke off and narrowly missed striking the Orb. I'm sure I don't have to tell all of you what that would have meant."

He didn't, because Jack knew perfectly well if the Orb was knocked away, so too would be the pressurized seals holding back millions of gallons of water. For anyone left on this ship, it would mean a certain and terrifying death.

"And there's another problem," Stark went on. "We've detected a magma chamber a few hundred meters beneath your position. That wouldn't normally pose a problem but these blast waves haven't only weakened the rocks above you. They've made the limestone foundation the USO is sitting on incredibly unstable. And by incredibly, I mean just one more of these things hits and you may all be dropped in the worst kind of frying pan. Since you're the ones in the greatest danger, I figured it was only right, given the monumental scale of your mission, that you have some small say in the matter."

Jack was growing more and more convinced that Stark wasn't nearly the asshole he pretended to be. "I can't speak for anyone else," he said. "But I'm staying for as long as we can."

"I was afraid you'd say that," Gabby replied. "Show Jack a cliff and he'll be the first to leap off it."

"That may be so, but never without a parachute," he countered.

"Or a really large umbrella," Grant said, eager to get in a Mary Poppins reference whenever he could.

One by one, each gave their consent, including Eugene, who stammered through his own reluctant approval.

Jack regarded a beleaguered Grant and an uneasy-looking Dag. "Tick, tock," he told them, before pushing on ahead.

Chapter 32

Mia was trying to do two things at once and failing badly at both. One part of her was hunting for recognizable words through pages and pages filled with blocks of random letters.

Meanwhile, another part of her was scrolling through a source of informational chaff. In this case, it was coming from the talking heads on TV who were working themselves into a frenzy. More than once she wondered why she didn't just turn the damn thing off, which in turn revealed a salient reality most of us faced at one time or another in today's age of information overload—turning it off meant disconnecting yourself from the outside world.

Based on what the major cable news channels were saying, social media had been inundated by a veritable cesspool of unfounded information and conspiracy theories. So many voices were speculating about the alien craft, who had built it and for what purpose that it made drawing any logical conclusions nearly impossible.

If the reports of an alien object were true, it was no doubt the most important story in human history, a discovery that only served to highlight several of humankind's most enduring questions. And not simply the old chestnut about whether or not we were alone in the universe. For Mia, it got to the heart of something far deeper. Namely, who were we? How had we gotten here? And what was our purpose, assuming there was one?

For thousands of years—maybe hundreds of thousands—humans had not only pondered these questions, but attempted to fill in the answers as best they could. To our ancestors, lightning was seen as the anger of the gods, or a punishment for perceived sins. During the Enlightenment, with God removed from the equation entirely, Zeus' lightning bolts had been reduced to the discharge of electrons which superheated the air.

As we continued our inevitable march into the future, our understanding would no doubt evolve. The point was, for a long, long time, we used artistic license to fill in the blank spots in our knowledge in order to fend off the delicious sense of fear that always accompanied the unknown. But the next part of what she saw on TV was where Mia had really been surprised. Although small pockets of the social media world were doing their best to spread fear, the bulk of humanity not only seemed open to the idea of alien contact, they eagerly awaited meeting beings from another world.

Since the first news stories broke, thousands of people in cities all across the globe had taken to the streets with signs which read 'Welcome back, E.T.,' 'Love thy neighbor' and 'If Kirk liked 'em green, why shouldn't we?'

Then there was Mia's personal favorite, a guy with red hotpants and a t-shirt proclaiming: 'Please probe me!'

In a rather heartwarming way, it didn't seem to matter to those assembling in the streets with a message of unity that so much uncertainty still surrounded that initial announcement. The Army denied that any such alien discovery had been made, while the Navy would neither confirm nor deny the story. For its part, the Air

Force, along with the White House, refused to comment.

Back on TV, the media had switched from the throngs pouring into Times Square in New York and Trafalgar Square in London to a panel of two astrophysicists and a disgruntled-looking head of SETI (the Search for Extraterrestrial Intelligence). Long ago, SETI had decided the best chances of finding life beyond the solar system lay in detecting radio signals emanating from a distant star. To this end, they'd built the Allen Telescope Array, a group of radio telescopes set up in Northern California. But in forty-plus years of searching, they had come up empty, which explained the rather sour look on the SETI guy's face. Even the host couldn't help but see the irony in looking far out into space for something that had been on earth all along.

And the disagreements didn't stop there, especially when it came to the strange pulsing lights that growing swaths of the planet's population had experienced twice already. The first time, the light had only touched sections of North and South America. But this second blast had gone much further, engulfing the entire planet. It didn't require much imagination to speculate that it too was somehow connected to the alien object the military had recently found. The timing made it impossible to ignore. Connected or not, the location of the object was still a closely held secret.

Both of the astrophysicist commentators were confident that satellites would soon be able to confirm whether the blasts were originating from outer space or from here on earth. If it was coming from somewhere outside, they said, an unusual solar event might be to blame. Or perhaps it was incoming messages from the alien home world. From there, each subsequent suggestion got more and more preposterous. But if the lights were originating from the surface of the planet itself, then they would be at a complete loss to explain how such a force was being generated and, more importantly, what effect it was having. Mia's own sense was that NASA already knew the source of the flashes and was keeping it a secret.

The final segment was a discussion with a panel of doctors from around the United States, all of them complaining about a sudden and dramatic rise in emergency room visits. Although few of the ailments had been life-threatening, all of them were life-altering. They ranged from porous bones, to sensitivity to the sun, mental impairments and rapid ageing. Perfectly healthy individuals were suddenly being struck down and left to wither away. If the doctors on TV had any idea Salzburg was somehow involved, they didn't say.

The host was about to cut to a reporter in the field when Ollie suddenly jumped up and shouted. The fright nearly made Mia spill her coffee over the papers strewn before her.

"I got something here," he cried, circling the words on the page.

Mia glanced down at those three simple words in a sea of gobbledygook and felt a cold hand move up the backs of her legs.

Chapter 33

MAN MUST FALL

All three of them stood staring at the words, their minds a witch's brew of thoughts and fears.

Mia and Armoni had worked through their respective piles without finding more than two nonsensical words next to one another. Ollie's discovery, on the other hand, was both simple and chilling. Had those three words been what Alan and others had died for? What some shadowy group wished to possess at all costs?

"What do you make of it?" Mia asked.

"Hard to tell," Armoni said. "From here it looks like a case of apophenia, if you ask me."

Ollie looked shaken. "Apo-what? You wanna fill the rest of us knuckleheads in?"

"Uh, speak for yourself," Mia shot back. "Apophenia is the tendency to see patterns and connections even when they don't exist. It's got something to do with how our brains are wired."

Ollie raised an eyebrow. "So you think these three words were just a coincidence?"

"Maybe," Mia conceded. "Or maybe the message is real. Either way, I have to admit, the meaning behind the statement is rather vague."

"Maybe it is to you," he countered, "but to me it's about as clear as a vodka martini." He pointed to the TV screen where they were once again showing the leaked video of the supposed USO. "It's clearly a threat. Made by them."

Mia was trying hard not to jump to conclusions. "Wait a second. Let's back up a bit. It was only three years ago that Dr. Alan Salzburg and his team discovered the genetic anomaly characterized by the appearance of an extra human chromatid."

"Maybe they created it," Armoni said, tossing out an idea even she didn't seem sold on.

Mia shook her head. "Not a chance. In their peer-reviewed research paper they were able to trace the emergence of the disorder to the mid-nineties. Well over twenty years ago. We didn't have the knowledge or the technology to pull something like that off. Even now, Salzburg's ability to integrate into an adult human body is light years ahead of the artificial chromosomes we've only recently come up with in the lab."

"The fall of man," Ollie said, mostly to himself. "Sounds almost biblical."

Mia held her hands up, worried they might be jumping to conclusions far too quickly. "Let's not get ahead of ourselves."

Ollie was far from interested in stepping back. "You said yourself this Salzburg thing is way beyond anything we're capable of. Can't you just admit that it's somehow connected to that giant UFO they found?"

For Mia, it was a difficult leap to make, perhaps one she didn't want to make, but she couldn't offer an alternate view that accounted for everything that was happening. "We know that Salzburg syndrome got worse after the first blast. What caused that? We don't know. Maybe it was merely a coincidence. Or maybe something else is causing the disorder to show up in people."

"See how you tie yourself in knots to explain away the things that make you uncomfortable?" Ollie said, waving the paper around. "Haven't you considered that maybe that thing is what's generating the pulse? If so, then it's not too far-fetched to think that maybe, just maybe the alien relic or whatever it is is changing us in ways we don't completely understand. For all we know it's part of a plan for them to wipe us out or take control of our minds."

"Most who see those three words are likely to imagine the worst," Mia said, trying to stay focused on the facts as they understood them. "You may be among them, whereas I see it as a call to change how we're living."

Ollie scoffed.

"Don't laugh. Maybe it's telling us we have to stop acting like we're somehow separate from the natural order. It doesn't say 'MAN WILL DIE' or 'WE'RE ABOUT TO DESTROY MANKIND.'"

"Sure, maybe they didn't spell out every little detail," Ollie argued.

"What I don't understand," Armoni said, "is how these aliens knew anything about ASCII or the English language?"

Mia and Ollie regarded her with blank expressions.

"I mean, the binary part makes sense," she went on. "Zero and one are basic principles of mathematics, so are prime numbers. I've read my fair share of articles on the challenges of communicating with an alien civilization. I guess one of the perks of being online all day long is you come across some really weird stuff. Maybe they've been watching us for a long time, knew everything about how we live and communicate..." Her voice trailed off.

"You mentioned something earlier," Mia said. "You were talking about the encryption on the USB. You said you'd seen it before."

She hesitated and ran her right hand down the side of her pant leg. "Yeah, I used to be part of a crew called the White Knights. Our MO was to break into government servers and see what we could find. We were looking for anything from who killed JFK to alien cover-ups and everything in between. I gained access using a rather simple phishing scam designed to get usernames and passwords from contractors working for the CIA. If you think the brightest minds are immune to a fake email from an irate IT administrator, you'd be dead wrong. Anyway, once inside, I trolled around for two full days before they knew I was even there. Didn't find anything about aliens or JFK, but I did find lots about a group called Sentinel."

"Sentinel?" Mia asked. She'd never heard the name before. Ollie was also curious.

"They had the CIA worried," she said. "That was what caught my attention and kept me reading. Turns out, Sentinel is a group of powerful men determined to squash any possible contact between humans and extraterrestrials. They apparently formed sometime in the 1940s when UFO sightings were becoming more and more commonplace. But it wasn't to help hide any crashed saucer. They were convinced that if humans ever encountered an alien race—peaceful or not—such a meeting would lead to our destruction.

"They began as a group of a dozen men, calling themselves the Majestic Twelve on account of the top-secret clearance they held. But soon others were brought in, tycoons and industrialists. They were men who had a stake in maintaining the status quo. But never politicians. No one who could be bought off, or bent to the will of the people. They worked behind the scenes, wielding great power.

"Soon the name Majestic no longer fit and the group

became known as Sentinel. Today, new faces have replaced the old, but their commitment is the same. I found other stuff too, scary documents about the organization's paramilitary arm—the people who did their dirty work, soldiers and assassins." Armoni's face was ashen. "If this threat is as real as you think it is, then the Brazilian police aren't the ones you should be worried about."

Chapter 34

Grant's pace was slow but steady as they descended three more levels. Between them and the Orb lay plenty of ship and at least a dozen floors. They could spend a decade on board without unraveling all of the craft's secrets. Dag was in the lead, followed by Grant. Jack brought up the rear, if for no other reason than to keep an eye on the biologist, who was too damned proud to know when enough was enough.

They were quiet as they plumbed deeper into the depths of the ship. Any concerns Jack held about a fresh blast wave sending the ship plummeting into the magma chamber beneath them came a distant second to finding answers to three main questions. Namely, who built this ship, where had they come from and, perhaps most important of all, what was it doing here?

"Hold up," Dag said, stopping suddenly.

Straight ahead was an archway, eight feet tall and wide enough for two grown men to pass through comfortably at the same time. Dag directed his lights beyond the threshold.

"I see something," he stammered.

Jack pressed forward, past Grant. He spotted the object at once, lying at an angle by the entrance to the room. It didn't appear to be part of a machine or an errant tool left on the floor. This was clearly something organic.

"What do you think it is?" Grant asked, breathing hard.

"I'm not sure," Jack replied, his eyes locked on the object. Carefully, so as not to disturb anything, he stepped no more than two feet into the room and bent down next to it. Grant and Dag followed suit. They remained in place for a while, staring, trying to make sense of what they were seeing. Jack's initial impressions were about color and texture. Dark brown, as thin as a child's arm and shriveled. But beyond that, it was long, two meters, maybe a little more and folded in half as though spring-loaded. Tiny hairs protruded along the length of it. At one end was a rounded edge—was it a socket?—and on the other a smaller fold, this one containing three narrow digits.

They were looking at what appeared to be the mummified arm of an alien creature. Did it belong to whoever built this ship or was this one of their pets, or maybe a meal?

Grant rose to his feet, sweat dotting his forehead and streaming down his face. A fat salty drop rolled into his eye and he blinked it painfully away, his lights flickering on and off with every third beat of his left lid.

"Take a deep breath," Jack told him. "This is what you've been waiting for your entire life."

Grant backed away, breathing hard, and Jack wasn't sure if the biologist was really panicking or if the blisters on his face were somehow to blame. Then without warning, Grant's lights jerked as the heel of his boot struck something, sending him falling backwards.

Jack sprang to his feet and as he did, a row of soft red lights slowly peeled away the darkness from above.

Grant sat on the floor, his arms bracing him from behind, his legs bent at the knees over another mummified body part, this one even larger. He squealed and scrambled to his feet.

"Don't move a muscle," Jack said. Scattered all around them were more mummified remains. Arms, legs, torsos. But Jack could only guess. Dag tapped him on the shoulder and pointed toward the recessed lights in the ceiling. Jack followed Dag's upturned finger and that was when he saw the nets, hanging from the ceiling. And inside were more remains. One of the nets had weakened with age and spilled its contents onto the floor, spreading arms, legs, and other bits in every direction.

"What is all this?" Dag asked, staring down in horror at one of the limbs.

Jack felt his fingers rubbing together, trying hard to push through the gloved fabric separating them. "Looks to me like a close encounter of the third kind."

Chapter 35

Armoni's warning about Sentinel was still settling in.

"If these guys are so against first contact, why wouldn't they go after SETI?" Mia asked, still trying to wrap her head around everything she'd heard.

"Where do you think SETI's funding comes from?" Armoni asked, fishing a Soylent out of the fridge and popping the lid off. "Most of the big donors are either part of the group or somehow connected to it. It's been going on for decades with nothing to show for it. They know it isn't going to work. The whole thing's a publicity stunt. But should an intelligent signal ever be detected, you better believe they'll do everything they can to bury it."

"Wouldn't the scientists just go to the media?" Ollie asked.

"Yes, but who controls the media? Sentinel would simply compromise them. Plant drugs in their cars, accuse them of pedophilia, rape. Just ask Julian Assange. Their other tool is ridicule and, when that doesn't work, straight-out misinformation. Flood the zone, as you Americans say, with contradictory information. Soon, no one knows what to believe.

"But it's with their propaganda arm that things get really scary. These days, fewer and fewer people trust the news, but everyone likes movies. Count up the number of feature films where aliens are portrayed as the good guys and then count up the ones where they're invaders, monsters and generally out to destroy us. Again, follow the money. That's what I did and nine times out of ten, the project led back to someone connected with Sentinel. If I'd known before you showed up this had anything to do with them, I would never have let you in."

"But contact with an advanced alien race would be the greatest event in human history," Mia said, imagining the possibilities. "Think about what they could teach us. Free energy. An end to war. The secrets of the universe. Maybe even the existence of God."

"That coin can always be flipped," Ollie replied, refilling his coffee mug, his thick fingers looping delicately through the handle. "What if they want something we have? Our water, minerals, or perhaps a resource we aren't even aware of? We only discovered uranium a couple hundred years ago and the periodic table continues to expand. It's hard enough figuring out what people in other countries are after, let alone beings from another solar system, galaxy, or even universe."

"Ollie has a point," Armoni said, settling onto the futon. "The people at Sentinel believe they're keeping us safe from a threat we don't understand."

"Maybe, but I'm not buying it." Mia's hands went to her hips. "You said yourself they were a bunch of rich industrialists. Can you imagine what would happen if humanity was given the means to produce free energy? Seems to me what they're really scared of is losing their cushy spot at the top of the pecking order."

"Free energy sounds great in theory," Ollie said. "But imagine the economic consequences. First the energy sector would go bust and before long everything else would follow."

"Wars big and small would be fought to fill those

vacated spots at the top," Armoni added. "Not to mention the tens of millions who would suddenly find themselves out of a job. It would be chaos."

Ollie's face hardened. "This message we found. It can never get out or fall into Sentinel's hands. You all saw the news. At the moment, the planet's on a high about meeting our cosmic neighbors." He turned to Mia. "You said yourself this message was prone to misinterpretation. And Armoni's right, there would be chaos, but not from the threat of free energy. It'll come from the fear and panic that takes hold the minute they realize these aliens aren't here to help us, but to wipe us out."

A buzzing sounded from Armoni's computer room.

Her brow furrowed. "Someone's here." She hurried to the monitor to see who it was.

Mia heard her curse from the other room a second before an explosion rocked the building. Cinderblock dust rained down on them in a fine drizzle, coating the tops of their shoulders. A jolt of terror shot through her. She ran to Armoni, who was watching one of the monitors. Armed men in black military gear were charging up her stairs.

Mia withdrew the USB and pushed it into her pocket. Where was the rest of her stuff? The panic pumping through her system was inhibiting her ability to think clearly. In the living room, Ollie drew his pistol and positioned himself along the narrow hallway.

"That door won't hold them for long," Armoni shouted, grabbing the back of Ollie's shirt and pulling him. "There's a way onto the roof, but we have to go now."

By the futon, Mia was scanning the couch, searching for her red knapsack. While they'd been waiting for the algorithm to run its course, she had slid the notebook back in place. The printed pages were also strewn about.

From down the hallway, she could hear the hollow boom as the men pounded against the door with a ram. Armoni called after her to hurry up, that it was now or never.

Fumbling through papers on the floor, Mia finally found the one she'd been looking for and shoved it into her pocket. Still unable to find the backpack, she ran for Armoni, who ushered her into a back room and closed the door behind them.

No sooner had they stepped inside than the clang of metal reverberated back to them, followed by the stomping of heavy boots through the apartment.

In the back room, Armoni drew aside thick curtains, revealing a pair of French doors and a burst of light from outside. She flung them open and charged onto a small patio. Sitting next to a wrought-iron table and chairs was a ladder that she began to climb. Mia was waiting to climb next, Ollie behind her, when the door in the room opened. Ollie leaned into the line of sight and fired off three rounds, striking the assailant twice in the helmet and once through the tactical goggles, painting them red.

As soon as Armoni had made it up, Mia began climbing, pumping arms and legs powered entirely by the horror of what would happen if they were caught. Seconds felt like hours as she heard Ollie continuing to exchange gunfire with the attackers. At last, he darted back toward the ladder and began scaling it. He was nearly at the top when the special ops soldier stepped onto the patio. Mia reached down, grabbed Ollie by his shirt collar and yanked on him with everything she had. Rounds from the soldier's automatic weapon riddled the ladder and the eaves, striking only inches from Ollie's feet as he jumped clear.

With all three of them up, Mia kicked the top of the ladder, sending it tumbling backwards off the patio and into the alley below.

The three of them clattered across tin rooftops, jumping from one to another, Ollie first, followed by Armoni and Mia. They needed to find a way down to street level soon. Once the armed men scaled onto the roof, they'd be sitting ducks.

At one point, Mia ran past Armoni, who pulled to a stop just shy of a two-meter gap between rooftops. The adrenaline pumping through Mia's veins meant she hadn't even considered stopping. To stop meant to die. After landing hard, Mia rolled, struggling to keep from sliding over the edge. Ollie reached out and caught her with one hand and waved Armoni on with the other.

The crack of a rifle made all of them turn at once. A soldier who had made it onto the roof was firing at them. Quickly, Armoni backed up and took a fresh run, building up speed. She reached the edge and thrust herself into the air, arms and legs bicycling wildly. For a moment, it appeared as though she was going to make it. Then with a boom she struck the edge of the roof, her fingers scrambling for purchase. Mia dove to catch her and managed to clamp down on Armoni's forearm. Rounds thudded all around them. Mia saw the white-hot fear in Armoni's eyes and then heard a final thump as a bullet struck her in the back. The scrambling stopped as Armoni's body went limp and slid over the edge. Mia shouted, only dimly aware it would do her no good.

In a single motion, Ollie scooped Mia up over his shoulder and moved along the downward slope of the roof. Nearby was a balcony. The drop couldn't be more than a dozen feet. He lowered her over a table, bullets whizzing around him. She landed, steadying herself before turning back to the roof. But Ollie was already gone. Mia called his name, her voice drowned out by the sound of rifle shots filling the air. He never answered and somewhere beneath the sharpened sense of terror still clawing at her, Mia wondered if she would ever see him again.

Chapter 36

Jack surveyed the evenly-spaced horizontal slats that ran along the walls.

Meanwhile, Dag was focused on the nets strung from the ceilings. Most contained mummified remains. "How can you be sure this wasn't some sort of abattoir?"

"This was no abattoir," Jack replied without elaborating.

"Should we not be calling this in?" Grant asked, bracing himself against a nearby container.

Jack ignored the proposal and headed for the bars he'd seen. "Only once we've figured out what we've got." He gripped the bars, dug in the toes of his boots and began climbing toward the closest net. It was no more than fifteen feet in the air, but in the biosuit, flexible as it was, it might as well have been a hundred.

"You're gonna fall and break your neck," Grant said.

Jack couldn't help but laugh. "You sound like my mother."

"Yeah, well, maybe you shoulda listened to her more."

I spent most of my life listening, Jack thought. *And most of what she said turned out to be a lie.*

Jack drew even with the mummified body in the net. He held on with one arm and dug in his sample kit for his scalpel with the other.

"This is no meat locker," Jack told the others.

"Really?" Dag said, sounding unconvinced. "What would you call it then?"

"Sleeping quarters."

They looked at him strangely.

"It wasn't so long ago sailors on wooden ships used hammocks," he argued. "For all we know, these things once lived in trees, or something comparable. As a biologist, you know firsthand how evolution can flavor behavioral traits."

"This is true," Grant acknowledged. "Take something as simple as eye contact. Whether we interpret it as a sign of love or a threat, the significance of the act has been hard-wired into our primate brains. Other species evolved along different lines. Anyone who doubts it need only stare in a cat's eyes, then do the same thing to a dog and see what happens."

"Precisely," Jack said. "Now get ready to catch this, will you?"

Both men moved into place, their arms outstretched.

Jack swung out a hand, wrangling the four cords attached to the ceiling. They felt springy and soft. Dag came over and pushed his legs against the wall, giving him use of both arms. Jack slashed at the cords until they frayed and finally gave way. Although the remains were mummified, they still had weight to them, much of which fell into Grant's waiting arms. The biologist staggered, but stayed upright.

189

They then pushed three waist-high containers end to end, using them as an improvised autopsy table. Given there was no way they'd be permitted to bring these bodies back to the Orb, much of their work would have to be done here, a decision born as much out of prudence as it was necessity. Any sequencing of DNA— assuming it was present and could be collected—as well as any isotopic analysis would be performed later on.

Jack got on the main channel and informed the others what they had uncovered. Degraded as the bodies were, it was nonetheless a monumental discovery, the first non-terrestrial biological beings ever found. Predictably, the reactions ranged from surprise to jubilation. While Gabby and Rajesh rushed down to witness the momentous occasion, Eugene chose instead to continue searching other levels.

Then Commander Hart piped in. "Doc, I suggest you don't touch anything until I've notified Admiral Stark."

"I'm sorry, Commander, but time is ticking—you heard the admiral." When Jack didn't hear a reply, he asked, "How's Olsen?"

"He's up now, although still a little groggy. Musta hit his head when all hell broke loose up here."

"We'll be filming the preliminary autopsy. Maybe you can pipe it up to Stark. Throw the admiral a bone so he can't accuse us of sitting on our hands." Jack still had a few minutes before Gabby and Rajesh arrived. "What about you, Anna? Interested in joining us?"

"I am occupied at the moment, Dr. Greer."

"It's not you, it's me, right?" he said, grinning. "Don't worry, you're not the first to give me that line."

The others laughed. So too did Anna, although Jack figured she couldn't possibly have understood the joke and was simply reacting to peer pressure. *What's next?* he wondered. *Smoking cigarettes? Skipping class?*

When all were assembled, Jack reached into his sample kit and removed a large pair of tweezers. Each of them decided to record what they were seeing just so that nothing was missed. Although none of them had any medical training, Grant's background in biology made him by far the most suited. Jack handed him the tweezers and a scalpel.

"All right, the subject appears to be wearing a delicate fabric of some sort," Grant said. He rubbed the thin material between his fingers and watched it disintegrate. "There it goes. Grab a sample of that, please, Dag. Hard to say for sure whether this was a uniform or some sort of ceremonial attire." Grant then moved on to the body itself. "The subject appears to be an arthropod." Which was to say, a large invertebrate with an exoskeleton. But to the average person, it looked like little more than a giant insect. "Large head, wide at the top and tapering to a narrow point at the... uh, mandible." He glanced over at Jack. "You know, I nearly said mouth."

"It happens," Jack said, trying to ease the tension. "Given this is a first, it's inevitable some of our own biases are bound to sneak in."

Grant nodded and carried on. "The subject appears to be a quadruped with an estimated length of eight or nine feet and a height of six or seven feet. Of course, in this state it's impossible to know for sure." He leaned in closer. "It also has what appears to be an advanced form of compound eye."

Compound eyes, found in insects and crustaceans, were formed by hundreds and sometimes thousands of photoreceptor units.

Gabby motioned to the ceiling. "You add up the soft lighting and the large eyes. I wouldn't be at all surprised if their home planet orbited a red dwarf."

Dimmer than our own star, red dwarfs were older and far more common throughout the galaxy. Still, many scientists questioned their ability to sustain life.

Gabby used her scalpel to collect some samples for potential DNA testing.

Grant and Dag then turned the body over. "Attached to the thorax are a pair of what appear to be wings. Though they look far too small for actual flight."

"You think they're vestigial?" Dag asked, meaning they once had a function in the creature's evolution.

"That's where I'd put my money." Grant raised one of the spring-loaded arms. "It has three six-inch digits at the end of each arm." He then turned to the creature's mouth, prying apart flaps of dried skin along with a small, perhaps vestigial, mandible he'd noted earlier. "Inside, I see two rows of small sharpened teeth."

"Ladies and gentlemen," Dag chimed in, "we've got a carnivore on our hands."

"The mandible and sharpened teeth certainly point in that direction," Grant admitted. "Although I'd say this creature evolved into an omnivore."

Jack smirked. "He's an enlightened meat-eater."

"Perhaps," Grant replied. "From what we know of animals on earth, carnivores tend to hunt in packs and as a result develop forms of planning and communication."

"The precursors to intelligence," Dag said.

"In some cases, yes."

"And what of the poor herbivores?" Jack threw out, standing up for the little guy.

"Well, consider our own planet," Grant said, glancing up from the body. "Of course, it's all we really have to go on, but most intelligent species tend to either be meat-eaters or congregate in groups. Dolphins, chimpanzees, elephants, dogs, crows..."

"Humans," Gabby said. "Don't forget we may be at the top of the food chain, but in many ways we're still just as much an animal as everything else."

They grew quiet. Jack's gaze settled on the creature's shriveled wings and the nets they slept in. Those two were perfect analogies, weren't they? No matter how far you travelled, you could never really outrun the forces that made you. These beings, with all of their technological advancement, were still prisoners of their own evolutionary history. Jack wasn't sure if the thought gave him solace or a resounding sense of despair.

Chapter 37

Mia exited the apartment building and ducked into an alley. Thankfully, the crowded housing and narrow passageways of Villa 1-11-14 aided in concealing her movements. Although the shooting on the roof had stopped, that didn't mean the men who'd come to kill them had left.

What had become clear was that both Armoni and Ollie were missing. One had been shot in the back and was likely dead, while the other, Ollie, had probably fled in an effort to lead the gunmen away from her.

She wrung her hands, heading toward the sunlit sliver of street up ahead. The alley was less than ten feet wide and marked by a series of stairwells leading to basement doorways. As she reached the street, Mia craned her head out far enough to see a group of black vehicles and an ambulance parked in front of Armoni's apartment. Noticeably absent were the flashing lights from the Buenos Aires police. The street was also mostly deserted, as though the locals knew from experience when to mind their own business and stay inside.

From the next alley over, four men appeared carrying a stretcher. Mia's heart leapt. Was it Armoni? Then another emotion struck her. Dread at the thought that maybe it was Ollie, also wounded or perhaps killed.

Were these men part of what Armoni had called Sentinel? Given their nondescript uniforms and vehicles, they didn't appear to be affiliated with any known government agency. If they were out to squash any signs of E.T. contact, it made sense that suppressing Alan's research would be high on their list. It also followed that they would be actively trying to locate the underwater object plastered all over the news these last few days.

An unusual sound drew her attention across the street. There she caught sight of a large hairless rat, lurking in the shadows. But rats didn't make noises like that. It sounded more like a cat. As the thought crossed her mind, the animal rose and hurried through a patch of sunlight. This wasn't your regular alley cat. This poor creature was emaciated, its furless body covered in red blisters. The sight reminded her at once of the patients crowding the emergency room at Santarem Municipal. Could it be this woeful cat was also suffering from a form of Salzburg?

She was still struggling to come to grips with this stunning revelation when she heard the shouting.

"Hey, you! Stay where you are." Three men in black uniforms broke into a run, racing in her direction. And in that split second of terror, all her staggering mind could register was:

They speak English.

As reality elbowed its way back in, Mia tore off, darting back into the alley. She reached the middle of the dimly lit space when a pair of powerful arms grabbed hold and yanked her off her feet. Before she knew it, she was being hustled through a doorway and into a sparsely furnished room where a black bag was put over her head.

Chapter 38

The dim red glow of what the team was now calling the ship's autopsy room was starting to make Jack feel like a passenger on a very spacious submarine.

The last few hours had been spent cutting down the rest of the alien remains and studying them. Like the first, nicknamed Harry, no internal incisions were made. To Jack's surprise, the Orb had already been stocked with biohazard body bags for this very possibility. In all, they found ten alien bodies. On the surface, most were very much like Harry. In some cases the uniforms they'd been wearing had disintegrated. In others, they'd been reduced to a substance as delicate as ash. The mere act of lowering the bodies had proven enough to dissipate the material.

For the science team, the lack of sleep was proving a far bigger problem. Nearby, Grant was slumped on the floor, his back pushed up against a crate. Above him, Dag was sprawled over the top of the same container, snoring loudly. With a snicker, the others switched to channel three to escape the rhythmic sound of logs being sawed. Still, Dag did have a point. From here on in, Jack would try to coordinate shifts where members of the science team could snatch handfuls of sleep whenever and wherever possible.

"Our time here is running out," Jack reminded them. He'd seen the tension creeping onto their faces in ever greater degrees, mostly in the brow and the jaw as their muscles performed an intricate little dance. The anxiety also came through in the slight quaver of their voices, a sound the mics picked up with excellent precision. And Jack couldn't blame them. The prospect of a war breaking out on the surface seemed to pale in comparison to the threat of the ship tumbling through a hole in the ocean floor.

"We still don't know what brought these beings here sixty-five million years ago," Grant said, laying out their dilemma as succinctly as he could.

"Maybe they were explorers," Gabby suggested. "Mapping nearby stars. Somehow they lost propulsion and crashed."

"The castaway theory," Jack said. "Yes, I've considered that. But this ship is far from broken." He shot a finger up. "Exhibit A: The groovy mood lighting. Not to mention the bridge appears to still be functioning—"

"I wish we knew their secret," Dag cut in, a groggy look on his face. "I bought a laptop and it crapped out on me after a year."

"Given what we've seen so far," Jack said, "I think they knew this was a one-way trip, the same way we know there's a chance we may never leave this ship alive."

"What are you saying?" Gabby asked.

"The nets were where they slept. I think they had a clear mission, one they knew could last a long time, hence the crates of food. And once they felt that mission was complete, they were probably too old to go home. One by one, they lay down and died."

Grant shuffled around to make himself more comfortable. "I know something about how they must have felt."

"That may be, but it still doesn't answer Grant's question," Dag said. "Why?"

"Perhaps they came to study life on earth," Rajesh offered. "Isn't that what we also do on other planets?"

"Would they need a ship this big?" Gabby asked. "Seems like overkill to me."

"Maybe they prefer Hummers over those dinky little smart cars," Dag said, casting out a line.

No one bit.

"Gabby's right," Grant replied, pressing up against the container. "A race that inefficient wouldn't get very far in a galaxy like ours. Then there's the tinkerer theory."

"Tinkerer?" Jack asked. "Enlighten us, please."

"You know how the story goes, they show up and tinker with earth DNA. Make a few modifications here and there."

"But why?" Gabby asked.

Jack wasn't buying it. "What group of responsible scientists, human or not, would trash a planet in the process? These weren't pot-smoking teenagers joyriding with Dad's Cadillac, nor do I think they came with the altruistic purpose of making a few genetic modifications."

"So what *are* you suggesting?" Dag asked, impatient.

"At first, given the size, I wondered if this was a generation ship."

"A what?" Gabby asked.

"It's a fairly old concept," Rajesh cut in. "I've read about it in science fiction novels. Even at the speed of light, crossing from one end of our galaxy to the other would take over a hundred thousand years. We are talking about mind-boggling stretches of space and time. If a civilization wanted to colonize another world, there are only a handful of options they can turn to. One of those is to populate a spaceship with a set number of astronauts handpicked for their strong genetic stock. During the long voyage, each of them would be paired off and expected to rear a large family. The idea is that by the time the ship arrives, a crew of a few hundred would eventually number in the thousands."

"I can already see a ton of problems," Gabby pointed out. "It would require the initial crew to have the utmost altruism, since they would know they had no chance of ever reaching the final destination. And it would be worse for those born during the voyage, since they never signed up for the journey in the first place. I can imagine revolts taking place."

"Clearly that wasn't the case here," Grant said. "We've only found ten of them."

"Maybe they weren't each other's type," Dag offered. He glanced at Jack, his face becoming serious. "There is another version of this story though. It's pretty much the same, except instead of growing an active population that requires food and produces waste, they put the astronauts into a state of suspended animation."

"That would require special cryogenic chambers," Jack said. "And we haven't seen anything like that yet."

"Maybe they stored the genetic blueprints to make their own settlers," Gabby said pensively.

"So this isn't as much a ship," he theorized, pointing his gloved finger at the body on the autopsy table, "as it is a factory for creating more of these."

"An invasion," Dag said. "But what went wrong?"

"It's only a working hypothesis," Jack made clear, trying to temper their growing concerns. "For all we know, we could find something that sends us in a totally different direction."

Just then Eugene's excited voice cut in. "Uh, guys, you might wanna look at this." He relayed the feed into their OHMDs. The right lens of Jack's glasses lit with a grainy video. In it were rows of glass tubes and beneath each of them a holographic display module.

Nobody asked and Jack didn't need to explain. They were looking at incubation chambers.

Chapter 39

Male voices, whispering nearby. Those were the only sounds Mia could make out, apart from the earthy smell of the black bag that had been pulled over her face.

"Who are you?" she asked in vain. "Why are you doing this?" There was a pathetic quality to her voice, one she was playing up on purpose. Maybe if she triggered her abductor's guilt reflex, they might decide to let her go. It was a long shot, but right now her options were diminishing with every passing second.

Villa 1-11-14 was one of the most dangerous neighborhoods in the world and here she sat blinded and awaiting her fate. They had zip-tied her hands behind her back and then in turn zip-tied that to the chair's lower spindle. Unlike in the movies, rocking backwards and toppling onto the ground would only fracture her wrists and render her even more vulnerable to attack.

Slowly, she began to form an image of how she could defend herself. As soon as they pulled the sack off her head, she would leap forward and latch onto the man's face with her teeth.

It sounded like a terrific plan, until she caught the tread of heavy boots heading toward her and felt her resolve begin to waver.

Off came the hood in one quick snap, but she didn't

lunge. Didn't move a muscle. Instead, she sat staring at the handsome face of a man who looked American.

"Untie me," she demanded.

Ignoring her plea, he instead pulled up a chair, turned it around and swung a leg over as he straddled the seat, a move that looked to Mia very much like a cowboy climbing onto his horse. He regarded her, his grey eyes intent, his arms folded over the wooden top rail. The wood creaked as he moved back and forth ever so slightly.

His short hair was dark and wavy. A clump hung over his forehead, threatening his face, but he didn't flick it away. Didn't seem to notice.

A muscular man in his late twenties stood behind him, arms crossed over his broad chest. His face was far less pleasing than that of his friend seated in the chair before her.

"You two gonna just stare or you gonna tell me what this is all about? You don't look like you're from around here." She started the same speech in Spanish before he cut her off.

"Save your breath." His voice was deep and he smelled vaguely of chocolate. "My name is Tom. The mean-looking junkyard dog behind me is Sven. He may not speak, but then why bother when looks can kill?"

Sven growled, baring a mouthful of crooked teeth. After a second of this, his lips curled into a skewed grin.

Tom motioned to the doorway and beyond. "Those men out there, you have any idea why they're after you?"

Mia batted her eyelashes. "Isn't it obvious?"

His chin dropped. "Cute. This may come as a surprise given the zip ties. But we're here to help you."

She shook her head. "I've been hearing that a lot lately."

"Have you also heard of a group called Sentinel?" he asked, cutting to the chase.

The muscles in her arms tensed. "I have," she affirmed, her voice now quiet and filled with apprehension. What could he tell her that she didn't already know?

"Then I take it you know what they're after?"

"Are you with Sentinel?" she asked, not entirely sure if she would believe him one way or another.

"We used to be," he said, nodding toward Sven, who grunted. "But not anymore."

Her head cocked to one side in confusion.

"Lately, there's been more and more of us who've come to see the organization for what it is. A state within a state. Their original mandate was to protect the world from outside threats. But with time, that unchecked power began to corrupt them. What started as a noble enterprise aimed at preventing the human race from killing itself soon became an excuse to create systems of dynastic power."

"Killing itself?" Mia asked, trying to figure how this story was lining up with the one Armoni had told her.

Tom drew closer. "It's not like the pre-Columbian natives were sending postcards to Europe. 'Weather here's great. And there's more gold than you can carry.' See, Columbus was a dimwit who thought he'd landed in India. From there things went from bad to worse. Either way, we can all agree they would have been better off had Columbus just stayed home.

"In the very same way, for billions of years, earth has enjoyed a relatively quiet existence on the outer edge of the galaxy. While there was nothing we could do to prevent being discovered by an inquisitive alien race, Sentinel didn't want a bunch of idiot scientists giving away our location. For all we know, our galactic neighborhood may be the equivalent of Compton or Villa 1-11-14."

Pimped-out UFOs and aliens with low-hanging space

pants fluttered across her mind's eye and she stifled a burst of laughter.

"Sounds like a joke, I know," Tom said, hardly cracking a smile. "That's because for a long time we did a great job turning anyone who uttered the word UFO into a laughing stock. It was a strategy designed to make it easier to sweep the problem away when they really did show up. But like the rest of the planet, Sentinel had taken its eye off the ball, looking to the stars, instead of down here on earth."

"If you're really here to help, then why didn't you stop them from taking Armoni away?" she said accusingly.

Tom's gaze was locked on hers. "I'm sorry to say that Armoni is little more than a casualty in a larger war. The information you possess can make a real difference. And we've come to disagree with far more than Sentinel's greed and heavy-handed methods. Those of us who have defected now believe that contact with another intelligent race should be embraced, not feared. That the real danger comes in trying to oppose it."

"How do I know I can trust you?" she asked, not entirely sure what Tom could possibly say to convince her. Sven, on the other hand, offered little more than a grunt.

"I know your full name is Mia Ward," he began. "That you live in Richmond and that you lost your job, your marriage and access to your daughter, largely in that order. I know the last four years you've battled an addiction to pharmaceuticals and have been clawing your way back to a normal life ever since. But more than any of that, I know you wanna talk to your daughter again, maybe even see her face." Tom held up a sat phone. "And if you trust us enough, we can help make those things happen."

Tears flowed from her eyes.

"Mia," Tom said, his voice taking on an uninterested, matter-of-fact tone. "If we were Sentinel, you would already have been stripped and tortured. And once we'd gotten anything and everything we deemed useful, you'd have been killed. Lucky for you we're not. But here is what's happening. Humanity is entering the greatest moment in its history, a time which will lead to either exaltation or extinction. We think you're the only one who can help get us through it."

The USB in Mia's pocket pressed against her thigh. Surely, if Tom and Sven were the bad guys, they would have snatched it from her and left her for dead once they had what they were after. She flashed back to Armoni's apartment, their frantic search for the encrypted message and Ollie's sudden burst of joy at finding it. She clenched her teeth, the rough contours of Ollie's face still etched in her mind's eye. Fearing the answer, she asked whether they had seen him.

Tom's eyes skittered away before swinging back.

Fresh tears fought their way to the surface. "Tell me he isn't dead."

Tom shook his head. "Ollie is one of them."

Chapter 40

Jack and Gabby arrived to find Eugene staring into one of the tubes. Rushing up those three levels in rapid succession had only accentuated Jack's concern over Grant's condition. Dag and Grant were still two levels behind. Once they finally arrived, Jack and the younger paleontologist would help Grant back to the Orb.

This new enclosed space Eugene had discovered looked very much like a dormant laboratory. The tubes were arranged in rows, like soldiers on parade, thirty-seven wide and thirty-seven deep. But unlike soldiers, the tubes varied in size. The ones at the front were tiny while those further back were large enough to fit a horse. But regardless of size, all of them had one thing in common. They were empty.

Gabby pressed her face close to one of the transparent enclosures. "I see a faint hint of residue at the bottom of this one," she said. "Whatever they made here, it's long gone."

Eugene waved them over to the tube at the far end he was staring into. "You should see this."

Jack peered in and saw a pink liquid pooled at the bottom.

"Was this the way you found it?" Jack asked, surprised and bewildered.

Eugene glanced up with a hint of guilt. "Uh, well, not exactly."

"You touched something?" Gabby said accusingly.

"Barely, I mean, I was looking around in amazement and my hand must have brushed up against one of these control panels." He moved his arm back and forth in short choppy motions. "I'm telling you, don't get too close because these things are on a hair trigger."

"Hair trigger for what?" Jack wondered.

The holographic display beneath the tube was showing what looked like cells splitting apart at a rapid rate.

Gabby caught Jack's eye. "I believe it's creating life."

Dag came on the channel. "Jack, I'm gonna need your help with Grant. He lost his footing and I think he might have broken something."

Jack started away and then turned to Eugene. "Keep an eye on this stuff, will you? And don't touch a damn thing. Gabby, watch him, will you?" She nodded. Then to Rajesh. "We may need your help."

Chapter 41

The news that Ollie was a Sentinel sent shockwaves charging through Mia's body. She shook her head, not wanting to believe it.

"I'm sorry, Mia," Tom said, clearly sensitive to how she must be feeling. He pulled out a knife and cut her restraints. "We were worried you'd run out of here and straight into a hail of bullets."

"Is it possible you've made a mistake?" she asked them, a heavy tinge of desperation on her lips.

Tom got up, went to the other room and returned with a folder. He handed it to Mia, who flipped through its pages. Clipped on the inside cover was a picture of Ollie along with his pertinent information. His name was the same and so was his Australian background and his work for *National Geographic*.

"So far, everything he told me was the truth."

"Keep going," Tom said.

More pictures followed. The first batch were long-distance shots of Ollie meeting with men in dark business suits.

"These are known high-level Sentinel operatives," Tom explained. "We've been following him for the last three years, which is how we found you and the package you received from Dr. Salzburg."

She turned the page and gasped when she saw the next set of photos. Ollie in a park meeting with Dr. Greg Abbott. Abbott had worked at Alan Salzburg's lab with them and had been the one to pack up the things from Mia's office after she was fired. "That rat! Did he have anything to do with Alan's murder?" she asked, a strange sense of anger and betrayal washing over her. Alan had done terrible things to her and yet she found herself feeling pity for the man. No one deserved to end up burned to a crisp in the trunk of a car.

"We believe so. He hasn't been heard from since Alan's death. But we're confident Abbott will pop up sooner or later."

Tom then reached over and flipped to the last page. On it were images of Ollie on the lawn of a suburban home playing with a young boy, no older than three or four. Nearby was a fetching woman with long blonde hair, watching them. Somehow, this one seemed to hurt the most.

"What was his mission?" she asked. "In relation to me."

Tom took the folder and set it on the table behind him. "To intercept the package by sneaking into your room that night."

"Was he ordered to kill me?"

Tom nodded. "From what we know, it was meant to look like a suicide. He was to leave pills by your bedside, as though you'd had a relapse."

The daggers kept plunging into her. She struggled to breathe. The room was spinning out of control.

Tom came in and touched her arm. "I know this is hard. Do you need a minute?"

"No," she said, determined. "I want to know everything."

"I believe the package arrived sooner than expected and headquarters sent in someone else."

She found Tom's gaze and held it. "You say you want my help to stop Sentinel from pushing the world into chaos?

"We do."

"Then I need something from you."

"Name it," Tom said, a streak of light illuminating his piercing eyes. Unlike Ollie, Tom was serious and intense. Horrible at a cocktail party, but indispensable in a crisis.

"Sentinel may try to get to me through my daughter. I want her and my ex-husband brought to a safe location until this whole mess is over with."

"It's already been done," he told her. "We moved in the same day you were attacked at the hotel. We would have grabbed you too, but Ollie reached you first."

"Thank goodness," Mia said, aware that a tremendous weight had been lifted off her shoulders. She brought a hand to her chest, feeling her heart beat normally for the first time in so many hours. Her gaze shifted to the satellite phone sitting by the file folder. "I wanna talk to them."

The muscles in his face made a subtle twitch. Something was wrong and he wasn't telling her.

"Please tell me they weren't hurt." Mia wasn't sure she could take much more of this.

"There's something you should know. It's about Zoey."

That old anxiety was back again in full force. "What did you do?" Mia rose out of her chair, her fists clenched into compact hammers.

Tom removed his phone and flicked through his photos. He held it up to her.

"Your ex reported she'd stopped talking a few days ago. He brought her to the family doctor, who found nothing wrong. Then a few hours ago, this began to show up."

Mia studied the image. Zoey was lying on the bed of a hotel room, sucking her thumb, something she had never done before. But there was more. The flesh on her forehead, face and the tops of her precious little hands were now a deep shade of red. When Mia enlarged the image, she noticed burn blisters up and down Zoey's arms. Any sense of urgency to stop Salzburg from affecting random people around the world had now been magnified by a factor of a million.

Finding a solution would mean tapping the greatest scientific minds. And in the world of cutting- edge biology, there was hardly a man Alan Salzburg hated more than Dr. Lars Van der Berg. A European eccentric with razor-sharp intelligence, Van der Berg possessed the kinds of insights into the field of genetics Alan could have only wished for.

Slowly, the fear and sadness had given way to anger and now staunch determination. Over the course of their discussion, even Tom appeared to notice the change.

Mia's steely gaze flitted from Tom to Sven. "Get me to Amsterdam."

Chapter 42

By the time all four men reached the Orb, they were wiped. Jack flung his helmet onto a nearby couch in the mess as the others brought a wincing Grant up to his bunk.

"How bad was it?" Hart asked, climbing up from comms.

Jack's shoulders slumped. "He broke his hip. I'm also worried he might have gotten hit with a dose of radiation during one or two of those blast waves."

Hart shook his head. "Radiation? I don't see how that's possible. None of our instruments have picked up anything like that. Besides, your biosuits are designed to detect and warn against any biological, chemical or nuclear threat. Maybe it's just a question of age."

"Didn't you know?" Jack said. "Sixty's the new forty. But you've seen his face. Something's not right."

"Yeah, well, he's not the only one. I was just speaking with Admiral Stark and he says a big chunk of the men in sick bay have some form of mystery ailment. I've also been monitoring the news feeds. It's the same everywhere. You think it could be connected to what's happening here?" He pointed downward, but Jack understood what he was getting at.

"I'm not a medical doctor, but I also don't believe in coincidences. You've seen what those blasts are capable of. Even Stark said the *Grapple* was nearly sucked into a giant vortex."

"Maybe it would be best for everyone if we just destroyed this thing," Hart said, his features set.

Lieutenant Olsen wandered by just then, wearing a jock strap over his Navy uniform.

Jack's brow furrowed. "Is there something I need to know?"

Hart shook his head and glanced back at his fellow SEAL. "He hasn't been the same since he got knocked out. Keeps asking the same questions over and over. His mind's got the retention of a sieve. I'm sending him topside as soon as the submersible docks with fresh supplies."

"Make sure Grant's with him. He's gonna bitch and moan, but he's not doing himself or us any good lying in his bunk. He needs medical attention."

Hart glanced down. "The Admiral said they're bringing in a hospital ship to care for all the sailors who are sick."

"Then how come we haven't caught it?" Jack asked, rhetorically.

Hart brushed his hands together and slid them into his pockets. "Maybe we have and just don't know it yet."

A moment later, Rajesh came down the spiral staircase. His gaze flitted between the two men. The computer engineer was clearly uneasy around military personnel. Jack recalled him explaining his reasons—how DARPA and other military branches had tried to co-opt his research in artificial intelligence for use on the battlefield. Rajesh wasn't a pacifist, although he was acutely aware of the potential dangers of a world dominated by a species of sentient killing machines. He felt as though one was already more than enough. "Do you have a minute?" he asked Jack.

"What's on your mind?"

Hart nodded and retreated back to comms.

"I was performing a routine diagnostic on Anna when I came across something rather disturbing."

"Disturbing? How so?"

"An anomaly in her subroutine." Rajesh rubbed his chin, growing thick with stubble. "These are small glitches she normally works out on her own. She's surprisingly self-sufficient."

"She's a fine woman," Jack said, "for a robot."

Rajesh's smile appeared and then faded just as quickly. "To make a long story short, I traced the anomaly I mentioned back to a Trojan exquisitely hidden in her primary operating system."

"I'm not following."

"Someone found a way to circumvent her firewalls and the multiple levels of security in order to plant a virus."

Jack swallowed. He had a sinking feeling he knew where this was headed. "Can you tell who did it?"

"No, but I have my suspicions. I have destroyed the bug and my team on the rig has increased her security protocols. But I'll need some time to track down how this happened and who was responsible."

"Well, keep me apprised of what you find."

Rajesh nodded and started to walk away before he stopped. "There's another reason I'm telling you this. You remember the leak to the media earlier? The one that got Stark all fired up? Well, I traced the outgoing signal back to her."

"Anna leaked the data on the craft?"

"In a manner of speaking, although the instructions to do so originated with the virus. It appears someone was trying to compromise the work we're doing here."

Chapter 43

Often referred to as 'The Venice of the North', Amsterdam was a European city ringed by over a hundred and sixty canals. Once home to famous painters like Monet and Rembrandt, the city was better recognized today for its red light district and the nearly three thousand house boats that floated atop its brown, murky riverways.

But steeped in history as the city was, Mia hardly got a chance to see much of it. Following a thirteen-hour flight, Tom and Sven had whisked her from the airport to a safehouse in the center of town. Seated on the edge of her new bed, Mia fished into her pocket and opened the passport they had given her. She'd left Buenos Aires under an assumed name, Diane Tanner. Tom had also confiscated her cell phone, to prevent the temptation to call her daughter and inadvertently give away their position.

Tom appeared holding a sat phone and dialed the number to the motel where Paul and Zoey were being kept. "Make it short, we leave for the university in ten," he instructed her. Someone on the other end answered and Tom said, "Put him on."

She took the phone. "Paul?"

The voice sounded groggy. "Mia, is that you?"

"Listen, Paul, I can't say much right now, but these people are there to keep you and Zoey safe."

"They keep saying that, but if I can't call the office and explain why I'm not coming to work, I'm gonna get fired, Mia."

"They'll see that doesn't happen. You're gonna have to trust me."

He was quiet. "Whatever it is you're mixed up in, I'm sure…"

"Have you seen the news lately?"

Paul hesitated. "You mean the folks getting sick?"

"What I'm doing isn't only about me."

"I know, Mi." It was the nickname he had given her when they were together, a name he'd stopped using after he found out about Alan. "Zoey's not doing well. I think she needs a doctor."

"You already took her to one, didn't you?"

"Dr. Brownstein's a nice old man, but for anything more serious than a flu shot he's pretty much useless. She needs a real doctor."

"Paul, I'm working on making everyone better. You're just gonna have to trust me." She knew it was a tall order. The trust had been the first thing to die in their relationship, a trajectory begun when Alan had spread word of their indiscretion and again when the ensuing divorce had led Mia to seek refuge in prescription painkillers. "When was the last time she spoke?"

Paul sighed. "I don't know, it's been days. Her eyes are open and she'll stare at me sometimes, but it's like no one's home."

"She isn't the only one, Paul…"

His breathing grew more rapid. "People are saying there's a disease going around. Is that what this is?" Calling Paul a germaphobe was like calling the Mad Hatter eccentric. While technically accurate, it did little to acknowledge the totality of his neurosis.

"This isn't a virus, Paul. I can assure you of that. But we're trying to figure out where it's coming from." Based on his labored breathing, she could tell her affirmations were doing little to calm his fears. "If there's any change with Zoey, please have the people you're with contact us."

"Yes, of course."

"Take care, Paul. And give Zoey my love."

"I will." He paused. "And Mi, take care of yourself."

•••

Minutes later, Tom accompanied Mia to the AGL (Amsterdam Genomics Laboratory) on the medical campus of the University of Amsterdam. Unlike the Renaissance and Baroque architecture in the city center, the AGL was modern with sleek lines, its façade covered in glass panels. Members from Tom's organization had already set up a meeting between Mia and the head of the laboratory by pretending to be from the WHO.

As they reached the faculty department, a woman in a white lab coat was waiting for them. "Dr. Ward?" she said, smiling, an expression that accentuated her high forehead and rounded facial features. She appeared to be in her early fifties and fit for her age. "I'm Dr. Merel Jansson."

They shook hands.

"I'm happy to meet you, Dr. Jansson—"

"How is it exactly we can help the WHO?"

"Well, you see, we were actually hoping to speak with Dr. Lars Van der Berg."

A saddened expression clouded her features. "I'm afraid Lars has been gone some three or four years now. A tragic turn for such a brilliant mind."

Mia felt the air being sucked out of her lungs. "Is he dead?"

"In a manner of speaking, he is. Lost his grip on reality. Had some sort of breakdown and had to be carried from the university on a stretcher."

"Where are they keeping him?" Mia asked, still reeling. Most of her hopes had been pinned on the insights she was certain Dr. Van der Berg could bring to the mysterious spread of Salzburg.

"I'm not sure," Jansson said, as though the idea had never occurred to her. "But I can certainly find out." She touched Mia's elbow. "Maybe there was something else we could help you with."

The cloudy film over Mia's eyes suddenly cleared. "We believe we may know what's behind the rash of medical ailments around the world."

Jansson's gaze narrowed. "I'd say a good thirty percent of my staff has been affected. The range of symptoms is quite broad. We've begun shifting the bulk of our work away from cancer research toward whatever's behind this."

"Is there somewhere we can speak in private?" Mia asked.

Jansson looked around, taken aback. "Of course, come with me."

She led them to her office and closed the door. The room was simple and well-kept. Nudged against the wall was a desk, on top of which sat a computer monitor and keyboard. Behind her was a bookcase stacked with Dutch medical tomes.

Mia proceeded to fill her in on Salzburg and everything else she'd learned about the disorder in the last few days.

219

Dr. Jansson appeared to take it all in. "You understand what you're describing is quite impossible. New chromosomes don't simply form on their own and they rarely, if ever, appear in toddlers or adults. What is the mechanism? And what are the genes it's carrying?"

"That's what we've come to find out," Mia told her. She understood Dr. Jansson's apprehension. For the most part, Salzburg was behaving in ways scientists had never previously observed. Cell duplication errors in the womb were one thing, but seeing such a thing in adults was something else entirely. Which was what made Salzburg so unique. There was no cell division that could account for its ubiquitous presence in a patient's system. Therefore there had to be another way in which the new chromosome and the genes it carried inserted itself into the DNA chain carried by every living cell. Had she remained in Brazil, that work might have continued, but that was before a man disguised as a bellboy had tried to kill her.

She then told the doctor about the stray cat she'd seen in Buenos Aires and how it had exhibited symptoms similar to the human patients with the disorder. That one really threw her for a loop. "If you're right," Jansson said, "then unraveling how this mysterious disorder works will lead to a quantum leap in our understanding of genetics."

Mia agreed. "That is, if it doesn't kill us first."

"I'll have samples from patients sent to the lab right away." Dr. Jansson studied her carefully. "So, Dr. Ward, what's your plan of attack?"

"Our focus should be on vectoring. If we can figure out how Salzburg is inserting that forty-seventh chromatid into individual cells, we may be able to beat this thing."

Chapter 44

After swapping out his old rebreather unit for a fresh one, Jack headed up to the bridge. There he found Anna studying several holographic displays at once, each cycling through a series of symbols.

"How's it going?" he asked, coming up behind her.

She backed out to face him. "Hello, Dr. Greer. I believe I am making progress."

"So what's it say?" he asked, motioning to the parade of green holographic characters dropping slowly from the top of the three-dimensional image.

A grin formed on her digital features, a slight pink glow on her cheeks. "I am not there just yet, but I can tell you a breakthrough might not be far off. The holographic displays are by no means a complete catalogue of their written language, but they have nevertheless provided several useful clues."

Jack was intrigued. "How so?"

"Allow me to explain. A language with twenty to thirty-five symbols is likely alphabetically based, a system where words represent simple sounds. On the other hand, a language based on syllables may contain anywhere from eighty to one hundred signs. To date, I have recorded close to seven hundred symbols, which indicates these beings are likely utilizing a logographic system in which symbols represent words and in some cases sounds and syllables. I have also compiled a list of objects and concepts these words are most likely to represent. It seems logical that the information on these displays relates to the operation and maintenance of this vessel and the systems on board her."

Jack raised his eyebrows. "Sounds like a lot of guesswork to me. Have you considered these beings might not think the way we do?"

"That may be so, Dr. Greer. However, it is not inconceivable that one or more of the symbols I have found represent this vessel. At least that is a starting point. There are many other examples I will not bore you with." She smiled and turned back to her work.

Changing the subject, he asked her, "You're not frightened at all, are you, Anna?"

She turned back and tilted her head. "I do not understand your question. Please provide further context."

"Well, we heard from Admiral Stark about the risk involved in staying on this mission. Everyone took a vote on whether to stay or go. Rajesh voted to stay. But no one asked you. If we continue our work, we could all die."

"Death," she replied. "A cessation of all neural activities. I am not sure I identify with the emotion you described. Although I hope to finish my work before that happens."

Jack paused. "Why is that?"

"I am not certain. I wish to find answers."

Fear might not be in her repertoire just yet, but curiosity certainly was, whether Anna recognized it or not.

Jack was facing the entrance to the bridge when Eugene appeared. "I thought I'd find you here," the theoretical physicist said.

"You look like you've got something on your mind," Jack noticed. He wouldn't be the first today.

Eugene shook his head as he approached. "The specimen's now encased in some sort of artificial womb."

"Specimen?" Jack said, surprised. "A few hours ago it was only a clump of cells."

Eugene threaded his fingers together over his abdomen. "It's been growing at an incredible rate." His face brightened, highlighting an old scar on his chin. "You can already see tiny arms and legs developing."

This time Jack's jaw came unhinged.

"Okay, maybe not arms and legs, more like appendages of one kind or another."

"That's why you never touch a button unless you know what it does," Jack scolded him.

"But that's the part I still don't understand," Eugene said. "Don't be angry, but after you left, Gabby accidentally brushed up against the console and nothing happened. Then I tried to re-enact the same clumsy mistake that got the whole thing started and still came up with nothing."

"So what are you saying?"

"I remember looking at the incubation chamber and then down at the control panel and thinking how badly I wanted to mash a few buttons. You know, see what would happen. It was pretty obvious the tubes had been used to house biological organisms at some point. That was when the machine started making noise. I panicked, hit the console to make it stop and that's when I called you guys over."

Jack stood staring at him, not quite sure what to think.

"When I was a kid," Eugene went on, "I was scared to death of my great-granny. She was my dad's grandmother and the family mostly tiptoed around her. They thought she was possessed. As far as I was concerned, they were wrong. She wasn't possessed, she was batshit crazy."

"Seems to run in the family."

Eugene smirked. "You might be right. But she was convinced she could talk with certain people without ever opening her mouth."

"So you activated the machine with your mind?" Jack shook his head and motioned to one of the consoles behind him. "Listen, I'm open-minded. Show me you can manipulate one of those holograms in any way, shape or form and I'll believe you."

"I'm not saying that's what it was," Eugene protested. "I'm just telling you I didn't touch anything."

"I still want you to try," Jack said. He noticed Anna had stopped what she was doing and was watching their interaction. "See, both of us are curious."

Eugene shook his head, padded over to the nearest console and glared intently at it for several seconds.

"If you can get that elevator going I'll really be impressed," Jack encouraged him.

Eugene threw him a scowl and then resumed his demonstration. Slowly his cheeks flared and his eyes bulged with the intense concentration. Jack also wondered if he was holding his breath. The hologram didn't so much as flinch. Finally, Eugene let out a lungful of air and staggered forward, bracing himself on the seat before him.

Jack studied the elevator column in the middle of the bridge. Eugene and Anna looked as well. Nothing about it had changed.

"'Extraordinary claims require extraordinary evidence,'" Anna said, quoting the famous astronomer Carl Sagan as she rolled over and patted the back of Eugene's biosuit.

"Hey, Jack," Hart said, breaking into the channel. "I thought you should know, we have visitors."

"Visitors?"

"The team from Naval Intelligence has just arrived."

Chapter 45

Piggybacking off an endless stream of espressos, Mia's mind might have been wired, but the rest of her was screaming for sleep.

In short order, Dr. Jansson had redirected all of the lab's personnel and resources to answering two fundamental questions. One, how was Salzburg able to create brand-new genes out of nowhere? And two, what vectors was the disorder using to introduce the chromatid into mature cells?

Mia pulled away from the microscope and rubbed at her tired eyes. The information on Salzburg's DNA sequence they'd pulled off the USB had been immensely helpful. At this very moment, a team of researchers down the hall was running the data through a genotyping program designed to highlight and identify potential genes. For her part, Mia was trying to understand the mechanism by which the chromosome was created in the first place.

A few meters away in the staff lounge, Tom was sprawled out on a couch catching up on some much-needed sleep. He had been awake for well over twenty-four hours. Rather than sleeping during the flight over from Buenos Aires as she had, he had decided instead to perform counter-surveillance to be sure Sentinel agents hadn't followed them aboard the aircraft.

But hours of research had passed and still Mia wasn't getting anywhere. Any time she tried to compare the DNA from Salzburg to the human genome, she found zero matches. How could one have come from the other? Something wasn't adding up. Wheeling her chair over to a nearby computer, she decided to change strategies. Rather than comparing the entire Salzburg DNA sequence at once, she instructed the algorithm to only use short lengths of DNA, no longer than ten base pairs long. If large chunks of genes hadn't been replicated, maybe she would find smaller pieces mixed together. With that in mind, she ran it again, watching the progress bar the way a child might watch a tray of chocolate-chip cookies in the oven.

The reflection in the screen of someone behind her made Mia gasp. She spun in fear, her arms held out protectively. But the sight which greeted her was shocking for a completely different reason. One of Dr. Jansson's technicians stood frozen, his hand outstretched, holding a paper. His eyes were wide with terror because a knife was at his throat. Tom pressed the blade deeper, forming a red line against the technician's neck.

"Dr. Ward," he stammered in a thick Dutch accent, his voice quivering along with the paper he'd come to deliver. "The genotyping results are in." The technician's name was stitched over the breast pocket of his lab coat: Klaus.

Mia reached over and coaxed Tom's knife away from the startled scientist's neck. "Down, boy."

Klaus was about to drop to the floor.

"Not you," she said, holding him steady. "I was talking to Jason Bourne's twin brother behind you."

Tom fixed the scientist's ruffled lab coat and retreated back to the staff lounge, yawning as he went.

After a rather shaken Klaus excused himself, Mia dove right into the data he had provided. To her astonishment, in spite of the vast amount of non-coding DNA in the chromatid, only four previously unknown genes were present. As was standard procedure with designating HUGO symbols, the lab had named the new genes after the proteins they produced. They were as follows:

COL1 encoded a protein that attacked bone density, mirroring the effects of diseases such as osteoporosis.

TRPP2 specified a protein that weakened the ability of DNA to repair damage from ultraviolet radiation, leading to albinism.

SER3 produced a protein that effectively shrank the frontal and temporal lobes, sections of the brain which controlled abilities such as speech and reasoning.

The fourth and final gene they'd sequenced, DAF4, mimicked the genetic disease progeria, which caused a rapid whittling down of chromosome tips, greatly accelerating the aging process.

This was an important breakthrough. Not only because it explained the myriad of symptoms occurring now all over the world, but also because it could help pave the way for possible treatment.

Mia was still focused on the four new genes when the computer pinged. She turned to see the progress bar stall at one hundred percent before disappearing. Up popped another window with the results from her attempts to match strips of Salzburg's DNA to the human genome. As Mia stared, her jaw fell open in shock.

Sure enough, the algorithm had found a match, but not one she had expected. As Dr. Jansson had pointed out earlier, brand-new genes didn't simply pop into existence from nowhere. In the realm of medicine and academia, the overriding scientific understanding was that new genes were always slightly modified versions of old genes.

One example was the gene LCT that coded for lactase, an enzyme that enabled humans to digest dairy. And yet in non-human mammals, LCT became non-active shortly after infancy. So why the difference? It was likely caused by a mutation that took place among the goat and cattle herders on the plains of Hungary more than seven thousand years ago. Humans had started drinking milk and over time it had changed our DNA.

But if most genes mutated slowly over time, then it meant what she was seeing on the computer screen now was simply impossible.

Chapter 46

Jack arrived back to find the Orb in a flurry of activity. Two men wearing blue-colored biosuits were carrying Grant on a stretcher across the mess deck and into a waiting submersible. Close behind were two other men ushering a disoriented Olsen in the same direction.

"You must be Dr. Greer," a voice called out next to him. "I'm Captain Mike Kelly from the Office of Naval Intelligence." The captain licked his lips, slung his helmet under the crook of his left arm and thrust out his hand. Early fifties with a narrow face and a fading head of hair combed strategically to one side, Captain Kelly had a practiced air of friendliness.

The men shook hands. Two firm pumps, straight up, straight down. Release. It was a soulless shake and Jack was glad to have his hand back.

"And this is my second-in-command, Lieutenant Brooks."

The woman's plastic smile lingered for a second, maybe two. Her auburn hair was plastered to her skull and tied at the back in a painful-looking knot. The skin on her forehead was shiny, which only mildly distracted from the fact that her eyes were almost an inch farther apart than they should be.

Out came her hand. Two firm pumps, straight up, straight down. Release.

She appeared to be a recent graduate from the Captain Mike Kelly School of Public Relations. A six-pack of beer and half as many Jägerbombs—that was the lubricant Jack figured these two would need in order to yank the sticks out of their butts.

"Captain Kelly will be taking over the operation from here," Brooks informed him. "Commander Hart is free to stay if he so chooses."

Hart nodded. "Sure, I'll stick around. Isn't every day you get to be in the history books."

She swiveled to Jack. "And we'll need you to turn over any and all data—digital and hard copy—as well as any samples you've collected to date."

The blood rushed up Jack's neck and into his cheeks. "I was never told we'd be required to hand over our findings. We never intended to hide what we found, but you can't just come in and take it."

"Listen, Doctor," Captain Kelly said, trying not to sound condescending, but doing a piss-poor job of it. "We aren't asking…"

Jack turned to Hart. "Get Admiral Stark on the line. He'll sort this out."

Kelly licked his lips. He didn't seem pleased that anyone, especially a civilian, was going over his head. "Stark has no authority here. I'm in charge. But I understand time is not a luxury we have to waste, so I'll tell you what. How about you provide us with a copy of the data you've collected so far and we'll go from there?"

"I can get them the intel they're looking for," Hart said, nudging between the two men like a referee at a boxing match.

"What's your mission here?" Jack asked.

"That's top-secret," Kelly said. "You should know that. As far as I'm concerned, you should all be packed up and sent topside. But Admiral Stark asked me for a favor and you wanna know what I told him?"

Jack moved in. "I'm all ears."

"I told him I'd babysit so long as none of you crawl up my ass and started a fire. We've known each other all of five minutes and I'm already smelling smoke."

Jack gritted his teeth. "Well, I'm smelling something else and it sure as hell isn't smoke."

Hart grinned.

Forcing a smile, Captain Kelly took a step back and motioned to the men in blue biosuits shuttling back and forth around him. "There are a half-dozen intelligence officers here to help prosecute this mission. Just make sure you stay out of their way and you won't have a problem."

Chapter 47

A hand nudged Mia awake. Opening her eyes, she saw Dr. Jansson, the glow from the lunch room lights crowning her like a halo.

"What time is it?"

"Seven in the morning," Jansson said, handing her a cup of coffee.

Mia waved it away. She'd had enough coffee to fill every canal in Amsterdam.

"An assistant came to see me this morning," Jansson began.

"Yes, I was going to tell you about that," Mia interrupted. "It was all a big misunderstanding."

Jansson's brow furrowed. "Misunderstanding? You mean about the four genes identified within Salzburg?"

Mia glanced over and saw Tom standing at the entrance to the staff lounge. He was holding a large bag of croissants. "No, I was talking about... anyway, it doesn't matter." She reached into the pocket of her lab coat and removed the printout with the results from her own research. "I think you should look at this."

Jansson set the coffee down and took the papers from Mia. "This can't be right," she said, her voice strained. "Have you run it again?"

"Three times," Mia replied, and she had the bags

under her eyes to prove it. "It keeps coming out the same way. What we found in Salzburg weren't existing genes that had been mutated—"

"You're suggesting they were assembled from bits and pieces of non-coding DNA," Jansson said, amazement in her voice. "But how?"

"I'm not sure, yet," Mia admitted. "But I think this opens up a whole new realm of possibilities. If some unknown environmental factor is promoting the assembly of new, never-seen-before genes from so-called 'junk DNA' in our genome, then what else might it be capable of?"

The smile on Dr. Jansson's face held for a second more before falling. She looked around the room. Only Tom was nearby, searching for blueberry jam in the fridge. "Could you give us a moment?" she asked him.

Tom glanced up, his hair still askew from a restless night's sleep on a neighboring sofa. He hesitated, before Mia motioned that she would be fine. "I'll be right outside if you need me."

He left and closed the door behind him.

"He's very protective of you," Jansson noticed.

"Is he?" Mia asked, recalling poor Klaus and the knife at his neck.

"I made a call to the WHO last night."

Mia's pulse quickened.

"It's normal protocol anytime we host a member of the U.N.'s science division, you understand. They transferred me to Isabella Silva, the Regional Director for Northern Brazil. And let me tell you, she had quite a tale to tell."

Mia's heartbeat was now moving at a full gallop.

"Isabella said you'd been kidnapped."

"Kidnapped?" Mia stuttered, as surprised to hear the words as Jansson had been to say them. Had Ollie been lying that the Brazilian authorities were after her? Maybe they had read the crime scene in her hotel room precisely for what it was: an attempt on her life. Had they been chasing after Gustavo's plane on that runway in an effort to prevent her abduction?

"I informed her you didn't appear to be here under duress. But they insisted we contact the local authorities to have this sorted out."

Mia had worried this was where the conversation was headed. How did you explain to a perfect stranger that an invisible, but immensely powerful group wanted you dead?

Mia leapt to her feet and swung open the door. Tom was leaning against the far wall. The look on Mia's face must have signaled something was very wrong. He straightened.

"The cops are on their way," she explained.

"Then we need to go."

She bit her lip hard. "We can't."

"What? If you get picked up, we won't be able to protect you. Sentinel agents could be anywhere."

"They could have been waiting for us here as well, but we came nevertheless. It was a chance we knew we had to take. And there's one more chance. I need you to buy me some time."

Sweat beaded on his forehead. "How much?"

"An hour? Stall the cops however you can."

Tom laughed. "You'll be lucky to get ten minutes."

Mia could feel the vein in her neck thumping a wild beat. Jansson was coming out of the staff room when Tom broke off, heading toward the lab's main entrance. She locked eyes with the woman and said, "I don't have long but I need your help." She thought of Zoey, lying in bed in some dank motel room. "Millions of lives are at stake. Including my daughter's."

Jansson followed Mia to the DNA sequencer. "I didn't mean for any of this to happen. I was only following protocol."

"It's not your fault," Mia said, her fingers flying over the keyboard as she input fresh search parameters. "I believe our immune system is somehow being co-opted as a vector to inject Salzburg into our cells."

"But how?"

Mia swallowed hard, double-checking she hadn't missed anything before hitting enter. "I think the instructions are being sent to the same parts of our non-coding DNA that created the genes. If so, then we can use those same instructions to implant a human artificial chromosome of our own, stuffed with genes to neutralize Salzburg's effects."

She tapped her foot as she watched the impossibly slow progress bar flick from four to five percent complete. There was no way she was going to finish this.

"If I'm right, I need you to pass the information on to the WHO and Dr. Scott Chapman in Santarem." She jotted this down on a scrap of paper. Mia stopped and looked in Jansson's eyes. The woman was scared. "Surely you've seen the flashes?"

"Flashes?"

"The blinding light, you must have seen it."

"Of course. Hasn't everyone?"

"Every time it happens," Mia told her, "Salzburg grows more powerful."

The program was at seven percent and Mia cursed. Loud voices swept down the long corridor. She stood to leave.

"I nearly forgot," Jansson said, breathless, her wrinkled fingers clutching the note with Scott's number. "I have a paper Dr. Van der Berg was working on before he left." She reached inside her lab coat and removed a few rolled-up sheets. "It's a little out-there and incoherent in places, but maybe you'll find something useful in it."

The voices were growing louder and Mia could make out Tom yelling, "You can't come in here."

"One last thing," Jansson said. "I pretended not to know where Dr. Van der Berg is staying, but it was a lie. He's far away, a place I can't imagine you'll be heading anytime soon."

"Try me," Mia said. She'd already flown halfway around the world. What was a few extra miles?

"Kopan Monastery in Kathmandu."

Chapter 48

"Son of a bitch," Jack shouted, narrowly pulling a punch aimed at one of the biotubes, a move that would surely have shattered the glass, his hand or both.

Eugene and Dag were in the USO's lab as well, looking noticeably uncomfortable.

"Don't let it get to you," Gabby said. "You knew they would show up sooner or later."

"He really got under your skin," Eugene observed.

Jack brushed imaginary dirt off the knuckles of his glove. "Maybe it's the way that smug bastard demanded all of our data like it belonged to him."

Gabby stepped in and settled her hands over his. "How many hours have you slept in the last couple of days?"

He pulled away. "Not nearly enough."

"You're not gonna do us any good losing your mind over one arrogant Navy officer."

"It's just…" His voice trailed off. "We're here trying to find answers to legitimate questions and I just know all they care about is scavenging as much technology as they can find in the hopes of fashioning some sort of weapon."

"And what's so wrong with that?" Her answer surprised him. She wasn't trying to be provocative. Gabby meant it. "Weren't you the one who raised the possibility that these things might've come here to create a colony, maybe populate the earth with insect people just like them?"

"It was only an idea," he countered. "We were spitballing, you know how those things go."

"But what if you were right?"

Her words hung in the air.

"You've been against this from the very beginning," Jack said, recalling their first argument back on the rig. "Don't get me wrong. I'm all for self-defense, but not when it becomes a pretext for an arms race. Look what's happening up there. The world's practically tearing itself apart and why? Because on one side you have a dispute over land and on the other a global population that thinks just like you do. For all we know, the only reason the world isn't populated by insect people is because they got an inkling about how screwed up this world was gonna be and said thanks, but no thanks."

Dag laughed out loud, struck by the imagery.

"I wish I was kidding," Jack said, trying to keep his blood pressure down. His eyes found the tube at the far end with the artificial womb. He stomped over to it and tapped on the glass. The thing inside had grown to the size of a rat, which was not too far off how it looked. Although furless, the creature had an elongated body, four short limbs and the narrow face of a shrew.

Jack pointed. "Is this how they intended to rule the planet, an army of hairless mice?" His eyes remained locked on the creature, his words echoing in his mind.

"Dr. Greer." A male voice with an accent broke in.

He spun around to find Rajesh. "What is it?"

"I need to speak with you about that thing." His eyes shifted from left to right.

"Oh, yes, of course. You pick the channel, I'll follow."

Rajesh held both hands in front of his chest, just out of sight from the others. A four and a five.

•••

"I realize that the moment isn't ideal," Rajesh began, "but I managed to trace part of the code used to infect Anna's systems."

"Let me guess, Naval Intelligence."

"That's what I thought at first too, but that was not the case. It is far worse, I'm afraid."

"I find that hard to believe."

"The core section of code is extremely common and often used in corporate espionage. Then I did a little more digging on the dark web."

"From the Orb?"

"Internet access is mostly the same no matter where you use it. Even where locks and barriers are present, they can be circumnavigated if one knows how. The nitty-gritty aspects aside, I was able to trace the rest of the Trojan's design to a group called Sentinel."

"Sentinel? Never heard of them."

"Not many have. They are a pervasive organization intent on preventing man's outreach toward possible extraterrestrial civilizations."

"So you're saying they aren't the biggest fans of what we're doing here."

Rajesh smiled, his head doing that little dance again. "You may be off by a factor of a million, Dr. Greer. It's beyond not liking the idea. They consider it the greatest existential threat the human race will ever face."

"More than superbugs and nuclear war?"

"Humankind will always find a way to claw its way out of the ash pile and rebuild. But not if a far superior race sterilizes the planet."

"That hardly makes any sense."

Rajesh touched Jack's shoulder. "It may not make sense to us. I am merely telling you what they believe."

"Yes, of course." Jack ran his fingers together. "You think they're somehow in cahoots with the ONI team?"

"That's not possible. Sentinel is mostly made up of powerful civilians. Besides, what the Naval Intelligence men are here for is perfectly obvious."

"Yeah, they want as much alien tech as they can find."

Rajesh shook his head. "You mean tech that will require decades, maybe lifetimes to fully understand? Don't get me wrong, they'll collect it. But that isn't the real prize they're after."

Jack considered the bodies down in the autopsy room. Then the creature growing in the incubation chamber behind them. "I give up. What are they here for?"

"Anna."

Chapter 49

Walking through the streets of Kathmandu was like stepping through a portal and into a fairytale. Rows of pagoda-style buildings lined rust-colored roads. Strolling in their shadow were crowds of Buddhist monks in maroon robes, tourists wearing Tilley hats, and Hindu holy men, covered in ash and chanting their devotion.

Fleets of buses and white taxi cabs jostled for dominance over motorbikes piled with people. The conflict continued in the air as clouds of incense and turmeric battled waves of pollution and human sewage. It was a world of contradictions, at once both divine and detestable.

Mia, Tom and Sven sped past a woman washing clothing at a water spigot in the street. She glanced up at them, indifferent. From here they spotted the majestic corners of Kopan Monastery projecting up from a nearby collection of trees. There they hoped to find Dr. Lars Van der Berg as well as answers to a growing number of questions. But like any mission of discovery, for every question answered, five more rose up to take its place.

Mia had spent at least part of the thirteen-hour flight from Europe to Nepal reading and absorbing Dr. Van der Berg's final research paper. Or at least the parts she could make sense of. Much like Alan, Lars had also become convinced the human genome was hiding secrets it was reluctant to reveal. But his reasoning had less to do with Salzburg syndrome and whatever unusual DNA it contained than it had to do with mathematics.

As he put it, the DNA of all living things contained "an ensemble of arithmetical and ideographical patterns of symbolic language"—essentially, a non-random structure which bore all the hallmarks of being designed. He drew on Rumer's transformation as one of many examples. In 1966, Rumer found that the genetic code could be divided neatly in half, between whole-family and split-family codons. Codons were a sequence of three DNA or RNA nucleotides that corresponded with a specific amino acid. The chance of this occurring naturally was astronomically low.

For his part, Lars used Rumer's transformation to describe twenty-eight 'swappable' codons with a combined atomic mass of one thousand, six hundred and sixty-five and a combined side chain atomic mass of seven hundred and three. Both of these numbers were divisible by a prime number.

In all, Dr. Van der Berg listed nine elegant examples within the human genome where the mass of the molecular core shared by all twenty amino acids or other groupings was divisible by a prime number. The problem? Lars never indicated what that prime number was. Perhaps he didn't know.

The vast majority of Lars' paper gave her a headache, but through the pain, Mia was beginning to see that maybe their initial attempts decrypting the DNA in Salzburg had been rather crude and lacking.

The three of them were passing an open-air café when Sven took Mia's arm and pulled her to a stop. He grumbled, motioning over the television that was hanging on the wall inside.

243

"Alien threat to exterminate mankind uncovered in our DNA," read the headline. Groups of monks, locals and foreigners alike shuffled before screens all along the avenue. People looked at one another in disbelief. Similar scenes of shock were playing out around the world. Shortly, the president of the United States was set to make his third address in so many days. Pundits in the media were referring to the discovery as an impending genocide of the human race and it was having a predictable effect.

Sales of weapons in countries that would allow them had already begun to soar. So too had reports of families plucking their kids out of schools and heading for places in the country. For reasons hard to understand, one guy from Tennessee led reporters on a tour of the bunker he'd built and stocked with food and weapons.

But among a vocal minority, the threat merely confirmed what they already knew. Fringe religious groups were positively apoplectic, had been since the first mention of the ship, whose location was still unknown. But for them, such details were inconsequential. The end was here and many of them rejoiced.

Already, authorities had discovered mass suicides by a number of cults with alien fixations and a lust for death, stirring up memories of Heaven's Gate and Solar Temple. Thankfully, none so far had reached the fever-pitch numbers of Jonestown in '78, although it was becoming abundantly clear that was only a question of time.

"I'm surprised it took this long for people to start losing their minds," Tom said, folding his bottom lip into a frown and doing much the same with his arms. Humanity going to pieces was precisely the type of situation he'd been trying to avoid.

None of them were saying it, even though they knew

it all the same. Sentinel had gotten its hands on the decoded message and was doing its best to spread the fear of an apocalypse across the airwaves.

"This is straight out of their playbook," Tom explained, reading Mia's mind. "But nimble as a group like Sentinel may be, it still takes time to get the message in the right hands and coordinate their plan of attack. Looks like your friend Ollie sold you down the river faster than we expected. He must be a real go-getter."

Mia fought the bile surging up her throat. She had trusted Ollie and he had betrayed her just like Alan.

News of the alien threat was going to spread like a prairie fire on a dry summer's day. Between the cable shows, Twitter and Facebook, nearly everyone with internet access would be discussing what to do and how long they had before the anticipated invasion. But after reading Lars' research paper, rambling though it was at times, Mia was growing more and more certain the message they had plucked from pages of gibberish had been a mistake. Just as Armoni had so rightly pointed out, our brains were wired to see patterns. Jesus' image on a piece of toast, the devil in the billows of smoke from the World Trade Center. For those eager to see them, the world was brimming with codes. Mia wasn't eager at all. But even so, she was becoming more and more convinced that the real message hidden in Salzburg's DNA had yet to be unlocked. With any luck, she was about to meet the one man who might just hold the key.

Chapter 50

After Jack's rather surprising conversation with Rajesh, he and Dag continued to venture deeper into the bowels of the ship. As they descended, almost on a whim, Jack searched until he found the channel the Naval Intelligence officers were working on. He listened in as they proceeded to systematically cart away nearly everything the team had discovered. First came the bodies down in the autopsy room. Hart had told them about those. Next came the workshop where Gabby had found parts of what they suspected were escape pods. In a way, it was very much like watching the sacking of Constantinople, centuries' worth of golden statues carted off for the sole purpose of melting them into coins. Only the creature incubating in the lab remained undetected, and perhaps only so because at least half of the ONI personnel were on the ship's bridge, ogling either the symbols scrolling by on the holographic displays or Anna's considerable ability to decipher what they meant.

It wouldn't be long before Naval Intelligence stumbled upon the lab, confiscating the only living specimen on board along with the mysterious process that had jumpstarted its DNA after millions of years in suspended animation.

Dag was ahead of him now, no more than a few feet, when Jack decided he'd finally had enough of Captain Kelly and his merry band. He flipped back to channel two to find Gabby calling his name.

"Dag and I are trying to reach the ground level," he told her. "See if we can't find the engine to this thing."

"The animal in the incubation tube," she said, her voice distorted by her heavy breathing.

"The ONI men have it," he said, jumping ahead. "Gabby, they're taking everything, but don't worry." He tapped the sample kit still slung over his shoulder. "I kept some backups and I hope you did too."

"No, Jack, it wasn't them. The thing just disappeared."

●●●

They hurried at once back to the lab, the muscles in Jack's legs burning nearly as much as his lungs. They arrived to find Eugene pacing by the entrance.

"Where's Rajesh?" he asked, struggling to catch his breath.

"Still on the bridge," Eugene said. "Trying to make sure no one messes with Anna."

"I don't blame him," Dag added. "Wouldn't surprise me one bit to hear they meant to cart her away along with everything else."

Jack went to the empty tube. "So what happened exactly?"

"It had grown nearly twice the size since you were last here," Gabby began. "Eugene and I were here watching it slosh around."

"It was moving?" Dag asked, amazed.

247

"Yeah," Eugene replied. "And it was covered in fur. Next thing we knew a grate at the bottom of the incubation chamber opened up and drained all the fluid away. It was sitting there wet and confused. All of the sudden, it got sucked up through the top." Eugene flung his arm up as if to demonstrate.

"What did it look like?" Jack asked.

He stuck his palms out, shaking them back and forth ever so slightly. "My background in zoology is very limited," he said, pleading.

Dag, ever the paleontologist and movie nut, jumped in to help. "Did it look like something that might latch onto your face and lay eggs in your belly?"

Jack threw him a look.

"It had a long tail…" Gabby began to explain before fumbling with her glasses to send them a short snippet of video she'd taken.

Dag's eyes went wide as he watched. "Call me crazy, but that looks a hell of a lot like a Plesiadapiformes."

A light behind Jack's eyes grew bright. "We need to find out where it went." His gaze went to the top of the chamber and the black pipe which fed into a network of other ducts above. They each hurried in a different direction, following a spaghetti of twists and turns.

"The heck is a plesidapaformez?" Eugene said, butchering the word beyond repair.

Jack spotted a collection point high up where they all seemed to begin curving down toward the lower levels. He hurried for the nearest down-facing ramp, the sample kit on his waist clanking as he ran. The others followed suit. At the rear was Eugene still demanding an explanation.

•••

They stopped one level below the autopsy room. This was an area they had bypassed several times in their race to the bottom of the ship, where they hoped to find an engineering room and the source of the craft's propulsion. Scanning the ceiling, Jack noticed how the pipes from the lab all seemed to converge on this floor.

The group pressed on with nothing but the ducts above to guide them.

"Maybe it got sucked into some kind of holding pen," Dag suggested.

Soon they reached the central column of the elevator shaft. They circled the base until they found the archway to an area they hadn't seen before. From inside, red, blue and green lights bled out, casting eerie shapes along the smooth metal surface. Cautiously, they passed over the threshold and stepped inside. Just like the tubes in the lab, here too were enclosures—pods really—arranged in rows, thirty-seven wide and an equal number deep. Same as the lab.

They came to a pod in the second row on the far left, the same position held by the incubation chamber with the Plesiadapiformes.

"There it is," Gabby said.

Hazy tendrils of smoke danced inside the pod. Eugene drew closer right as the animal threw itself against the glass and let out a shriek. He recoiled and fell backwards.

"It's gone insane," Dag said.

"There's enough room in there if you wanted to join him," Gabby teased Eugene, who shrugged off the comment.

The animal was desperate to escape, but none of them were foolish enough to release it from captivity, even if they knew how.

249

A set of green holographic symbols shot out from a console next to the pod. The strange alien text rotated before them for less than sixty seconds before the room began to shake and the pod disappeared in a hail of swirling mist.

"Where'd it go?" Dag asked, shocked.

Jack raised a solitary finger. "Topside," he said with certainty.

"Will someone for the love of God please tell me what's so special about these plesi-things?" Eugene asked.

"It's Plesiadapiformes," Jack said, still absorbing the enormity of the situation. "A furry squirrel-like mammal with a long bushy tail that spent most of its time in trees."

Eugene put his hands on his knees and shook his head in disbelief. "We ran all this way for that?"

"Not just that," Jack explained, turning and heading back toward the ramp. "It also happens to be one of man's earliest ancestors."

Chapter 51

From the outside, Kopan Monastery looked more like a glittering Eastern palace than it did a place of worship. The temple featured five stories of fine, intricate craftsmanship, flanked on both sides by even taller pagoda-style towers and wide terraces. Groups of monks in saffron-colored robes shuffled toward a courtyard where a series of stupas were located. Stupas were large Buddhist shrines commemorating important monks or containing mantras, texts or other sacred relics.

Mia stopped a young monk to ask him what was happening. He smiled and bowed slightly, but said nothing.

An older monk spotted them and approached.

"I'm sorry, but the trapas are forbidden from speaking at the moment."

"Trapas?" Tom asked.

"Student monks." Clasping his hands together, he began to move away.

"Wait a moment," she called after him. "I'm looking for Dr. Lars Van der Berg."

"I'm sorry, but the monastery is closed to visitors." He turned and melted back into the crowd.

"Lars is sure to stick out like a sore thumb in a place

like this," Tom said, trying to be consoling.

"Dr. Jansson made it sound like he'd gone off the deep end. How do we know he won't be locked away somewhere? I say we follow the monks and see if we can't spot him in the crowd."

Sven grunted his approval.

Tom glanced over at the big guy. "Try not to scare anyone."

Matching the monks' careful pace, they merged into the river of saffron robes that flowed toward the courtyard. Even with the considerable height advantage they enjoyed, they were still having little luck finding anyone who matched Lars' description.

Until Sven cupped the back of Mia's neck with one powerful hand and used the other to point to an older white male in monk's robes about ten meters away.

With profuse apologies, they maneuvered through the throngs, working toward someone who looked very much like Dr. Van der Berg. Soon, as more monks joined, the crowd swelled and pushed back, and they lost sight of him. It was like moving through waist-high water.

"I can't see him," Mia called out. She was getting separated from Tom and the others. Then the man appeared again, this time closer to the monastery. He was moving away. Had he seen them? Glancing back, Mia had lost sight of both Tom and Sven.

She persevered, pushing upstream now, worried if she didn't get through she might not get another chance. The white figure disappeared into the monastery. If she could only break free from the crowd, she might be able to catch up. Monks both young and old were staring past her, at the ceremony that was about to begin. Feeling a surge of panic, Mia laced her fingers and stuck out her elbows, creating a wedge. Dispensing with all manner of politeness, she charged ahead. Minutes later, she had broken through, finding an open space closer to the temple. At last she could breathe. And, more importantly, she could continue her pursuit of the man she hoped was Lars.

She followed the outer wall until she arrived before a pair of solid and colorfully decorated oak doors. Her fingers wrapped around the brass handle and she pulled it open. Inside was an enormous and dazzling space that smelled of incense and ancient history. Cherry-colored pillars supported a high-beamed ceiling and a wraparound upper balcony.

Every square inch was covered in a rich tapestry of vibrant eastern colors. On the floor were prayer mats. Impressive as all those things were, none could compete with the golden statue of Buddha, twenty feet tall and adorned with a beautifully embroidered robe.

Following what she knew of Buddhist custom, Mia slipped off her shoes and proceeded inside. The prayer room was empty, except for a single figure seated next to one of the pillars.

As she drew closer, she noticed he was a Caucasian male, his chin lowered in meditation. But he was dressed differently than the person she'd seen entering the temple moments before. Surely Lars wasn't the only white guy around. In the last few decades, a growing number of westerners, disillusioned with the hectic pace of industrialized society, had begun flocking to the simpler way of life eastern monasteries afforded. Apparently, Lars had been one of them. But whether or not this was him or merely another western pilgrim in search of Nirvana remained to be seen.

"Dr. Van der Berg?" she whispered.

A man in his mid-seventies turned his head and regarded her without saying anything.

"I'm sorry to disturb you, but I'm looking for Lars…"

"Lars Van der Berg has passed on," the man said.

That old familiar frustration was bubbling up inside her again. "When did he die?" she asked, no longer bothering to hide her despair.

"The death was rapid and occurred the moment he arrived," the man explained.

Mia watched him, unsure.

"For the path to transcendence means you must relinquish everything you once were."

Mia feigned understanding as she noted the tattoos poking out from the collar of his robe. They looked like the faces of Buddhist religious figures along with bits of sacred text.

"Were you at one time Dr. Lars Van der Berg?" she asked, still wondering if this old guy was high on incense.

He nodded. "I was, but I am known now as Wangchuk Bhattarai trapa."

Mia sat next to him, folding her legs. Outside, the volume of monks beating drums and clanging symbols rose.

"What's going on out there?" she asked.

"A funeral for the head lama, Thubten Zopa Rinpoche," the man now known as Wangchuk explained.

Mia removed the research paper Lars had written back in Amsterdam. "I need to talk to you about this," she said, handing it to him. Wangchuk took the papers and glanced over them amid the growing cacophony of noise from the funeral service in the courtyard. "You wrote about a pattern of symbolic language you observed within human DNA and—"

He raised his left hand, for a moment resembling the statue of Buddha behind her. "Not only human," Wangchuk corrected. "The symmetry exists within all creatures."

Mia found herself speaking louder against the racket,

just to be heard. "Yes, but in your paper you mentioned those symmetries were connected by a single prime number, but you never revealed what that number was."

Perhaps resisting the urge to shout, Wangchuk began raising his other hand, this time his right. He was halfway into the action when gunshots rang out, the bulk of it lost in the overall din. The first two bullets struck Wangchuk's neck and then his temple, spraying the cherry pillar next to him a deeper color of red. Instinctively, Mia rolled backwards and behind the post, placing it between herself and the shooter.

Rounds tore chunks from the wooden floor on either side of her. She could see from the way the wood was splintering that the shooter was perched on the upper balcony. Mia felt a surge of fear and adrenaline rush through her body. She was breathing hard, her chest struggling to provide oxygen to her muscles. But more than that, she was trapped like a rat.

The sound of a magazine hitting the floor signaled an opportunity Mia couldn't pass up. She bolted from cover and dove behind the next pillar. Ten feet to her right was a set of double doors and her only chance to escape. Undeterred, the shooter remained in place, firing out whenever she peeked at him from around the corner. From the glimpses she was able to steal, she could tell he was a Caucasian male dressed in monk's robes, the same individual she'd been following earlier. More rounds ricocheted next to her, others thudding into the pillar. It was only a question of time before he repositioned and found the right angle.

Her senses on high alert, Mia caught the sound of a door opening on the second level. Was the assassin fleeing at last? Then another noise, this one as though two people were in a struggle. She glanced out and saw the gun clatter to the floor as two men engaged in hand-to-hand combat. Relief swept over her with the realization that Tom or Sven had finally come to her rescue. The larger man grabbed the assassin in a chokehold and jerked his body, breaking his neck. When he let go the dead man slid to the floor and out of Mia's sight.

Locking eyes with her rescuer, she saw now that it was not Tom or Sven.

It was Ollie.

Chapter 52

By the time Jack got back to the Orb, Commander Hart was on the comms line in a heated conversation.

"Is that Admiral Stark?" Jack said, struggling to calm his burning lungs. Who needed a gym membership, he thought, when you could scale a dozen ramps on an alien mothership?

Hart put a hand over his mic. "Ten minutes ago they detected an unidentified object exiting the water and heading for the coast."

"Tell him it's a pod and—"

"Jack, he's losing it. You better talk to him."

Nodding, Jack told Hart to patch him through. A second later, Jack said, "Rear Admiral Stark?"

"This is the Secretary of Defense, Ford Myers."

Jack inhaled a sharp breath. Had Myers come to personally oversee the operation? If so that meant the situation topside must be worse than he thought.

"Who am I speaking to?"

"Dr. Jack Greer, sir. I'm with an element investigating the USO. What you tracked leaving the Gulf contains a biological entity."

"You have got to be kidding me." The secretary's Virginia twang was growing stronger by the second.

"No, sir. Originally the specimen was in an incubation chamber and gestated at an incredibly rapid rate. Before we had a chance to remove it, the ship somehow took matters into its own hands and jettisoned it. You need to track where it lands and send a team to bring it back alive."

Myers sounded incredulous. "Are you telling me there's an alien on the loose somewhere on the Peninsula?"

"Not if you can get your people there quickly."

"Mexico's a sovereign nation, Dr. Greer. They teach you anything about borders at that fancy school you attended? We can't just go swooping in and—"

"Pardon my saying, Mr. Secretary, but there isn't time to argue about this."

He grew quiet. "Please tell me you haven't unleashed some sort of monster."

"No, least I don't believe so. But it may hold answers to questions we've been asking for a very long time."

Jack felt the seconds slipping away. If they waited any longer, there was no telling where the creature might be.

"I'll send them, but if anything goes wrong, it'll be on you."

The line went dead.

"How dare you withhold information," Captain Kelly shouted as he clambered through the airlock. Lieutenant Brooks and two other ONI agents were close behind. The agents struggled under the weight of a large duffle bag. The top was unzipped and inside were components clearly scavenged from the bridge.

The captain tried to make a beeline for Commander Hart, but Jack stepped in his way.

"I've got nothing to say to you. Now move!" Kelly ordered him.

"Not until you tell me what's in the bag."

"We don't have to tell you a damned thing," Kelly said, nudging past him.

When he saw parts from the bridge, a terrible fear swept over him. Jack recalled Rajesh's concerns that the ONI was here for Anna. Could some or all of her have been shoved in that duffle bag? Jack went to the master frequency and called out for Rajesh.

After watching the men load the bag into an empty submersible, he called out again and Rajesh's voice finally replied.

"Are you still on the bridge?" Jack asked.

"Yeah, but—"

He felt the veins at his temples starting to throb. "Is Anna with you?"

"She is and she's safe. Although Captain Kelly and his men gutted half the consoles here. But there's something else you need to know."

Jack waited for it, although somehow a part of him already knew.

"The countdown clock," Rajesh said, breathless. "It's started again."

Chapter 53

The monastery door swung open as Tom and Sven rushed in, guns drawn. At first they eyed the body of the dead monk before they found Mia. She was steadying herself on wobbly legs, staring at the balcony upstairs. A group of monks rushed in, hesitated when they witnessed the chaotic scene, then ran to Lars' body.

"We were searching the crowd for you when we heard the shooting," Tom said.

Sven swung her around and patted plaster dust off her shoulders and back.

"I'm fine," she said, checking the upper level again. It was empty. "He was here," she told them, not interested in keeping what she had seen a secret.

"Van der Berg?" Tom asked, not entirely sure who Mia meant.

She glanced at his body. The monks had laid him on his back and were preparing to carry him away. A pool of blood had collected by his side. "I was speaking to Lars when someone shot him from up there."

The two men listened intently.

"The shooter had me pinned down. Then from out of nowhere, Ollie appeared, knocked the gun out of his hand and killed him."

An angry sound emanated from the back of Sven's

throat as the big man turned and took off at a run.

"Ollie better hope Sven doesn't find him," Tom said.

Mia wasn't sure what to hope for.

The young monks moved past carrying Lars' body, a sight which hit Mia twice as hard. Insane or not, the man had been a genius in the field of bio-informatics. But more than that, she had become convinced he held a vital piece of the puzzle, a piece now lost forever. Her eye caught one of the tattoos on his neck and it reminded her of how Lars had been lifting his right hand to silence her a second before he was shot.

She went to the monks and asked them to stop.

"Mia, what are you doing?"

What if Lars hadn't been calling for her silence, but preparing to show her something? His limp arms were folded over his chest. She lifted the right one and studied the top of his hand before turning it over. And that was when she saw it. Tattooed on his wrist, just below the heel of his palm, were two digits. Could this be the prime number they'd been looking for? The key to unlocking the real message hidden in the Salzburg syndrome?

Tom swung around for a better look.

His voice, couched in reverence, now fell to a whisper as he spoke the words. "Thirty-seven."

Chapter 54

As the minutes and seconds to the next blast wave ticked down, Jack summoned the science team to the top berthing quarters. Whatever they were going to decide, it would have to be quick. Many of the bunks were covered in discarded t-shirts, sweatpants and other casual clothes the team had changed out of during those rare moments of rest. Needless to say, the sleeping quarters had quickly taken on the funky odor of a locker room.

Right now, the stench of body odor was the least of Jack's concerns. Once all were assembled before him he began.

"I want all of you to leave," Jack said, not mincing words. "Load your things onto the submersible and get topside while you still can."

"Shouldn't we be allowed to make that determination ourselves?" Gabby asked, defiance in her voice.

Standing with his back against one of the bunks, Rajesh said, "What about Anna and her work? She's so close to piecing together the alien language."

"She'll stay and so will I. I'll keep an eye on her, I promise," Jack assured him. "The scientist we could use most right now is Grant. Given his medical situation, we had no option but to evacuate him. I'm hoping there's someone else up there Stark can send down to us."

Hart crossed his arms, rippled with muscle. "Admiral Stark said they're putting together at least a dozen robotic rovers that can be controlled from topside. That way they can be used to explore the rest of the ship without risking any more lives than we need to."

"Makes sense to me," Dag said, peeling off his biosuit right in front of everyone.

"As head of the Office for Outer Space Affairs," Eugene said, stepping forward, "I should also stay."

Jack was impressed by the gesture, but quickly reminded him about the magma bubble beneath the ship.

"On second thought, I should probably go... might be easier to oversee the rest of the operation from the USS *Grapple*."

Gabby caught Jack's eye and shook her head. "That didn't take much convincing."

"What about Captain Happy and his band of merry men?" Dag asked.

"As far as I can tell they're going to stay," Hart said. "And so am I."

Jack met his eyes and saw the steely determination in them.

"After all, this expedition is under Navy jurisdiction," Hart explained. "And I should stay to make sure things run smoothly."

Gabby let out a soft chuckle. "By smoothly, you mean so Jack and Captain Kelly don't tear each other to pieces?"

The others joined in.

Hart winked. "Something like that."

"I don't need the backup," Jack told him. "But it'll be nice to have someone to talk to other than Navy so-called Intelligence folks." He turned to Rajesh. "There's no time for you to head back to the bridge. I'm afraid you'll have to give Anna your goodbyes from here. She's on channel three, I believe."

He shook his head and buried it in his hands. "I just hate the idea of leaving her."

Jack laid a hand on Rajesh's shoulder. "If it makes you feel any better, I spoke with her right before our little get-together. She agreed to stay, but only on condition that you went topside."

The computer engineer's eyes clouded with tears.

"I gave you my word she'd be fine," Jack reminded him. "Now grab your stuff and say your farewells, 'cause the sub leaves in five."

•••

Forty-five minutes later, with the sub away, Jack and Commander Hart waited on the bridge. It had taken some convincing for Hart to leave mission control on the Orb. Even the threat of falling debris knocking the habitat off the ship and into the murky depths had had little effect. In the end, Jack had been forced to remind him what being outside the USO during the last event had done to Lieutenant Olsen.

Jack sat on one of the large console chairs, trying to imagine what it must have looked like to see one of the alien creatures operating the controls here. How they might have communicated with one another. Was he right about them opting to die once their mission was complete, whatever that mission had been?

"Dr. Greer," Anna said, pulling away from a console on the other side of the bridge.

"Yes, Anna? What is it?"

"I am glad that you and Commander Hart chose to stay," she said, rolling over to him.

Hart, who was leaning against the bridge's entryway, nudged himself straight.

"We're glad too," Jack said, eyeing the SEAL, who probably wasn't used to hearing computers talk about feelings.

"It would have been nice if Dr. Viswanathan had

264

been here," she went on.

Jack swiveled to face her. "You miss him?"

"I believe so. Though I am sure he will regret not being here for the breakthrough."

His back straightened, the pitch of his voice peaking with excitement. "What breakthrough? Have you cracked the alien language?"

"Not all of it," she corrected him. "Enough, however, to know you are sitting in the navigator's seat."

Jack was about to pull Anna into a hug when the consoles began to flicker. That ringing came to his ears again, a low throbbing sound as though a giant electrical transformer were charging up before a massive release. He thought of Gabby and the others in the submersible, hopeful they'd had enough time to get away. Then the blast came and Jack was no longer worried about the others' safety. He was suddenly worried about his own.

Chapter 55

Rain pelted the safehouse windows, drawing streaks along the glass. Now back in Amsterdam, Mia was feeling upbeat and energized in spite of the soggy weather outside. No doubt about it, she was hopeful that the number thirty-seven might soon prove useful in their search for a solution to the worldwide health crisis. Of course, it was easy to assume that only humans had a stake in the discovery, but a handful of animal species were also showing signs. And not just any animals. Most of them were creatures that shared our personal space. Tests had revealed that certain farm animals and house pets also had Salzburg in their genome. And yet few if any wild animals bore the extra chromatid, except for bears, raccoons and crows. But even there, those three lived in relative close proximity to humans. Somewhere was the missing link and Mia was determined to find it.

As soon as they had arrived, Mia had contacted Dr. Jansson to get an update. The two women had spoken for close to thirty minutes. Under different circumstances this was an exchange of information that would normally have occurred via email, but with Sentinel actively hunting them, an encrypted sat phone was the only safe option.

Following Mia's departure, Dr. Jansson's lab had

taken her suggestions to heart while adding a few touches of their own. For starters, they decided rather than co-opting the body's immune system to deliver the HAC, they would instead use a retroviral vector. This meant repurposing a virus—such as VSV G-pseudotyped lentivirus—and coating it with proteins. Normally this was the preferred method among geneticists since VSV infected a large range of cells.

Mia had considered this option, but had worried that only humans could be treated and not the millions of animals who were also suffering from the disorder. Hesitations aside, Mia understood that where first steps were concerned, one needed to start somewhere.

But introducing the HAC into the body's cells was only part of the challenge. The larger issue was figuring out which genes might stop Salzburg dead in its tracks.

For that, Jansson's lab turned to a solution already found in nature. Female mammals carried a gene called XIST designed to silence one of the two X chromosomes women carried inside of them. Jansson's team duplicated the gene and reprogrammed the copy—naming it XIST2. When introduced, XIST2 would produce an RNA molecule that coated the surface of the forty-seventh chromatid, Salzburg, and effectively block its genes from being expressed.

So far, the limited test run had shown terrific and almost immediate results. For many patients, the new gene therapy was like flipping a light switch. But there was one more piece of good news from Dr. Jansson and it made all of the hardship Mia had faced these last few days feel worth it.

Tom entered her room with the sat phone. Mia pushed her back against the headboard as he handed it to her.

"Hello?"

"Mommy?"

Mia's heart leapt. She laughed, fat tears rolling down her cheeks. "Oh, honey, you had us so worried." Tom had apparently left a special order for Dr. Jansson that if she deemed it safe, she was to include Mia's daughter in the initial round of testing.

"Daddy says I was sick."

"I know, sweetie," she said, crying and laughing at the same time. "He's right, you were very sick, but you're better now. And that's all that matters."

"When are you coming home?"

Mia bit down on her lip. "As soon as I can."

When they were done, Tom took the phone and left the room. Wiping at her eyes, Mia was struck by just how strange Tom sometimes acted. Some moments he was capable of extreme kindness, like when he'd instructed Dr. Jansson to include Zoey in the first round of an expedited gene therapy trial. And yet he had also watched as her eyes filled with tears without offering so much as a...

Sven stood before her, holding out a box of Kleenex. A single tissue fluttered gently in the breeze from the ceiling fan.

"Thank you," she said, taking one and blowing her nose. There was no polite way of going about the act if you intended to do the job properly. He twitched as she gave it a final honk. She leaned back, dabbing away the last few specks. "I really needed that."

He settled onto the end of her bed, the springs of her mattress whining in protest.

Mia's gaze drifted slightly. "I'm not sure I'll ever have my family back," she told him, happy to have someone who knew how to listen. "Least, not the way things used to be."

He regarded her intently, the corners of his eyes curved downward like the sad eyes of a Saint Bernard.

"You know, they say life is like being at sea in a very

small boat. The wind and the waves will push you all over. Up and down, left and right. Sometimes it gets so bad all you see are giant watery hands falling on top of you, trying to flip you over and drag you to the bottom. Then before you know it, you're cresting the wave, high above it all, and for a moment you can breathe again. I guess it's mostly true. Peaks and valleys, you know."

Sven's head tilted slightly.

"My life has mostly been chaos interrupted by brief moments of order. Paul represented that order for me. And for a while I was good at it. But I kept asking myself when that other shoe was gonna drop. Kept wondering when the chaos was gonna come surging back in to pull me down and sink my boat. Figured it was only a matter of time." Mia let out a humorless spate of laughter. "You know how I got myself through school?"

The big man shook his head.

"I was a nude model." Images from the past whizzed by at supersonic speeds. Mia cackled and this time the joy was real. "Yeah, I took my clothes off for students in painting classes. Wasn't easy at first, but I sure as hell wasn't gonna wait tables. I'd already tried that one and it left me with nothing but shin splints and sore feet. The money modeling wasn't bad either. Only problem was the professor. He didn't give off the sleazeball vibe, not at first. But I caught the way his eyes lingered a little too long. And he was no spring chicken either. The man had eyebrows with more volume than some men have on their scalp. The clincher was when he asked me out. You're in a rough spot at that age. Pissing your boss off is never a great strategy, believe me. Needless to say, I told him no. He stopped bothering me after that. In fact, he stopped calling altogether. I'd been working those modeling gigs for two full semesters before he built up the courage and then couldn't take the rejection. I was forced to find a private school in town. I never realized it then, but there was something in me that drove older men wild. Paul is older than me by five years and Alan by at least twenty. Maybe that's what I should study next, when this is all over. The encrypted language of the human libido." She laughed again and so did Sven. "You're easy to talk to. I suppose that's because I know a guy who doesn't speak will never go blabbing my business to Tom or anyone else who'll listen."

He slid his index finger and thumb across his lips in a zipper gesture. "Your secrets are safe with me." His voice was so deep it seemed to rumble.

Mia's eyes saucered. "Whaaa? You speak?"

"Course he speaks," Tom said from the doorway, a dishtowel slung over his shoulder. She could tell by the devilish look on his face he was loving this far too much. "What'd you think, the big man was mute?"

"Um, kinda."

"He doesn't fancy talking, that's all," Tom clarified. "But that doesn't mean the man's incapable of the act." He winked. "And don't worry, I didn't hear a thing about your days as a nude model."

Mia was still processing her surprise over Sven's ability to speak and the voice that came with it when the room disappeared in a flashbulb of pain. Each of them rubbed at their eyes, blinking away any lingering white spots from their vision. This was the third event in less than a week. And it was after each that more and more people had begun showing symptoms of that rare genetic disorder she'd been fighting so hard to understand and stop dead in its tracks. But even before her sight had been fully restored, a concern had popped into Mia's mind, one she couldn't let go of. How would the HACs they'd implanted in the gene therapy test subjects hold out?

And more to the point, was Zoey still okay?

Chapter 56

An uneasy look passed between Mia, Tom and Sven.

"Those flashes are coming sooner each time," Mia said, rising to her feet. "We need to find out where they're coming from and how to stop them. And I want each of the test subjects closely monitored for any signs of backsliding."

Sven agreed and left to see to her last point.

If there had been any wheels turning in her mind over the prime number Lars had given them, the wheels had since ground to a halt. Even if the gene therapy they had administered managed to hold, she knew this latest event meant that a whole slew of new patients would require treatment.

"Haven't your people figured out where this is coming from?" she asked. "I thought you used to be part of Sentinel."

Tom bristled at Mia's comment. "Where Sentinel has hundreds and maybe even thousands of agents and personnel, we have dozens and nowhere near the cash."

"You're right, I'm sorry." They were all frustrated.

"We've been monitoring as many of Sentinel's lines of communication as we can," Tom told her. "If they know, they're either being very quiet about it or they're passing the info along by means we aren't aware of."

Mia had an idea. "How about you cut out the middleman?"

"Ignore Sentinel?" Tom was not liking the idea.

"Don't ignore them, but shift some of your assets. You guys keep following Sentinel and you'll always be a few steps behind. Look how long it took you to find me."

He shook his head, although the glare in his eye spoke volumes. She was right and he knew it. "So what are you proposing?"

"There must be satellites from the military as well as NASA that monitor these sorts of things. Have your people hack in and see what they can find." It was far too much of a coincidence to believe that the discovery of that alien ship and the explosion of Salzburg weren't somehow related. Finding that ship and putting an end to the flashes mutating our DNA had become her top priority.

•••

Tom returned two hours later with some news. She grew worried when he refused to make eye contact with her.

"Did your people find anything?" she asked, not sure if she wanted to hear the answer.

He handed her a number of satellite printouts. The first image showed a spot off what appeared to be the Yucatán Peninsula. The next showed an oil rig surrounded by a half-dozen US Navy ships.

"What you're seeing started out as an expedition led by a geophysicist named Dr. Jack Greer and an astrophysicist named Dr. Gabby Bishop. From what our hackers and sources close to the Navy were able to uncover, these scientists were digging for a meteorite when they found the ship. The moment of discovery matches up with the very first flash."

"They must have woken it up," Mia said almost to

herself.

Tom regarded her quizzically. "Woken it up?"

"It may have taken some time, but don't you see? Whoever left that ship behind wanted us to find it."

"But why?"

Mia's eyes searched the room as her mind raced. "Who knows? Maybe they were waiting until we were ready."

"Ready for what?"

"I'm not sure," she replied. "But that's what worries me." Her gaze fell on Tom again. "When do we head to Mexico?"

"I'm not sure. We're using our contacts in the Navy I mentioned to reach out to the task force in the Gulf. Needless to say, it's been extremely difficult. The whole area's under lockdown and patrolled by an armada of warships, not all of them American."

Every sector of people's lives was being affected by these events. And it wasn't merely those suffering medically. The corners of the political, religious and economic fabric of society were becoming more than frayed. They were being torn apart. And they would soon find themselves in a state that civilizations throughout history had sought to stave off. That state was one of chaos.

The slippery slope between order and chaos was well understood, even among the ancient Egyptians, and more recently in parts of the world such as Venezuela, Mogadishu and Syria. Only recently had the West gotten a fresh taste of it.

"All I need is for you to get me on the phone with someone," Mia told him, wringing her hands. "Give me a chance to explain we have a piece of the puzzle they can't do without. If these symptoms are occurring all over the world, then surely the Navy has been affected as well."

Tom nodded, clearly hesitant about the next bit of news he had. "There's something else." Everything about his body language told her he wished he could stop now.

"P-please tell me it isn't about Zoey," she stammered, pushing against the knot that was forcing its way up her throat.

His eyes flickered with sadness.

"She's relapsed again, hasn't she?"

He remained quiet. But his silence said enough.

•••

More hours passed as Mia tried to distract herself from the heartache tearing at her insides.

Tom entered with the sat phone and handed it to her.

Please don't let it be Paul with more bad news. With an almost imperceptible wince, she brought it to her ear.

"Hello, Dr. Ward. This is Jack Greer."

Chapter 57

After a rather surprising conversation with Dr. Mia Ward, Jack headed for the bridge. Apparently, seismic surveys conducted by the military confirmed a stubborn outcropping of limestone was the only thing keeping the ship from plummeting into the depths. If the countdown started again, they'd been ordered to follow the emergency protocol—which was to say, they were to head to the Orb, release it from the forward airlock and then fill the habitat's ballast tanks with compressed air in the hopes they might make it to the surface in time.

Like his introduction to Mia, the Navy's escape plan left Jack feeling less than optimistic. As for the geneticist, she had confirmed several of his emerging hypotheses: namely, that the blast waves were affecting people on a genetic level and that the intensity was growing stronger with each event. She was adamant they needed to be stopped at any cost.

Mia made cryptic comments about a group she said was out to stop any attempts at initiating first contact with an alien race. Any other time she might have sounded like a member of the tinfoil hat brigade, but Jack was quick to recall his conversation with Rajesh and the virus planted in Anna's software by a group calling themselves Sentinel.

If she could get here in time, Jack was confident her background in genetics would be of great service.

But there was another subject she had mentioned, one that had intrigued him a great deal. She said the genetic mutation appearing in people contained some sort of message. That after decoding it, Sentinel agents had leaked it to the media. She'd been talking about the 'MAN WILL FALL' Jack had heard from news reports. Perhaps the more surprising news was that Mia had begun to doubt the results of her own decryption. She claimed to have discovered a key that with the right algorithm might reveal something entirely different.

Even after Jack had explained the dangers, he was impressed with how quickly she had accepted his invitation to come help. It spoke to her bravery, sure, but it also told him she had an emotional stake in finding answers before the ship slipped away forever.

He'd informed her that a military transport was ready to fly her here from Europe, the details of which he would leave for the Secretary of Defense and his staff.

For now, he had other fish to fry.

Jack was scaling the final ramp to the bridge when he glanced to his left and noticed the trail of fuchsia and powder-blue colored lights dancing up the ship's central column. He passed through the archway a moment later and spotted Anna, perched before one of the consoles.

She perked up at his arrival. "Dr. Greer, you will be pleased to know that things are progressing nicely."

"No kidding!" he said, exuberant. "You got the elevator working. Anna, you are truly amazing. When Rajesh first unveiled you, I gotta say I wasn't sure." His expression softened. "I'm sorry I ever doubted you."

Her digital cheeks flushed. "Those are kind words, Dr. Greer, and they are greatly appreciated." She pointed to the panel. "I should let you know that the master controls for many of the ship's functions can be accessed through this terminal." She paused and her expression turned quizzical. "Please forgive my intrusiveness, but I accessed your personnel file on the rig's servers."

"Those are meant to be private," Jack said, unclear where this was going. "Why'd you do that?"

"Curiosity, I suppose. There did not appear to be a restriction on the information."

Although a little miffed, Jack understood that Anna was still new to cultural norms. The idea that an activity was frowned upon or considered inappropriate was just as foreign to her as expecting a westerner to understand the nuances of a Japanese tea-pouring ceremony.

"You wrote that you were unmarried and hoped to remain so. Why have you committed to remaining single, Dr. Greer?"

No doubt a great, if slightly insensitive question, one Gabby had often peppered him with. "I chalk it up to a string of bad luck."

"I am not clear on what role chance has to play," she said, her head tilting slightly. "Can you please elaborate?"

"Let's just say there were a few women in my life I was ready to settle down with. But in the end, it turned out I didn't know them half as well as I thought I did."

Anna didn't seem satisfied. It was tough being questioned about your love life, or lack thereof, by a robot with the emotional intelligence of a ten-year-old.

"Maybe once this is over," he told her, "I'll take you out for a beer and explain it all."

She smiled. "I would like that."

"All right, it's a date."

Those pixelated pink cheeks again.

"In the meantime, we have work to do." His tone grew serious and Anna straightened. "Our number one priority right now is finding a way to stop those blast waves."

"I have performed millions of searches on the

subject, Dr. Greer, and have found no explanation for the explosion of high-energy particles or a way to stop them from being periodically released."

Jack rubbed the tips of his fingers together.

"Are you itchy?" she asked him.

"Huh?" He glanced down at his right hand. "Oh, this. It's just a habit when I'm thinking."

Anna glanced down at her own fingers and began rubbing them. "I fail to observe any noticeable benefit." She stopped moving her fingers. "There is something else I came across during my exploration of the ship's computer systems." It was an audio sound-bite she fed into his helmet. At once his ears were assaulted by an unearthly racket of clicks and high-pitched whines. His hands rose up involuntarily to the sides of his head. The features of his face distorted in torment.

"What the hell is that?" he asked. "You trying to deafen me?"

"My apologies, Dr. Greer," Anna replied, cutting it off and reaching out with her robotic arm. "I believe it is a sample of speech, left over by the extraterrestrial race who operated this ship."

"Coulda fooled me. Sounded more like a room filled with thousands of angry cicadas." He took a moment to gather his wits about him. "What are the chances you could figure out what they're saying?"

"In the time we have left?" she said, seeming to contemplate the idea. "The probability is point zero zero zero one percent. There is, however, another file you might find interesting. It was created recently and do not worry, this one will not cause you any pain."

Jack wasn't so sure.

Anna manipulated the console. "This next file is a three-dimensional video, although the colors of familiar objects may appear strange because of the way humans process images."

This was interesting. "The aliens who ran this ship didn't use the same color spectrum as humans?"

"That is the most likely explanation. Allow me to play the recording." Anna raised her hands to the console and flicked through a series of displays, all of which looked to Jack like gibberish. She had already uploaded her decryption results to the servers topside, which meant if they didn't make it out, at least that vital breakthrough would live on.

Seconds later, a mostly green and blue holographic video began to play. He took a large step back to get a better look. He saw the rush of clouds as the earth raced up to meet the object falling through the air. A violent shudder shook the image, followed by a billowing wave of earth sent out by the shockwave.

Slowly the surroundings settled and a tropical forest came into view. Jack wondered what the time period was, a question soon answered by the distant shape of a farmer's shack. Had the video been transmitted from the pod that was recently released? He watched as the transparent partition slid back and the 'plesi' rushed from the capsule. Jack expected it to tear off into the jungle, but it didn't get five feet before it began writhing on the ground. A moment later, it grew still, dead on the jungle floor. Soon, a swarm of men in bulky hazmat suits rushed in and scooped it into a container.

Just then, Commander Hart radioed Jack to announce the creature had been found.

"Dead," Jack said, finishing Hart's sentence.

"How did you know?"

"It wasn't designed to breathe twenty-first-century air," he explained.

Hart fell silent for a minute. "I'm not following."

"The atmosphere today is composed of roughly seventy-eight percent nitrogen, twenty-one percent oxygen. The rest is made up of argon and traces of other gases. But sixty-five million years ago, when the ship impacted the planet, the atmosphere was very different. Scientists studying plant matter trapped in amber—sticky tree resin—have discovered oxygen levels on the prehistoric earth were somewhere between ten and fifteen percent. In a nutshell, these aliens not only produced a creature that would one day lead to *Homo sapiens*, but tweaked its DNA to be perfectly compatible with the environment at the time. But the ship contained thirty-six other pods, which means there's probably a DNA databank somewhere on this ship."

"So you're saying this ship was some sort of interplanetary zoo."

Jack shook his head. "Not a zoo, it was an ark."

Chapter 58

Jack was in the middle of changing the carbon dioxide filter on his rebreather unit when the submersible docked with the Orb's outer airlock.

Thankfully, Captain Kelly and the rest of the ONI team was down in the ship somewhere, likely hunting for more tech they could pillage. Jack understood military intelligence had their own agenda. But that didn't mean he had to like it.

The inner airlock door swung open and out stepped a woman he presumed was Dr. Ward, dressed in an orange biosuit. She was far more attractive than he'd expected and suddenly Jack felt the temperature on the Orb becoming uncomfortably warm. Two men in similar biosuits exited the submersible, the first larger and more muscular than the second. To Jack's eye, they looked more like bodyguards than they did scientists.

Jack extended a hand and introduced himself, as well as Commander Hart, who stood nearby.

Mia shook their hands and then introduced her colleagues. "This is Dr. Smith and Dr. Jones."

"Tom is fine," the slightly shorter man said, correcting the record. He motioned to his colleague. "And this is Sven."

Sven grunted.

"A man of few words," Hart said, shaking his hand. "I like you guys already."

Sven's full lips curled into a smile.

Despite their jovial air, Jack took careful note of the dangerous glint in the men's eyes. Real doctors or not, they meant business. "I hate to break up the party," he said, tapping his wrist, "but the sooner we get started, folks, the sooner we're able to get off this tin can."

Mia stepped closer to Jack. "I need to speak with you first. Is there somewhere we can go?"

"Of course. Follow me." He led her down two decks to the Orb's small science lab.

"There's so much you need to know," Mia began.

"Let's start with your two fake doctor friends."

She fell into a nearby seat, struggling with where to begin. How could she ever hope to condense everything that had happened over the last few days into a five-minute conversation? "You're right, they aren't doctors. They're here to stop Sentinel."

Jack sat as well and rolled over to her. Mia's hair was tied in a ponytail. Even in her biosuit, she somehow managed to smell of lavender. "I didn't mention it before, but I'm familiar with Sentinel," he said, telling her about the bug in Anna's software.

"Anna?"

He laughed. "Don't worry, you'll meet her soon enough. But watch out, she's the jealous type."

Mia smiled and raised her hands. "She's got nothing to worry about from me. I'm here strictly on business." Her face fell slightly with those final words.

Jack saw the change. "This is very personal for you, isn't it?"

"My daughter," she explained. "I've been searching for a way to treat the effects of Salzburg, but it seems every time I get close, fate has a way of snatching victory right out of my hands." She glared down at her palms in something resembling despair.

"Then you agree the ship's triggering changes in people's DNA?"

"That's the confusing part," she said. "I mean, Salzburg syndrome's been around since at least the nineties. These flashes only just began. If an extraterrestrial intelligence has been tinkering with our genome, then why would the extra chromatid appear so late in our genetic history? Here's what we do know. A year ago, Salzburg was present in one in five million people. Today, that's closer to one in a hundred and it's not even including animals."

Jack told her how some of the animals on his rescue farm had also been affected. "Skin rash, weak bones, aging and forgetfulness," Jack said, recounting the signs he'd also seen in Grant and Olsen.

"Yes, and in some cases it's far worse."

"So you're here to figure out how the ship is reassembling people's genes."

Mia straightened her back. "A good scientist would want to study the phenomenon, understand how it works and what it can teach us about our own genetic makeup."

Jack agreed.

She fixed him with a determined stare. "I just want to make it stop."

Jack's features shifted. "Anna's managed to teach herself part of the alien language and has gained access to the ship's computer system. If there's a way to shut it off, I'm sure she'll find it."

"She sounds like a quite a woman."

A smile tugged at Jack's lips. "She's very special, although she does have her limitations."

"Do you think if I showed her the Salzburg genome she'd be able to search through it?"

"If you're asking if she can find a hidden message, I

couldn't think of anyone better to ask."

"In the beginning I assumed it would be a message," Mia told him. "But now I'm not so sure."

Over the phone she had mentioned the rather ominous 'MAN MUST FALL' she claimed to have deciphered from the DNA in the Salzburg chromatid. "I think you have good reason to doubt the message is real. I mean, this ship has been down here for millions of years. Long before humans, let alone language, were even a twinkle."

Her eyes flared with surprise. "I had no idea it was that long ago. Nothing on the news…"

"Course the news got it wrong. Those same Sentinel creeps have done everything they could to spread scary videos and half-truths for no other reason than to scare people witless."

Mia drummed her fingers against the sample kit on her belt. "I'm not sure how much you know, but up there, civilization is pretty much falling apart. Sentinel's got everyone convinced the world is about to end because aliens are coming to kill or enslave them. Has Anna seen anything in the ship's computer systems that might shed light on why they're here?"

"No memo yet, although that would be nice." Dimples formed in Jack's cheeks. "Here's what we do know. When this craft crashed into the planet it led to a mass extinction, killing off not only the dinosaurs but nearly all life on earth."

Mia shook her head. "So the asteroid story we were all taught—"

"Was only partly right. Scientists have speculated the extinction rate following the event was close to seventy-five percent, but I believe it was much higher, closer to ninety-nine percent."

"Then how did life bounce back so quickly?"

"We believe much of the life was replaced by this

284

ship." He explained the pods they had found. "It only took a few centuries for the planet to begin recovering."

"I'm sorry," she argued, shaking her head. "But that doesn't match with the genetic evidence. We can trace the evolution of life all the way back to single-celled organisms. If an intelligent race wiped out life on earth and replaced it, there would be a pretty glaring line of discontinuity."

Jack acknowledged her point. "I don't pretend to have all the answers. We're still putting the pieces together. Which is why you're here."

Mia opened her sample kit and removed a test tube filled with a pinkish substance.

Jack studied it, drawing a blank. "What is that?"

"A piece of the dead animal they retrieved near the pod," she said. "They asked me to draw up a genetic profile while they ran their own battery of tests up top. We were being outfitted for the trip down here when I overheard a Dr. Bishop suggest the creature might represent an undocumented species, perhaps the earliest known primate."

Jack opened his own kit and grinned. "You're not the only one with gifts." He unsnapped a vial of his own, one that contained a brown fibrous material. "If we're about to start drawing up genetic profiles, then here's the first one on our list."

She took the glass tube and studied it. "This looks old."

"Sixty-five million years, to be precise," Jack said. "It's from one of the extraterrestrial crew."

Chapter 59

When the human genome first began to be sequenced in 1990, it cost hundreds of millions of dollars and took over a decade to complete. The Human Genome Project had also established a template that helped speed up future work in the field. Nearly three decades later, what had once required years could now be completed in less than thirty minutes.

These were precisely the thoughts coursing through Mia's head as she tapped her foot, impatiently awaiting the results to come in. Her frustration said something about human nature, didn't it? About how quickly we grew accustomed to the conveniences technology provided us. Anyone who thought otherwise was free to toss their television set in the dump and listen to the radio instead. Still don't agree? Then donate your microwave to Goodwill and fire up the stove whenever you needed to reheat your leftover pasta. Ironically, in the end, the joke had been on us, since the seconds and hours freed up by one modern gadget were often spent staring like a zombie at another.

Already, Mia had sequenced the plesi's genome, a rather quick affair compared to the genome for the arthropod race the team had recovered from the ship. While waiting, she had watched the autopsy video over her OHMD glasses, giving her a vague idea what the aliens might have once looked like. She still couldn't help looking at her situation from the outside and shaking her head. Had someone told her while landing in Brazil that she would soon find herself swept up in an international game of espionage, she would have laughed. Had they followed that up with the notion she'd soon find herself in an underwater habitat sequencing an alien genome, she would have wondered what drugs they were on.

Still, ever since the Navy helicopter had brought her to the rig, she'd been overwhelmed by the scale of the operation. She was sure even Jack was unaware of how many ships and aircraft were in the area. It looked like a warzone. And in more ways than one, it was.

Once the ship's location had become common knowledge, news helicopters had raced to catch a glimpse of whatever they could. They didn't seem to care that the military had declared a no-fly zone over the entire western part of the Gulf. Why should they? This was the biggest news event of the century. Heck, it was the biggest news story ever. And weren't reporters ravenous for Pulitzers and Peabodies the way actors craved Oscars and Golden Globes?

The accidents that had followed were hardly a surprise. Yesterday, a chopper for Miami's WPLG News had collided with New Orleans' FOX8 chopper a few miles from the rig. All on board were killed, including a top reporter from each station. The resulting blame game had only made a bad situation worse and fed the online conspiracies that the military had shot them down for straying too close.

These were crazy times, made far crazier by the public's insatiable need to know. It didn't matter that only dribbles of truth were being served up with an abundance of theory and conjecture. And it was the same pattern Mia had witnessed from the moment those images of the ship had first showed up in the news and online. To put it bluntly, the world was shitting itself and she was partly to blame.

In moments like these, when she had time to be alone with her thoughts, the role she might have played in stirring the insanity pot began to meld with her anxiety over Zoey's health. It was then that she took a deep breath and tried to keep her eyes on the prize. Oh, how a Xanax or a Valium would help take that searing edge off. She could feel her physiology begin to react at the mere thought of self-medicating. The muscles in her stomach began to seize into a painful knot. Bolts of electricity shot up her legs. Mia had been down that road before, more than once, and every time it had always ended in the same dark place.

Speaking of dark places, there was another one not too far away, a real place referred to as the lab—a spot down in the bowels of that monstrous gunmetal ship she'd eyed through the submersible's porthole window. That was where Jack, Tom and Sven were right now, searching for a DNA databank Anna suggested they would find there. Understanding which species had been grown in those tubes and sent to the surface might better help them figure out why these beings had come here in the first place.

When it came to sequencing the alien genome, she hadn't expected the biological matter Jack found to provide much of a genetic signature. Not only on account of its age—sixty-five million years was a heck of a long time—but also because there was nothing to say that all life in the universe was carbon-based. And no carbon meant no DNA.

The sequencer made a low beeping sound, indicating that it was finished. Mia scanned the results and as she did the color began to slowly drain from her face. She had been wrong. The aliens' genetic material was carbon-

288

based. But more than that, when she compared their genome to ours, she saw that seventy-five percent of our DNA was the same.

Then, with the comparison complete, the computer spat out one additional point of commonality. Mia slumped into the chair, not at all ready for what she was seeing. The alien had Salzburg.

Chapter 60

Mia climbed up one level to find Hart at comms.

"You're white as a sheet," he said, rising to his feet. "Everything all right?"

"I'm not sure." She stumbled up the circular stairwell that led to the Orb's mess, clawing at the railing as she went. She braced herself against the bulkhead, drawing in a deep breath, the muscles in her chest constricting painfully. When she had things at least partially under control, Mia broadcast to Tom and the others. "Are you guys still in the lab?"

"Affirmative," Tom replied, jovially. "We're heading back now. Mia, you will not believe this place."

"Did you find what you were looking for?" she asked, still struggling to control her breathing.

"You sound stressed," Sven said, his deep voice even lower over the radio. "Are you hurt?"

"No, but I need to know if you found the library you were looking for."

"We did," Jack assured her. "Anna's sent the elevator down to get us. We won't be long."

Mia caught a rustling behind her. She turned to see a woman in a blue biosuit emerging from the submersible.

"Dr. Ward, is it?" the woman asked.

"Did you just arrive?" Mia replied, still feeling a

touch disoriented. The implications of what she'd stumbled upon moments ago were so vast she was having trouble processing it.

"We've been here a while," the woman said. "I'm Lieutenant Brooks with the ONI." Strands of her hair were waving free from her bun at the back. It looked as though she'd been asleep or engaged in some challenging manual labor. "I expect while you're here that any and all pertinent discoveries will be shared with Naval Intelligence."

Mia swallowed. "Yes, of course." As far as she was concerned, she had no reason to hold onto the secret. Surely the military could be trusted. But that nagging feeling kept creeping back in. She'd learned the hard way what happened when you trusted the wrong person. The ONI had their own mission and for all Mia knew, classifying her discovery as top-secret could stifle any future research into fighting Salzburg.

"We're all on the same team," Brooks assured her.

Mia watched as she spoke, noticing how the woman's gums were more prominent than her teeth. She remembered seeing the same thing among great white sharks on a Discovery program.

"We have files on everyone here," Brooks went on, scooping her helmet off the table.

"I'm only here to study biological samples," Mia protested. She wasn't looking for trouble and wasn't sure why the woman was sizing her up like this. "Once we know what we have, we'll be happy to share it with you."

"So you have something?" Brooks' eyes narrowed.

"I didn't say that."

"No, but you implied it. Let's cut the bull. We know very well why you're here, Mia. You wanna save your daughter."

Mia felt heat rise up her neck and into her face. "Excuse me?"

"We also know about your little stint in rehab. Yes, of course, why wouldn't we know? Don't think you weren't vetted before the Navy allowed you to come to a highly sensitive facility."

Mia put her hand to her head. The room was starting to spin. Was she having trouble adjusting to the change in pressure in the Orb? "I-I'm not sure what any of this has to do with my daughter."

"It has everything to do with your objectivity," Brooks said, folding the helmet under her arm. "The human race is at the most critical crossroads in its history and you've got one person on your mind. What about the rest of the country?"

"Or the rest of the world," Mia added, suddenly wondering if Brooks was right. Had she been so laser-focused on finding a treatment for Salzburg that she'd lost her way?

The whoosh of the inner airlock opening sounded behind her. Brooks leaned in. "Like I said, we're in the intelligence business. We know what you're going to do even before you do. When the time comes, make sure you remember whose side you're on."

Brooks strode toward the airlock, acknowledging Jack and the others as she went by.

"What was that all about?" Tom asked, alarm growing in his voice when he saw Mia's face.

Mia spun and watched Brooks close the airlock behind her. "I think she was threatening me."

Chapter 61

Jack followed Mia down to the Orb's lab to process the DNA samples he'd retrieved from the ship's library. He had suspected for quite some time that if such a database existed, it would likely be located close to the chamber the animal was incubated in, a DNA master file of sorts that could be copied whenever a particular species was "ordered up". The tricky part was waiting for Anna, still on the bridge, to remotely open the tray door housed beneath the glass enclosure. She repeated the commands for two additional pods. Since arriving, they had only seen a single source of activity in the alien lab. If other species had also been manufactured, recognizable or not, Jack felt it was important to know.

Mia inserted all three samples and set the machine to sequence the genome for each.

"I saw what Brooks did back there," Jack said, half-seated on the table before her.

Mia's expression hardened. "If you'd arrived sooner you would have caught the whole show."

"Intimidation's her only weapon," he said. "She's trying to remind you who's in charge."

Tom and Sven came down, the larger man having trouble navigating the narrow stairwell.

"Hope we're not interrupting anything," Tom said,

not sounding very genuine.

"The more the merrier," Jack offered, waving them into the tight space. He turned back to her. "You wanna fill us in on what's got you so spooked?"

She ran her hand along the table's surface, distinctly aware of the hardened plastic it was molded from. She then told them what she had found.

Jack remained quiet, then asked, "What do you suppose it means?"

"As far as I can tell, it's pretty clear," she replied, her hands clasped together now. "Genetically speaking, those praying mantis people you found mummified in the hold of the ship are our distant cousins."

"Not only us," Jack said. "That means they're related to all life on earth."

Tom cleared his throat, painfully aware he was in over his head. "How's that even possible?"

"Panspermia," Sven said, the word surprising even himself.

"It's the idea that microbes blasted into space could seed other planets," Jack explained. "Some have theorized that was how life may have got started on earth. I think what Dr. Smith—er, I mean Sven—is suggesting is that process may have happened in reverse."

Mia wasn't sure. "So a piece of Earth rock gets blasted into orbit and somehow lands on a planet in another solar system, laying the foundations for an insectoid race?"

"Saw it in a movie once," Sven said, grinning sheepishly. "The aliens came back to reclaim their old home. Then a big war broke out."

Just then results for the first two specimens came back. They studied the screen as the computer searched for a match among animal species on earth. The first sample returned no known matches. The second found a name: Mesonyx.

Jack's eyebrows rose up. Mia too looked surprised. Tom and Sven were lost.

"Is that a good thing?" Tom asked, his gaze bouncing between them.

"Neither good nor bad," Mia told them. "But definitely a surprise. See, fifty million years ago, Mesonyx was a wolf-like creature that lived and hunted on land. Perhaps due to environmental pressures, such as changes in climate, scarcity of prey or threats from larger mammals, they began spending more time in the sea. Slowly, over millions of years of natural selection, they evolved into the aquatic species we know today as dolphins."

"First early man," Jack said under his breath, "and now early dolphins." A picture was beginning to form.

That was when the computer finished analyzing the template DNA belonging to the proto-primate plesi. On a hunch, Mia asked the computer to compare this template sample from the alien lab to the genome she'd developed earlier from the plesi ejected from the ship.

Mia filled them in on what she was doing. "The incubation chamber used this very sample as the template to create the archaic primate species you watched grow to near adulthood."

"That was before it was sucked out of the artificial womb," Jack added. "And fired from the ship in one of those pods. But if one is merely a template, then they should be identical, so why are you comparing the two?"

The computer zeroed in on a segment of DNA, flashing a red light.

"There's a section that doesn't match," Mia said. She ran a further test to isolate the discrepancy.

"Could it be a mistake during the replication phase?" Jack wondered.

Mia felt the breath catch in her throat. "The error

occurred in a single gene, altering the protein it produced and its effects on the organism."

"A mutation," Jack said, watching in awe as Mia's fingers flowed across the keyboard. "But what was the new gene that formed?"

A moment later they had their answer.

"Monoamine oxidase A," she said, her pulse fluttering. "Otherwise known as MAOA."

"That's all great," Tom said, wringing his hands. "But what is it?"

Jack turned and regarded both men. "The gene that controls violence and aggression."

Chapter 62

The normally smooth skin on Mia's brow wrinkled as it always did when confronting a big discovery. "It's nicknamed 'the warrior gene'," she said. "Monoamine oxidase A is an enzyme that breaks down neurotransmitters in the brain—dopamine, norepinephrine, serotonin. The MAOA gene helps to regulate this enzyme. Humans carry various forms of the gene, resulting in different levels of enzymatic activity. In other words, people with one type, MAOA-L, produce less of the enzyme and thus show a far greater tendency toward violent behavior while those with the MAOA-H version produce more of the enzyme and demonstrate far more empathy and kindness."

"A good versus evil gene," Tom said, gripping the armrests of the chair he was sitting in.

"Certainly looks that way," she replied.

Jack scratched his chin. "What about the second specimen you tested from the alien lab? The template for the Mesonyx. Did it show any signs of MAOA?"

"None whatsoever," she replied. "But we would need to run through every DNA template the ship has in order to rule them all out."

"Dr. Greer?" Anna called over the radio.

The muscles in Jack's jaw seized up. "Anna, is

everything all right?"

"It is, Dr. Greer. Although I must admit to listening in."

Although they were on the Orb, Jack became distinctly aware he was still wearing his OHMD glasses, which had allowed her to listen in on the conversation. "That's fine, Anna. Would you like to add something to the discussion?"

"Not at the moment," she replied. "But given your recent discovery, there is a file in the ship's archive that you may find particularly illuminating."

They all exchanged a curious glance.

• • •

After suiting up, Jack found Commander Hart at the comms center and asked if he'd seen or heard from the ONI team.

The edges of the SEAL's mouth turned down as he shook his head. "Can't say that I have, Doc. Last I heard they were searching for the ship's propulsion system. I did see Lieutenant Brooks was in the Orb about an hour ago. Want me to scan the radio channels and send them a message?"

Jack considered the idea. "I may not be their biggest fan, but I do want to make sure they're not in any kind of trouble."

"You think they may have found something big and are keeping it quiet?" he asked, cocking an eye.

"The thought had crossed my mind," he admitted. "It's not like them to keep out of sight."

Hart laughed. "You do have a point. Most of the time they're banging around with salvaged tech and stuffing it into the submersible."

"Appreciate it," Jack said walking away. By the time he reached the mess, a vague sense of uneasiness was stirring deep inside his gut, a feeling that would continue to nag him long after they reached the bridge.

Chapter 63

While Jack was wrestling with an uneasy feeling he couldn't quite put his finger on, Mia was in the process of stepping into a strange new world. Her vitals spiked as the inner airlock door sealed shut and the one leading down the ladder into the ship swung open. She had grown used to the biosuit, opting to keep it on even while on the Orb for that very purpose.

Her breathing came in short, ragged bursts. On the main platform, she stood frozen in place, her knees weakened by the immensity of the structure. Inevitably, her gaze was drawn to the central column and the narrow walkways radiating out from each level. But it was the pastel-colored lights shimmering up the body of the cylinder she found hypnotic to behold. The sensation was similar to finding yourself in a wonderful dream, the kind you hated waking up from.

Jack reached out and touched her arm. Despite the suit's robust organic polymer, his touch was welcomed and reassuring. When their eyes met, she caught a hint of envy.

"I wish I could join you in seeing it again for the first time," he said.

They headed toward the closest bulkhead and a set of ramps which led up several levels to the bridge.

The muscles in Mia's legs began to burn. "Why not take the elevator?" she asked.

Jack smiled. "I figured you'd want to get a look around on your first trip inside."

Soon they reached the bridge. Anna was there to greet them. She rolled forward, extending one of her robotic arms, her digital features lit with a beaming smile. Jack introduced them, one at a time.

"She's a robot," Mia said, shocked.

"A glorified toaster," Jack admitted, grinning. "Yeah, that was my first reaction too. At least before I got to know her. You'll find she's so much more than what you expect."

Mia contemplated this as she shook Anna's hand.

"Dr. Ward has a special project for you, Anna," Jack told her. "One that I'm sure you'll enjoy."

"I cannot wait to hear about this special project," she replied, leading them back to the main console.

"But first, what is it you have to show us?" Jack asked.

Anna tapped the screen and then waved her arms, scrolling through the holographic options swirling before them. "If you recall, Dr. Greer, the lab specimen ejected from the craft was tracked by a recording system."

"The specimen that died soon after breathing twenty-first-century air," Jack said.

Anna nodded. "Yes. I considered this as I listened in on your conversation about the MAOA gene you found in the deceased animal's genome. If the pod had made a recording of that event, why would pods ejected earlier not have done the same?"

Jack was intrigued. "That would give us a visual record of the species dispersed from the ship."

"Correct. After rolling back through the archives, it became abundantly clear that the bulk of the ship's activity occurred within a few hundred years after the impact and the resulting mass extinction."

Mia found the idea of images from sixty-five million years ago fascinating. "How many pods were sent out at the time?" she asked.

"One thousand five hundred," Anna replied. "Although there were two to four creatures of the same species in each pod, often two males and two females. It should also be noted that some of the pods travelled vast distances."

"The aliens were repopulating the planet," Tom said. "Like some sort of technological Noah."

"How many video records have you found?" Jack asked, feeling the excitement dancing along every nerve ending.

"I have found recordings for each of the one thousand five hundred ejections. However, there is one in particular worth viewing." Anna made a swiping motion with her robotic arm. The green glowing hologram disappeared, soon replaced by a flat moving image that seemed to curve in on itself. It was as though the video were being projected on the inside of a sphere, with the effect that it could be viewed perfectly from any position on the bridge.

Images appeared of a pod speeding toward the earth, slicing through thick white clouds. Moments later, a sparse landscape came into view. From this high up it was obvious the earth had already been blackened and ravaged by the tremendous impact. But it was also clear that life, resilient as it was, had begun to reclaim the devastated lands. Among the ruins, oases of green foliage dotted the area. And it was into one of these islands of life that the pod landed. Clouds of dust rose up as it struck the supple earth. A door opened and two furry plesis charged out. Several seconds passed before two more followed. This last pair approached their new surroundings with caution. They skulked around, listening intently for danger. Anna flipped ahead a few days. By now the animals had all climbed into a nearby tree and created a nest. But only one male and two females were visible.

"Wait a minute," Jack said, noticing the numbers were off. "Where's the other male?"

Anna scrolled back several hours to reveal a scene where one of the males was chasing the other, squealing and biting. The scene continued for several minutes, those on the bridge feeling as though they were watching a PBS nature show set sixty-five million years in the past. Then it happened. The more aggressive plesi caught up with his wounded brother and sank a mouthful of sharpened teeth into his opponent's furry neck, staining the jungle floor red with blood. The animal twitched a final time before his body grew still.

"Do you understand?" Anna asked, as the video ended.

Jack stared at the image of the dead creature frozen on the holographic display. "It seemed that only one of the males had the aggressive version of the MAOA gene," he said, the full impact only starting to dawn on him.

"The violent one wanted both of the females for himself." Tom said. "Wanted to be top dog and decided to wipe out his competition."

"Were any other proto-primates sent out?" Jack asked. So much would hinge on the answer Anna gave next.

Slowly, Anna shook her head. "No other pods with plesiadapiformes were released."

"So you're telling us," Tom said, unable to hide his own sense of astonishment, "that the aggressive little bastard who did the killing…"

"Is man's earliest ancestor," Mia said, completing Tom's thought.

"And if the other had lived instead?" Sven asked.

Jack raised his eyebrows. "Then the human race might have been vastly different."

Mia thought of the chaos going on in the world above them. "We sure as heck wouldn't be so eager to murder one another, that's for sure."

Tom ran his hands through his hair. "So man's legacy of murder and conquest all comes down to a snippet of DNA that got copied wrong."

"History has turned on far less," Jack offered.

Mia grew quiet, unable to stop thinking about her time spent in Sunday school as a child. There was something about what they'd seen just now that bore a familiar ring to it. She thought of Sven's question about what the world might have been like had the more peaceful plesi lived instead. And that was when it came to her. "This was man's fall from grace," she blurted out.

They regarded her with surprise, except for Anna, who remained stoic.

"What are you saying?" Jack asked.

"I remember the pastor at my church discussing how man's lust for power and greed had led to his banishment from the Garden of Eden, a fall from grace which has haunted us ever since. I recall wondering even then how I could possibly be held responsible for an original sin I had no part in committing. As a teenager, I discarded what I considered an archaic and outdated belief system without realizing the grain of truth it contained. By killing his rival, the real Adam ensured that his violent genetic tendencies would be passed to his descendants, tainting the entire primate and human family tree."

Chapter 64

They were still reeling from what Mia had told them when the holographic display retreated, revealing the countdown clock.

"Wait a minute! When did that pop up?" Jack said with alarm.

Anna studied the alien symbols she now recognized were numbers, counting down to the next blast wave. "I am afraid there is no way to be certain. It must have been obstructed by the video."

"That means we have an hour," Jack told everyone, quickly explaining the clock and its significance.

"I am sorry to disagree with you, Dr. Greer, but there are only twenty-eight minutes until the next event."

A mix of fear and despair lodged in Mia's chest. "But there's still so much to do," she said. She was thinking not only about any insights they might have gained about Salzburg and how to beat it, but also about the other secrets of earth's evolution yet to be discovered on board.

They heard a crackle in their ear as Commander Hart joined the radio channel. "Jack, are you there?"

Was this about the timer? And if so, how could Hart have known about it? "I'm here, go ahead."

"You need to get back to the Orb right away," he

said.

"I know," Jack replied. "The countdown started again and this time I don't think the ship will make it through another blast."

Jack caught a thread of fear in Hart's voice. "That's not our biggest problem," the SEAL told them. "I just got done speaking with Admiral Stark when he told me the team from the ONI had arrived from Maryland, said they got held up a few days to receive specialized training."

"I'm not following you," Jack replied. "Captain Kelly and the Naval Intelligence team have been here for days."

"No, Jack. They're scrambling up there to figure out what the hell's going on. There was a Captain Kelly and a Lieutenant Brooks, but they died in Iraq more than ten years ago. Whoever those people are, I can assure you they aren't Naval Intelligence."

"Are we in danger, Dr. Greer?" Anna asked, with the innocence of a young child.

"More than you know," Jack replied. Then to Hart. "We're heading back to the Orb now. Do we have anything to defend ourselves with in case Kelly and the others show up?"

"I've got a pistol," Hart said.

Jack couldn't help but laugh. When he'd asked Hart earlier about weapons, the SEAL had told him there would be no need for them down here. Jack was happy he'd lied.

Anna summoned the lift up to the bridge. Heavy vibrations rattled their bones. A low hum crawled through their helmets and into their ears. The lift was on its way.

Jack knew there was still time to escape the ship. But that wasn't what worried him. It was the imposters on board, a group he could only imagine was made up of

305

Sentinel agents. He gritted his teeth, remembering how they had systematically pillaged everything they could lay their hands on. And then when most of it was gone, they too had disappeared down below.

"Jack, it's Hart. I'm prepping the submersible. I need you and your team to double-time it."

"Working on it," Jack replied, feeling the bridge rattle beneath his feet as the lift worked its way up the long column.

Hart started to say something else when his voice cut off. A split second later, they heard a loud explosion three levels beneath them.

"Hart, are you there?" Jack asked, concerned. The lift doors squealed open and they stepped in. In a moment, they were heading down to where the Orb was docked. But despite repeated calls, Hart didn't respond and Jack was powerless to claw back the sinking feeling all of them were about to die.

Chapter 65

When the lift opened, Mia charged along the catwalk and stopped halfway to the platform. Below her, the central core of the ship descended into incredible darkness. Before her, in the distance, was the ladder that led to the Orb. Although her helmet blocked most of the ambient sound, she didn't need sound to see the water collecting along the bottom rung.

They continued on, if only to be sure. As they proceeded, Jack gave them hand signals, indicating the alternate channel they should switch to. There was hardly a question that Kelly's people would be listening in.

Once at the stairwell, Tom leapt up the ladder in quick order to check on the Orb. Salt water foamed at their feet as the others backed away and waited for him to return. A moment later he came sliding back down, gripping the ladder's edges.

"It's gone," Tom said, in shock. By the sound of his speech, it was clear the moisture in Tom's mouth was gone too. "The airlock door connected to the ship is still in place, but it's been severely damaged. There's no telling how long before it gives way and the sea comes pouring in."

Tom had no sooner finished what he was saying than they felt tremors from a fresh explosion down below.

Jack went to the railing along the platform and peered down to see an orange glow on one of the lower levels.

"They meant to trap us here," he said, searching around frantically for options.

None of them needed to ask why. The answer was obvious. Sentinel knew that it was only a matter of time before someone saw through their charade. And there was only one way to make sure the truth of what was discovered stayed buried forever. Like so many fanatical groups before them, they were hell-bent on seeing it through, even if that meant sacrificing their own lives in the process.

"Commander Hart never mentioned them leaving in the submersible," Mia said.

Sven balled his hands into fists. "Which means they're still here somewhere."

"They want to make sure we don't find a way out," Tom said, seething.

For Mia, the sadness of failing Zoey was just as devastating as the idea of dying two thousand feet beneath the ocean. She was battling the sense of panic growing inside of her when she had an idea. "Maybe there is a way off the ship."

Jack caught on at once. They could use one of the pods in the lab down below.

Another explosion shook them.

"Then we need to get down there before they destroy our only hope of escape," Jack told them.

"Hold on," Tom said, calling them back. "If Sentinel managed to sneak bombs on board, then there's a good chance they're armed."

He was right, Jack realized with growing alarm. They had already lost their most viable way off the ship, now they had to contend with bombs and firearms. He turned to Anna. "When you were searching through the ship's computer, did you come across any information on a weapons locker or anything else we could use?"

"I'm afraid not, Dr. Greer," she replied, a sullen expression on her face.

"Wait a minute," Mia blurted out with excitement. "Didn't you say Dr. Bishop found a pile of junk a few levels beneath us?"

Jack nodded. "It was a repair depot. What about it?"

"Maybe it will have something we can use."

With traces of smoke wafting past them, the group hurried back on the lift and headed three levels down.

"What do you think the chances are they'll have a laser gun hanging around?" Sven asked, hopeful.

Mia wanted to smile, but couldn't. "I don't know about you, but right now, I'd be happy with a wrench."

•••

Another explosion rocked the ship as they scoured the workshop for anything useful. With laser guns and wrenches in short supply, they each grabbed a patchwork of discarded metal pieces. They were looking for anything with a sharpened tip to stab with or a rounded end they could swing as a club. The irony of their situation was not lost on Jack. They were on the most technologically advanced craft on earth and were reduced to wielding medieval weaponry.

Within minutes, they were back on the lift, heading down to where the man pretending to be Captain Kelly and the other Sentinel agents were surely awaiting them.

Jack fought hard to silence the nervous energy coursing through his limbs. They would get one shot at this. And if anything went wrong, all of them were sure to die. "Anna, how long before that next blast wave?"

"Nine minutes, forty-three seconds and—"

"That's good enough." Addressing the others, Jack said, "Any suggestions on how to handle these Sentinel goons?"

"Find the biggest one among them," Tom said,

clenching his fist. "And take him out first."

The lift door slid open. Through the clouds of black smoke they spotted the archway that led to the pod room. But beyond that appeared the vague outline of a human figure. As they suspected, Captain Kelly had known they would come, known there was no other choice. Behind them, sea water came splashing down the ramp. The airlock door must have blown. Jack wondered whether it was better to be shot or to drown. Something told him he was about to find out.

Chapter 66

With time slipping away, they entered the pod chamber, ready to roll the dice.

Captain Kelly stood before the first row of pods. The composite glass doors were cracked and in some cases completely shattered.

Jack's eyes drifted to the control panels. They too had been smashed.

Kelly caught Jack's gaze, then tapped the side of his helmet and raised an index finger. They switched to channel one.

"Took us a while to break the glass," Captain Kelly told them. He seemed calm, like a man who was resigned to his fate. "Turned out the stuff was a hell of a lot stronger than we thought. The control panels too. What I wouldn't have given for a material that strong on my dad's Buick when I wrapped it around that telephone pole. I was young and drunk and might have saved myself from losing my girlfriend and doing six years for manslaughter. It's amazing how you can turn your life around when you have the time to consider what you've done."

Lieutenant Brooks appeared from out of the smoke, along with four of Kelly's men. They moved close to their boss. Jack spun to find the last two Sentinel agents.

Each was armed, the barrels of their pistols pointed right at them. They were trapped, but Jack hadn't expected anything less. As the two groups stood facing one another, water continued to rush in, splashing down the ramps as it collected in the lower levels.

"I don't have to tell you your chances of making it out alive aren't looking good," Kelly informed them, a sick grin on his face. He pointed to a block of C4 wedged between two pods. "But I'm prepared to make a deal with you." He turned to Mia. "All the pods are broken," he told her. "Except for one. Number thirty-seven, way at the back." The grin on his face showed he knew about her trip to Kathmandu. "Go ahead and hand me Dr. Salzburg's USB and I'll let you take your chances on lucky number thirty-seven."

"And the rest of us?" Tom asked.

Kelly snickered. "Traitors to the cause don't get special treatment. People like you never understood. We're doing this because we love the human race. Want to prevent the holocaust we know is coming. Fear is man's greatest weakness, but it can also be his greatest strength, the only shield our species possesses against its own demise."

As Captain Kelly justified his lunacy, letters began to appear one by one on the inside of Jack's glasses.

S-W-I-T-C-H… T-O… C-H-A-N-N-E-L… T-W-O.

He glanced over at Anna, who glared back at him expectantly.

Jack and the others did as they were told. And almost immediately Captain Kelly and his Sentinel agents clasped the sides of their helmets. Then a burst of light shot out from the OHMD glasses they were wearing. Anna was piping in an audio sample of the alien language as well as blinding them with a dizzying array of visuals. Jack and the others charged in at once, darting through the ever-thickening smoke to strike out.

Jack brought the curved metallic bar in his hands down on the man standing before him, shearing his collarbone in two. The gun dropped from his hand and skittered across the floor, lost in the haze. Wild shots rang out as they clashed in brutal hand-to-hand combat.

Mia caught sight of Brooks fleeing toward the back of the room and ran after her, a sharpened spike in her hand. Brooks turned and fired as she fled. Mia ducked behind one of the pods, watching sparks fly off the machine's shattered surface. When Brooks' weapon clicked empty, Mia swung around the other side to cut her off. They met in the middle, caught between two rows of pods. The auditory and visual assault was still underway in Brooks' helmet and Mia moved in to take full advantage. She wasn't much of a fighter, but perhaps the distraction might help even the playing field.

Mia thrust at Brooks' chest, embedding the point no more than an inch into her suit. Brooks recoiled in pain as the tip lodged into one of her ribs. She swept her hand down and knocked the weapon out of Mia's hand. Light winked off the end as it fell to the ground and out of sight. Mia moved in to strike with her fists, but Brooks raised an arm to thwart the blows and countered with one of her own. The force struck Mia in the chest, knocking the wind out of her. She stumbled back as more gunshots rang out just beyond view.

Now it was Brooks' turn to charge and both women exchanged a flurry of blows to one another's torso. When Brooks over-extended with a sweeping attack, Mia hooked a leg behind her feet and pushed with all her might. Brooks tumbled to the floor. No sooner had she fallen than Mia was on top of her, wrapping her hands around Brooks' neck.

From the corner of her eye, she caught sight of Brooks' left hand, searching for the spike. A second later Brooks' fingers closed round the blunt end and she drove it into Mia's leg. A burst of pain rose in Mia's throat as the stinging point sank into her thigh. She shrieked and used both hands to force it out. Kicking forward with her left knee, Mia used it to pin Brooks' arm down as she forced the blade's edge toward Brooks' face. When it was nearly there, Mia closed her eyes and pushed her body forward, shoving it instead through Brooks' neck. The Sentinel agent's eyes went wide before slowly fading away.

Mia rolled off of her and struggled against the overwhelming urge to throw up. Close by, other individual battles were still underway. One Sentinel agent lay sprawled at Sven's feet. The other was receiving copious blows to the midsection.

A few feet away, through the swirl of smoke, Jack and Captain Kelly were locked in their own deadly struggle. Like many of the others, their weapons had been the first to go. Now only fists and sheer willpower would prevail. If ever there was a time when the warrior gene might have come in handy, this was it. But Kelly wasn't exactly rolling over and playing dead. In spite of the auditory distraction and partial blindness Anna was blaring into their helmets, he was still able to fend off Jack's attacks. And it wasn't long before Jack understood Kelly's game plan. He didn't need to beat them, he only needed to delay until it was too late.

Suddenly, the ground began to vibrate, followed by that low hum which always signaled a final blast wave was powering up. But once that happened, the rock shelf the ship was balanced on would surely give way, sliding them into a fiery abyss.

Kelly charged out of the haze, pinning Jack up against one of the pods. The captain's forearm pressed against Jack's throat, threatening to choke him out. Jack struggled for air, pounding uselessly against the side of Kelly's helmet, the only area he could reach. The world began to swim away from him, his punches throwing less and less power with each passing second. The blood pooled in his head, engorging his features into a mask of fear. In a final desperate act, Jack swung his arm across, striking the faceplate on Kelly's helmet. The sudden look of worry on his opponent's face told him to do it again, this time with everything he had. Jack cocked his elbow and struck again, this time shattering Kelly's visor. At once, Kelly released his grip and stumbled back against the wall. The brutal nature of the fight had tired both men. Kelly's lungs drew in, searching frantically for breathable air, but finding instead only a cocktail of toxic gases. The Sentinel leader slumped to the floor, clutching at his throat.

Chapter 67

The humming sound had nearly reached its peak when Jack ran back to the pod room's entrance. In a corner was Anna, trying to reattach one of her broken arms. Scattered around were the bodies of Sentinel agents, their glasses still lit with a blinding display. But they weren't the only ones hurt. Mia emerged, shaking and covered in blood. A few paces away, Jack saw a large figure that looked a lot like Sven slumped over. He rushed over and pulled him back. Sven gazed up at him, his eyes filled with tears. Jack's own eyes fell to the floor where he saw Tom, dead from two bullet wounds to the chest.

The humming ended and that was when the rumbling began.

"Pick him up," Jack told Sven, nudging the big man's shoulder when he didn't respond. They needed to hurry for pod thirty-seven and hope that it was still working.

Anna and the others were already heading in that direction. When they got there, Jack ordered Anna to open the pod door.

"I'm sorry, I can't do that, Dave."

Biting back the rising panic, Jack paused as the reference sank in. "Yes, good one, Anna, save it for later, would you?"

"My apologies, Dr. Greer," Anna said as she used her one good arm to activate the console and enter the command.

Mia and Sven exchanged looks of fear and confusion.

"She was quoting Hal 9000," Jack explained as the glass door slid open.

They piled inside as Anna plugged in the final commands. The shaking was getting worse. In the distance, water sloshed onto their level, racing toward the pod room. Anna tried to roll forward, but the pod entrance was a foot off the ground. She wasn't going to make it in. But worse, the rover they'd attached her to was too large to fit inside. With water now gushing around their feet, Sven set Tom's body down and grasped Anna by the shoulders and twisted her torso off the rover's base. When she was inside, the glass door slid shut. Then a violent burst of g-forces followed as the pod shot up the tube. Soon they were out of the ship, bubbles roiling past their eyes. But it was only when they burst forth from the ocean and spotted the sun shining down on them that they truly felt safe. For Jack, he had never been happier to fly in all his life.

Chapter 68

USS *Grapple*
Gulf of Mexico

Jack and Mia stood on the deck of the salvage ship, USS *Grapple*. Military blankets were draped over their shoulders, steaming mugs in their hands. He sipped at his coffee, peering over to see what she was drinking.

"Green tea," she said, tilting the mug just enough for him to catch a glimpse of the light brown liquid.

He smiled and went back to the blaze of beautiful colors cast off by the setting sun.

Shortly after the pod had landed, a group of military men in hazmat suits had descended on them. Predictably, a battery of medical tests had followed. What lay ahead were the endless debriefings as the Navy sought to understand not only the full extent of what they had discovered on the ship, but also how things had gone so horribly wrong.

Mia didn't pretend to have answers to all of those questions. Besides, there were several she was still grappling with herself. Unsettling as some of their discoveries had been, it was clear that much of what we understood of human origins on this planet would need to be rewritten. And yet far from bringing the world closer together, Sentinel's campaign of disinformation had only driven it further apart.

But Sentinel hadn't only sown dissent. They had taken the life of Tom, a man she hadn't known for long. But what she knew of him, she had liked a great deal. At one time a member of Sentinel, Tom had had the strength to challenge his faith in that corrupt organization and lay down his life for a noble cause he believed in. She knew Jack had felt a similar respect for Commander Hart.

A hatch opened and out came Rajesh, Anna nestled in the crook of his arm. If someone didn't know any better, they might mistake him for a ventriloquist.

"We owe you one," Jack told her.

Anna's face brightened as she reached out with her new arm. "We are even, Dr. Greer."

"Even? How so?"

Her expression grew serious. "It was largely through our interactions that I began mapping alternate neural pathways, discovering areas of myself I did not know existed."

"For better or for worse, I think we all left a bit of ourselves down there," Mia said, distinctly aware of the weight she would carry for what she had done to Brooks, even if it had been in self-defense.

"It's called growing up," Jack told Anna, lifting his mug to her in a silent cheers.

Rajesh nodded his thanks as well. "The Navy has offered to help get Anna back on her feet, so to speak. No strings attached."

"What does that mean?" Mia wondered.

He bobbed his head and grinned. "I'm not sure, but I suppose the two of us will soon find out."

They turned and headed back inside, leaving Jack and Mia alone once again.

"There's an old adage that for every answer you

receive three more questions arise," Jack said, feeling the sun's warmth wash over him.

Mia laughed. "Story of my life. You starting to have regrets?"

He thought about it. "Right now, only one, although others are bound to follow."

"Really? And what's that?" She peered at him through narrowed eyes.

Jack leaned in slightly, tilting his head. And for a brief moment, Mia wondered if he was about to kiss her.

Instead, he said, "I wanna know why. Why an advanced race would bother with all of this. The ship, wiping out an entire biosphere eons ago, only to repopulate the earth. I've been racking my brain and can't come up with a single explanation that makes any sense. And for some reason I just know the answer was somewhere on that ship." His gaze fell. "I guess we'll never know."

Mia's eyes sparkled as a grin formed on her soft lips. "Maybe the answer hasn't been lost." She held her battered USB key before him. "Maybe the answer is right here."

Chapter 69

The Pentagon
Washington, D.C.

The Emergency Conference Room inside the
Pentagon's National Military Command Center was
unusually spacious. Rectangular and with thirty-foot
ceilings, it seemed almost wasteful that the only furniture
present was a long oak table—a remnant from the
Truman era—along with a dozen or so leather chairs.
The lighting here was dim, some of it pooling in the
corners, the rest strung low over the men in uniform
waiting patiently to begin the briefing. Hung on the walls
were enormous display screens packed with maps of the
United States and the world.

Secretary of Defense Ford Myers, only just recently
back from his time in the Gulf of Mexico, sat at the head
of the table, drumming the fingers of one hand, sipping
an espresso with the other. When he was finished, Myers
deposited the mug, dabbed the edges of his mouth and
stared out at the Joint Chiefs of Staff. "I'm ready."

General James F. Dunham cleared his throat and
began. "At zero eight hundred hours today, NASA
satellites detected a small gamma ray burst emanating
from the planet's surface."

"Yes, I'm aware," Secretary Myers replied, pushing his mug off to the side, making sure the spoon stayed squarely on the saucer. "The USO was lost shortly after that. Fell into a chasm, I believe."

Always the consummate professional, General Dunham squared his shoulders and carried on. "The burst I'm referring to came after that and was a localized event."

Myers wasn't annoyed anymore, he was confused. "Are you saying we've got another USO on our hands?"

"I'm afraid so, Mr. Secretary," Dunham replied. "This time we determined the blast wave's area of effect was less than fifty miles. We believe it's in the beginning stages."

"Where's it located?"

"Greenland," General Dunham said. "So far satellite imagery hasn't revealed an object. Our best guess is that it's buried somewhere under the ice sheet."

The Secretary swore and rubbed the palms of his hands up and down his forehead. "Do we have any more information on the individuals who gained access to the USO by impersonating Naval Intelligence officers?"

A crack appeared in Dunham's steely composure. The other generals looked on, expressionless, although their deep embarrassment was on full display for anyone who knew how to spot such feelings on hardened men.

"We're working on that," Dunham said, clearly anticipating the response that was to come.

"Not good enough, General. A group of terrorists—because that's what they were, terrorists—managed to enter a restricted, top-secret area and steal invaluable technology right from under our noses. You're not going to tell me they didn't have help on the inside. We need to know how they did it and we need to know now."

Dunham clicked his teeth with annoyance. "We'll get to the bottom of it, you have my word. But there's something else you need to know, Mr. Secretary. Something more important than the infiltration."

"I doubt that very much," Myers said, his tone spelling out his suspicions clearly enough. If the generals thought they could distract him from their incompetence, they had another thing coming.

General Dunham produced a black and white photograph and passed it down along the chain of generals on his side of the table. When it arrived before Secretary Myers, he plucked the glasses from his inside jacket pocket, slid them on and peered down at the image. "What the hell am I looking at?"

"Voyager One, sir. Launched in 1977. It left our solar system sometime in 2012. She is now travelling through interstellar space and expected to reach the nearest star system sometime in the next forty thousand years. She does periodically peer back at earth, however, and send us a snapshot or two. The scientists' idea of keeping us humble, I suppose. The image you're looking at was taken twenty-four hours ago."

Secretary Myers stared long and hard. Slowly, his eyes began to make sense of the smudges of light set against the dark interstellar background. And as that happened, his gaze was drawn to one particular part of the image. A blemish, larger than the others, closer. Then all at once, the realization struck him with sudden and overwhelming force, the shock so powerful it was enough to make the blood drain from his face. Even the caffeine-fueled anger once pumping through his veins dissipated like a fine mist.

Without needing to be told, Myers now understood the reason for the general's deep concern. The object in the photograph was silver, shaped like a giant diamond, and headed straight for earth.

Real life versus fiction

While *Extinction Code* is a work of fiction, several of the elements that went into building the story were drawn directly from newspaper headlines and magazine articles as well as from medical and academic journals. Here are just a few.

Drilling the impact crater:
In 2016, an international team of scientists descended on the Chicxulub impact crater in the Yucatán Peninsula. This was the location where sixty-five million years ago a meteor struck the planet and ended life not only for the dinosaurs, but for seventy-five percent of the species on earth. Their goal was to drill down into one of the 'peak rings' to learn more about what happened in the days and years following the meteor strike. To my knowledge, no expedition has ever set out in search of the meteorite itself.

Galactic Cosmic Rays:
Cosmic rays are bursts of high-energy particles originating from outside of our solar system. Although the source is still somewhat unclear, many scientists believe they are created by supernovae. Since they contain radiation, direct exposure to cosmic rays can alter segments of our DNA and lead to health issues. Astronauts working in space often reported seeing flashes of light whenever their eyes were closed. The cause was eventually attributed to cosmic ray particles striking their optic nerves. Such rays also pose a challenge for the prospect of long-distance manned spaceflight. In the future, spacecraft hoping to travel the vast distances between stars will require some form of

shielding against various forms of radiation.

Sentinel:
For a variety of reasons, there are several groups and prominent individuals who believe that contact with an intelligent alien species might lead to humanity's demise. Among them is theoretical physicist Stephen Hawking, who suggested recently that "meeting an advanced civilization could be like Native Americans encountering Columbus. That didn't turn out so well." In my research, I also came across an organization called Lifeboat which seeks ways to mitigate the impact of future extinction-level events. In regards to first contact, they say, "We are against any efforts to purposely provide our technological level and location to potentially hostile aliens."

Silencing chromosomes:
As with the fictional Salzburg, scientists using gene therapy have recently learned to 'muzzle' the extra chromosome (twenty-one) which causes Down syndrome using a gene called XIST. In women, XIST is used to silence one of the two X chromosomes they carry, a built-in function which made repurposing the gene that much easier.

Office for Outer Space Affairs:
Yes, it sounds made up, but it really exists and is actually part of the UN (not the US). The full name is the UNOOSA (United Nations Office for Outer Space Affairs). The department's staff is larger than one person (sorry, Eugene) and also deals with more than the prospect of first contact. See the UN's website for any additional information.

MAOA gene:
The 'warrior gene' is real and exists largely as it was described in the book. However, more research is needed in the area of human aggression to fully understand the interplay between genetic and environmental influences.

Magma pockets beneath impact craters:
Large enough asteroid impacts on earth, like the one in Sudbury, Canada, have been known to create pockets of magma beneath the earth's surface, forming what is known as an igneous intrusion.

Prosimians:
It should come as no surprise that several debates are currently raging within the field of primate origins. Identifying animals from the fossil record that look and behave like modern primates is easy. The challenge for most scientists is that the links between distant primate ancestors becomes more and more tenuous, especially since there was an explosion of mammalian species in the years following the extinction of the dinosaurs. So if anyone claims they can draw a precise line from proto-primates through to *Homo sapiens*, you should be very skeptical. As additional species are uncovered, however, that picture will become clearer.

The number 37:
In a peer-reviewed work entitled "The 'Wow! Signal' of the Terrestrial Genetic Code," scientists Vladimir I. Shcherbak and Maxim A. Makukov have suggested there are mysterious patterns of mathematical symmetry within the human genome. They've identified at least nine occasions in which the number thirty-seven occurs. They believe this lends weight to the idea that humans were bio-engineered by an intelligent species.

Similarly, other scientists such as Paul Davies have argued for a concept called 'Biological SETI,' the idea being that if humans were engineered by an advanced alien species, signs of such a manipulation would likely reside in our DNA.